CAPITAL
VOLUME ONE

First published in 1997 by
Allen & Unwin

This edition published in 2013 by
UWA Publishing
Crawley, Western Australia 6009
www.uwap.uwa.edu.au

UWAP is an imprint of UWA Publishing
a division of The University of Western Australia

THE UNIVERSITY OF
WESTERN AUSTRALIA
Achieve International Excellence

National Library of Australia Cataloguing-in-Publication entry
        Author: Macris, Anthony, 1962- author.
        Title: Capital volume one / Anthony Macris.
        Edition: New edition.
        ISBN: 9781742585666 (paperback)
        Dewey Number: A823.3

Cover photograph by Markku Nurmikari.

CAPITAL
VOLUME ONE

ANTHONY MACRIS

UWA PUBLISHING

One

The young man in the fawn trench coat can't wait to get off the train. He stands in front of the grey metal doors and runs the tip of his index finger up and down the worn rubber strips where they meet. It is approaching rush hour; all the seats are taken, the standing areas are half full and the warm carriage air smells of recycled dust, perfume, and naphthalene. The overhead fluorescent lights, diffused by their rectangular casings of white plastic, flicker in time with the uneven slowing down of the train and cast a fluctuating glow onto the passengers' faces, the shadows that mould the fabric of the young man's fawn trench coat also fading and strengthening with the light's intensity. An outbreak of high-pitched laughter makes him glance around towards the centre of the carriage: a group of schoolgirls in maroon dresses and navy blue blazers, their brightly coloured bags strewn over their laps and the floor, giggle at each other under the blank stares of the surrounding passengers.

The lights suddenly fail, and the carriage plunges into artificial night. The train stops with the jolt of metal and the rattle of windows, the passengers impassive as they are swallowed up by the darkness and roughly jerked forward then back. The silence that follows is immediately broken by renewed snorts of laughter from the schoolgirls. Moments later the lights flicker back to life, revealing their giggling faces.

The young man in the trench coat tisks in exasperation at the train stopping yet again, the chances of realising his plan for the afternoon – meeting up with a friend in a pub near King's Cross then going on to see a film in Islington – becoming more and more remote. He presses his forehead against the cold metal of the door and feels the vibration of the idling engine transmitted to his skin. Even though he left the house in good time, every step of his journey has been dogged by a slight delay: a conversation with a garrulous neighbour, a footpath disrupted by road works, a slow-moving queue at the ticket office, a broken down escalator at Liverpool Street and now a Tube train that constantly stops and starts, subdividing the final part of his journey from Russell Square to King's Cross into seemingly countless tiny journeys that have no destination other than the tunnel itself.

The train creaks into motion, going so slowly, so infuriatingly slowly, that he screws his eyes shut and presses his forehead harder against the thick metal, the engine's vibrations penetrating his skull. He opens his eyes, straightens up and, balancing his weight, rocks from side to side. To occupy himself he reaches into the pocket of his brown woollen trousers and takes out the red plastic card holder he acquired earlier this afternoon, not without some difficulty, the surly ticket seller at his local station demanding to see that the holder he wished to replace had reached a sufficient level of decrepitude to warrant a new one (it had), even then only parting with the new folder as if she were doing him a favour he in no way deserved.

Keeping the folder open with his thumb, he stares for the thousandth time at the map of the Underground network, an orderly circuit board of coloured lines reduced to the size of a credit card, the city's polluted river flowing along the bottom section in a thin blue band that rises and falls like a graph representing the peaks and troughs of an unstable economy's inflation fluctuations. In the other sleeve of the holder is a public transport identity card onto which a passport-size picture of himself has been glued, one of four taken in an automatic photo booth in Victoria Station. Printed onto the thin film of plastic laminating the card is a broken red line made up of a repetition of the British Rail logo – two parallel dashes crossed by a zigzag – that cuts diagonally across his face. He studies the colour of his skin which, usually a pale olive, has come out a muddy brown, the expression on his face blank, even dazed, giving no hint of the smile he mustered only a split second later, one of these latter images now sitting in a tiny tortoiseshell frame on his mother's mantelpiece. He admires what he always admires about his face, but soon notices the features that annoy him. He tilts the card until his image is covered in a pool of milky light, then closes the plastic holder and stows it back in his pocket.

He resumes running his finger up and down the groove formed by the meeting of the strips of rubber, and stares out the window at the tunnel wall only a few centimetres away, its cracked and flaking surface dimly lit by the carriage lights. Pipes and cables and wires drift by, twining round each other and spreading along the wall like creeper vines, their yellow, blue, and violet casings partially covered by charcoal-like dust. Cold air streams in through a gap between the strips of rubber, direct blasts sometimes stinging his eyes as if to further irritate him.

He steps back and looks up at the map of the Piccadilly line that runs along the wall of the carriage, the same map repeated along its entire length so that passengers, no matter where they are positioned, can plan their journeys. His gaze flicks from one station to the next, Finsbury Park, Arsenal, Holloway Road, Caledonian Road, finally jumping back and forth between the names marking the boundaries of his current location, somewhere between King's Cross and Russell Square, his eyes moving so quickly that the letters begin to float against their shiny white background.

He shakes his head and tells himself that it may not be as late as he thinks, that he could still be on time, and curses himself for not wearing a watch. He scans the carriage in search of one, but all nearby wrists are covered by winter coats. Frustrated, he tries to find an empty space where his eyes can rest. He looks down at the carriage floor, at the wooden slats that make it look like a pen for dumb animals, but immediately misses having something to read, his mind feeling as if it had been cut adrift and left to feed senselessly upon itself. He looks up at one of the advertisements mounted above the map of the Piccadilly line and reads:

12 HOURS, 15 MINUTES.
A thousand Broiler turkeys to produce six pounds of manure.
The Common garden snail to cover a total distance of 319 feet.
The world's population to grow by 132,300.
To fly from Paris to Miami.
The period of daylight on March 30th and September 15th.
A Blue-fin tuna or a Blue shark to swim 735 miles.
The British worker to earn enough to feed his family for 11 days.
490 flights to take off from Heathrow.
A Fresian cow to produce 10.2 litres of milk.
The human heart to pulsate an average of 55,000 times.
Sputnik to circle the Earth 7.73 times.
The wings of a hummingbird to beat 3.08 million times.
The average time a computer spreadsheet user will save
every working week by switching to Microsoft Excel.

Light suddenly fills the window as the train crawls into the station. Passengers move towards the doors and he finds himself pushed forward, not by any physical contact, but by the feeling that the space is contracting around him in a mixture of sudden and stealthy gestures: seated passengers stand, others lift suitcases or handbags, others still adjust scarves or tighten their hands around umbrella handles. Within seconds the space around him is full and he has merged with them into a single entity, a pack animal poised to escape the carriage while the train hovers at some point between movement and stillness.

A tall man squeezes up beside him and rests his hand on the grey metal door. The sleeve of his leather jacket rides back to reveal a chunky diver's watch strapped to his wrist; its stainless steel band gleams against the background of his broad, hairy arm. The man in the trench coat cranes his neck for a better view, hoping that he may yet still be able to meet up with his friend and get to the cinema, but discovers, to his disappointment, that while he can vaguely identify the digital display, the main watch face, and even the two smaller faces, they are tilted at an angle so extreme as to be unreadable.

He is about to ask the man for the time when the train stops with a jerk. The grey metal doors roll open and the black rubber strips part slowly, clumsily, to reveal a curtain of tightly packed bodies restraining themselves from crowding into the open doorway. The momentum of the passengers from behind sweeps him out of the carriage and into the wall of people, this barrier instantly breaking up as he steps onto the platform. Faces glide past him, centimetres away from his own, smears of flesh and hair and material whose glances sometimes meet his as they try to avoid knocking into him. He shoulders his way forward, protected by his trench coat and by the coats most of the passengers are wearing, the layers of leather and fabric and the reinforced shoulder pads absorbing the blows the crowd inflicts upon itself. He glances up at the electronic signal board that juts out imperiously over the swarm of people on the platform, a heavy black rectangular box with a display screen of tiny amber lights, similar to the type used to jazz up the neo-classical façades of bank buildings and department stores, the bulbs forming the message UXBRIDGE..........2mins.

All the while on the lookout for a watch, he walks close to the edge of the platform to avoid the main confusion and get out of the station as quickly as possible. The train doors roll shut, a whistle blows and the train departs, for a few moments clattering beside him at the same pace. He finds himself walking faster as the train picks up speed. Through the glass panes of the doors gliding beside him faces gaze out, their attention seemingly absorbed by the layers of dirt that have been allowed to build up on the windows, stuck to the dried swabs of disinfectant that can be made out when the light reflects on the glass at a certain angle. He continues increasing speed along with the carriage until he is almost running, for a time level with the face of a woman who looks at him in surprise as if he were bidding a dramatic farewell to the wrong person, his shoulder bumping against the dusty grey metal as he tries to keep to the narrow path delimited by the carriage and the crowd of passengers until, accompanied by a powerful whining from its engine, the train surges ahead. He drops back to a normal pace, his heart pounding in his chest, the last carriages rattling past him nearly empty. He pauses, panting slightly, breathing in a faint odour that smells like a mixture of scorched hair and gas.

He falls into step beside a schoolgirl in a navy blue blazer, one of the group on the train he has just got off. He glances over at her and their eyes meet; she turns her sullen face away immediately. He notices that her blazer is a little too small for her, the sleeve revealing a brightly coloured Swatch with a crotchet and quaver for arms, their forms so confusing that it is impossible for him to read the time, no matter how much he tilts his head. He is about to ask her the time when she, perhaps realising that he is about to approach her, quickens her pace and vanishes into the crowd.

He catches sight of his platform exit, marked by a small sign that says WAY OUT THAMESLINK, above these words an old-fashioned stick arrow pointing left. Relieved to be finally leaving the chaos on the platform, he enters a short passageway with walls covered by rows of advertisements locked away in aluminium housings. Now that it has been diverted into the narrower space of a linking tunnel, the crowd has begun, by some mysterious natural process, to form itself into lanes, which makes progress much quicker, giving the man in the trench coat renewed hope that he may have just enough time to collect his friend at the pub and immediately go on to the cinema, foregoing their usual drinks, which he may be able to persuade his friend to indulge in after the film, although he doubts it, knowing what a creature of habit he is.

His path, however, is blocked by the person in front of him, a short, balding man in a dark blue pinstriped suit, who comes to an abrupt halt and, to the surprise of the man in the trench coat, kneels down and proceeds to open an extremely thick briefcase, his elbows waving in the air like the wings of a crippled bird as he rummages through its contents. Walled off by the traffic that has formed around him, the man in the trench coat is forced to wait beside one of the framed advertisements. Through a dirty plane of glass a young woman looks over her naked shoulder and smiles at him. Her face has been enlarged to double life size, its skin tones going from bland pink to tanned orange, her lips a weak red. In her right hand, level with her dimpled cheeks and enormous smile, she holds a plastic bottle of a deep blue colour, the words SUN IN printed on it in white. The background of the poster is a light sky-blue, the sort of colour that, if stared at long enough, makes the spectator feel disoriented, out of body, just a pair of eyes and a nervous system floating in featureless blue space. Against this background the words SUN IN have been repeated in larger letters, this time in the flowing script usually found in greeting cards with feel-good messages. Underneath the headline a small text explains how you can simply wash the sun into your hair instead of going to the trouble of home dye-kits or the expense of salon treatments. Her hair has been carefully done, each wave full of the residues of the photographer's studio lights, which are now being lit by the tunnel's fluorescent tubes. Even though the colour of her hair is meant to be natural and spontaneous, it is precisely these elements that have been filtered out, leaving only a muted chemical lustre against the sky-blue background.

The short businessman rises and moves on, slowly, still preoccupied with some all-important detail. The man in the trench coat is prevented from overtaking him by the uninterrupted stream of passengers. Following close on the balding businessman's heels, he takes a few more steps forward but is once more pulled up short as the businessman stops again, this time so abruptly that he nearly runs into him. Rather than go to the trouble of kneeling again, the businessman leans against the wall and lifts his leg into the air, balancing the briefcase on his thigh and continuing his search. Exasperated by his behaviour, the man in the trench coat is about to complain when, from around the approaching corner, only a few metres away, he hears the distant but nevertheless clear sound of an accordion.

The melody is instantly recognisable, one of those Gypsy or central European folk songs that was regularly played by the local Greek cabaret band at New Year's dances when he was a child – the lead singer's thick black greasy hair flecked with steel wool, a large medallion set into his sweaty tuft of chest hair exposed by a shiny white synthetic shirt, its thin vertical strips of even shinier crossweave swelling out as they follow the contours of his pot belly, his chunky platform shoes partially covered by the cuffs of his black flares low at the hips, tight at the groin, the accordionist dressed in an identical outfit save for a pair of aqua-blue flares – whose repertoire went from 'Rollink down the Rivet' and 'Runnink Bear and Leetle Ouite Dove' to the Kalamatino, 'Zorba the Greek' and also this dramatic, sensual melody, now being played to an indifferent crowd of people.

The accordion music suddenly stops, its absence for a moment making more pronounced the muffled pounding of hundreds of footfalls. The man in the trench coat, still blocked by the businessman, starts to lose patience and, his gaze taking on the clarity brought about by a surge of intense dislike, stares down at him, noticing how short he is, a repulsive, gnome-like figure in fact, the shoulders of his jacket sprinkled with dandruff, the white flecks of dead skin lying there motionless, seemingly fused to the fabric, his head strangely still, as if it were too small, or too heavy, made of solid bone or perhaps solid flesh that had been stuck directly onto the torso. His grey hair is plastered down at the back, the side sections grown into long layers and swept over his bald patch, a taut dome of purplish brown skin mottled with pink. Many of the longer hairs have become unstuck and, heavy with hair oil, sag and curl around a pool of light that reflects off this bald patch, the pool's shape varying as the businessman, clearly losing balance, moves his head from side to side, showing the back curve of one ear, then the other, more and more of the thick briefcase becoming visible as it slips down his thigh.

The accordion starts up again with loud choppy bursts, the musician now seeming to be hitting keys at random. Spurred on by the burst of sound, the man in the trench coat pushes his way into the moving wall of passengers and skirts around the man in the blue suit who, in a posture that seems to defy gravity, his thigh trembling with the effort of supporting its heavy weight, is running his fingers over the top edges of the sleeves of a large, portable stretch file, in feverish pursuit of some stray piece of paper, his eyes peering into the individual sections with a mixture of panic and anger. As he passes by, the man in the trench coat sees a watch strapped to his arm, an old-fashioned time piece of obviously excellent quality, the protective glass acting as a lens that magnifies and to some extent distorts the watch's face. Despite this distortion he instantly recognises the exact position of the arms, which tell him that he is nearly forty-five minutes late, a figure that exceeds his worst expectations and causes him to abandon any thought of meeting up with his friend who, although a likeable person in every other respect, flatly refuses to wait more than thirty minutes for anyone.

Two

Every morning I leave the house for school. Every morning I pause for a moment on the footpath outside the front door, right in the middle of one of its square blocks of white concrete. I look down at the tips of my school shoes, then slowly up, as if I'm standing on a diving board that continues forever.

My house is on the top of a hill that slowly falls for miles. The footpath descends, square concrete block after square concrete block, into the haze of the suburbs, into the blur of light greys, dirty olive greens and bruised bitumen that my vision has reduced the distance to. The footpath cuts through this haze, a ribbon shining with heat and light. It glows a chemical white, like the robes of Marlon Brando, Trevor Howard and the other members of the High Council of Krypton in the first Superman movie.

I walk this endless footpath every day, from my white wooden house to my redbrick school. Little pieces of the black acrylic paint I'd used to paint my leather shoes flake off onto the hot white concrete. My mother shouted at me for painting my shoes with black acrylic. She'd be glad it was flaking off.

The dark blue vinyl bag I carry is light because I don't take most of the books I need for the day. I don't care and the teachers don't notice. When they do I make excuses and look at my neighbour's. This shuts them up. They like quick solutions. A minimum of fuss. Of effort.

In my pocket is a clump of sticky copper coins. I found them in my parents' shop, under the cabinet that holds the till. The coins have piled up there over the years, a dank rock-like formation growing in the dark, glued together by cooking fat, particles of food and dust. By the time I discovered it there were blotches of blue and green on the coins, the same green that forms on the copper statues of colonial heroes and statesmen. They dangle in the deep pocket next to my genitals, their bulk hitting my thigh in time with my lethargic steps.

The footpath is the source of this lethargy. I pass along this surface of white concrete, the spark of a harmless fuse leading to no explosion, only six hours of timetabled boredom. The sun is behind me, my shadow precedes me. I stare into my shadow so the white concrete doesn't blind me. My bleached violet stain mutates with every step, flickering over this wrinkled surface, the skin of a petrified animal.

I space my footsteps so that I never walk on the lines dividing the squares. I'm usually so absorbed in this that I often don't look when crossing a side street, and cars have nearly hit me. I sometimes pretend that the lines between the squares have been electrified, that if I step on them I'll be fried alive, a prisoner on an electric fence, a fruit bat on a power cable. Or that, like electronic eyes, they activate trap doors that will slide back and bury me alive. Most of the time though I avoid them because they're there to be avoided. Like vicious dogs and people I don't like.

I don't often pass anyone on the footpath; most people here travel by car, even for the shortest distances. When I do come across somebody, there's no surprise. They can be seen a long way off, a speck slowly moving towards me, me a speck slowly moving towards them. The specks gradually turn into people: man, old, light grey shirt; woman, oldish, blue shopping bag;

woman, young, boob-tube, dog. I only step off the footpath if there's no room left– if two people are walking together, for example. I usually drift over to the left side, and wait for them to take the right. And we pass by each other, avoiding eye contact at all costs. I enjoy this moment, the idea that with all this space we are nearly forced to brush up against one another, that we could be miles apart but sooner or later the concrete path will make sure we meet.

The traffic on the road is light, regular, fast. The chrome details of the cars, the fenders, hubcaps, door handles and radio aerials, reflect chunks of sun; soon they'll be too hot to touch. Most of the cars have only one driver, figures whose faces can't be made out in the darkness of the car's interior. The contact of rubber spinning at 45 mph on the hot bitumen makes a heavy whooshing noise, whoosh following whoosh when a few cars pass. I only notice it on very still days, when the emptiness is so strong I can feel it. It's the sound of the suburbs whispering to themselves, thinking to themselves. From time to time radio music is mixed in with the whooshing sound, but this is rare. Everything is usually silent.

The sun is higher now, my stunted shadow precedes me. I stare into it, into the particles of acid blue swarming over the shining concrete, my feet kicking it along the metre-wide strip, causing it to buckle, to warp. The shadow of my head stays fairly constant, though. Sharp tufts of hair. Now one ear, now the other.

The houses on either side of the road are made up of horizontal strips of weatherboard, mostly painted white. Dulux. Taubmans. TRUST BRITISH PAINTS? SURE CAN! Most have corrugated iron roofs painted rust-red. There's hardly any decoration, and when there is it's either simple or practical: a hanging plant, a wrought iron door number.

The uniform I'm wearing is like the houses: a minimum of decoration. We wear uniforms because in that way everyone will be equal. On the same level. Or just the same. My shirt is ligh blue cotton with two big square pockets. I have one with maroon pocket flaps and dark blue piping. My shorts are made of long-wearing light grey material that all school shorts seem to be made of. They're held up with elastic. When my shirt gets undone the bunched up strip of material digs into my skin. Sometimes I notice it and leave it and then go to the toilets at little lunch or big lunch to inspect the damage; my finger wanders over the red marks that make me think of a convict's lashed back. My long grey school socks have two thin bands at the top, maroon and yellow, a goldy yellow. They start off just below my knees and end up somewhere around my ankles on the way home, because during the day I always take out the elastic garters my mother makes me wear. My black Bata Scouts have animal track soles. I hardly feel my body, my smooth, hairless body. I am the white concrete path. I am the uniform.

I imagine the concrete path is a thousand feet up in the air, stretching in either direction for as far as the eye can see. The sky feels like the thick piano opening of John Lennon's 'Imagine'. I'm calm, ecstatic. I'm not afraid; after all, I do this every day, walk along a metre-wide strip of concrete. I never fell off it when it was on the ground, why should I fall off it when it's in the sky?

When I put my hand into my right pocket, the clump of coins hits my genitals as I take out a one-cent piece. My genitals are darker than the rest of my body. My testicles are close to my body, my scrotum is smooth and tight, as is my foreskin. I like this smoothness. I'm told that my body is not yet developed. If it means my genitals have to change, I don't want it to develop. They start to sweat bunched up in my underpants. I wish I didn't have to wear any.

The film of copper, dust and fat feels sticky. I balance the coin in the crook of my index finger, let my arm fall, pull it back and then pitch the coin onto the path. It hits the concrete on its rim and spins forward in a fairly straight line for a few sections, before veering to the right. On the left face of the coin

14

spins the image of a possum with a long bushy tail, big staring eyes and long stiff whiskers. On the right face, revolving ever closer to the ground as the coin loses speed, is an image of the Queen. She wears a crown and is staring with the appropriate aristocratic dignity at the letter R, a part of the sequence of words ELIZABETH II AUSTRALIA 1968 printed just inside the diameter.

When I pass the coin where it has fallen I don't pick it up, but pitch another one, a two-cent piece. This time it doesn't wobble on impact. It shoots straight down the middle of the path for ten or fifteen squares, giving a little jump every time it hits a dividing line, with each jump losing a little more momentum. On the right face spins another image of the Queen, only this time she's younger. She's staring with the same cool dignity at the letter T. Her crown is lighter than the other one, and the neckline of her dress lower, showing the curve of her spine down to the shoulder blades. On the left face spins the image of a frilly lizard, its jaws open, the frill around its throat flaring out, its tail flicking over its head like a whip. The coin's spinning shadow precedes it, acid grey swarming with amber particles over the hot white concrete.

Three

Once he realises that his plans for the afternoon are ruined, the young man in the trench coat feels strangely disoriented, his presence in the tunnel irrelevant now that he has no specific destination. As he draws closer to the end of the first section of tunnel, various options for salvaging the afternoon pass through his mind: a different film, a museum or art gallery, a walk in one of the larger parks. But the thought of negotiating these city spaces alone, without a companion to take the edge off their impersonality, depresses him. He is about to stop by the tunnel wall, to take pause, then decides against it, afraid that he might block someone else's path, just as the man in the blue pinstripe suit had blocked his.

Becoming more dispirited by the second, he continues his journey, the leather soles of his shiny black leather brogues rapping against the stone floor, arcs of light reflecting off the edges of the holes punched into the leather. He stares down at the grimy yellow floor, a surface that runs through hundreds of kilometres of tunnel, into toilets, locked staff rooms, ticket halls, over the concourses of cavernous mass-transit interchanges such as King's Cross, Charing Cross, Victoria, Liverpool Street, Paddington and Clapham Junction. Unable to think of an alternative destination, and vaguely horrified at the thought of finding himself yet again in a music store around Piccadilly Circus looking at boxed sets of the complete works of Beethoven, or in a Charing Cross Road bookshop sifting through tables of remaindered hardbacks, he lets himself be borne along by the crowd, staring down at the endless yellow path, trying to collect his thoughts.

As he walks his attention is drawn to the grid of fine, dirt-filled lines that cuts the surface of the floor into individual sections. Each tile is approximately 30 cm², composed of different varieties of shattered stone that have been set into a lemon-yellow binding medium. As his gaze jumps from one square to the next (the simple, geometric shapes soothing after the constant bombardment of faces and advertising he has had to suffer), it occurs to him that he has seen the same type of tile in many places: on the floor of the local bakery, the concourse of Sydney's Central Station, a shopping arcade in suburban Athens, and – he is sure, even if he can't specify exactly at what point – in the film he saw last night with a woman he hopes to keep as a friend despite her determination to become his lover, her behaviour in the largely deserted cinema ranging from stroking his hand to rubbing her leg against his, these attentions temporarily stopped by her shedding of tears at various points in the film, a review of which is listed in the entertainment magazine *Time Out* rolled up inside his trench coat:

> **'Freedom is Paradise'** (Serge Bodrov, 1989, USSR)
> Volody Kozyrev, Alexander Bureyev, Svetlana Gaiten,
> Vitautus Tomkus. 76 mins. Bodrov's excellent
> movie has no more flab that its young hero, a tough
> but doe-eyed teenager in a black-leather jacket who
> escapes from reform school and traverses the USSR
> in search of his father—who is also in prison. Like
> other kids in the reform school, 13-year-old Sasha
> has tattooed the title message on his arm as a badge
> of hope. His quest takes him from Alma Ata to
> Archangel'sk on the White Sea. It's an ideal itinerary

for a road movie, full of regional and ethnic variety and rich in political associations. Bodrov, a one-time satirical journalist, starts from the assumption that everyone in the USSR is conditioned to think and behave like a prisoner. But his focus is squarely on Sasha's resilience, imagination and emotional needs; as a picture of childhood's end, it's strong enough to stand alongside genre classics like 'My Life as a Dog' and Hou Xiaoxian's 'Summer at Granpa's', and the fluency and simplicity of Bodrov's film language makes it a pleasure to watch. It's the most likeable of recent Soviet films, and the one that sets the standards for the coming difficult years. (Tony Rayns).

the text highlighted with a fluorescent pink pen, as are various other listings for films, plays, art exhibitions, concerts, dances, clubs, talks and courses, this procedure of marking cultural events, most of which he never attends, one of his favourite activities. Ever since he was unexpectedly laid off from work three weeks ago ('The war in the Gulf, I'm afraid,' were the only words of explanation), his days have been spent keeping his spirits up by arranging outings – preferably those that are either cheap or free – with his scant supply of friends and acquaintances who he has, at times, literally had to beg to accompany him (with the exception of his determined female friend), the solitude of the city so unbearable that the only way he can cope with it is by effacing it with the distractions it provides.

He comes to the end of the first section of tunnel, still having made no decision what to do next. As he turns the corner his leather soles pound against the yellow stone floor, their impact sending small shocks up through his heels and the balls of his feet into his body, each shock telling him that there is no way he can inscribe himself on this space, that there is no way it will yield, that the only mark his presence will leave is a transference of abrasive grit from shoe to floor, an infinitesimal wearing away of stone or, at best, and only as a result of thousands of previous footfalls, the beginning of a hairline crack or the chipping away of an entire fragment of stone.

He turns into the second part of the Thameslink, a short section of tunnel that looks as if its construction had been only partially completed: the walls and ceiling are made up of a continuous surface of rough, grainy concrete that has been so unevenly laid it could be mistaken for a cave. The task of giving it a finished appearance has been left to a coat of flesh pink acrylic paint, the type of colour used for cheap dolls or comic book illustrations. Grime and dust have settled into the lower parts of the wall's undulations, creating a bizarre chiaroscuro effect, the play of light and dark making the tunnel look vaguely organic. A pink light washes over the passengers, their skin taking on the rosy tint of sausages in butcher shop displays, the gridded floor they walk on a virulent yellow, the jagged pieces of stone – off-white suffused with yellow, green or black – glowing like a river bed of broken teeth that winds its way through a pink grotto.

He crosses the floor, the noise and density of the crowd dispersing in this small, high-ceilinged cavern, racking his brains for a suitable destination. The more he tries to decide, the more confused he becomes. Blocks of pink highlighted text from *Time Out*, colour-coded Tube lines, bloated classical façades, interiors of coffee shops, rows of book and cassette covers, snarls of cars and pedestrians, all these and countless other images swirl around his mind and smother each other as he advances across the floor. He wants to stop, to turn back, to go home, but is unable to; his only certainty seems to be the impact of his shoes on the stone, the sensation of crunching grit, the pounding of leather on broken teeth.

At the foot of the stairs he is forced to lengthen his stride in order to clear a small pile of rubbish that has accumulated against the bottom step: a crushed Ribena tetrapak, a torn blue foil crisps packet, a small red and white chocolate wrapper, and a piece of apple green A4 paper, creased and folded by the footsteps of Underground customers. Blackcurrant juice dribbles out of the Ribena tetrapak, soaking into the rubbish and spreading out in front of the stairs in a translucent, reddish puddle. The young man is not entirely successful in clearing the pile of rubbish; his heel comes down on the capital K of the word Kebab printed onto the sheet of paper in large black letters, alongside a line drawing of what looks like a plastic cup on a skewer, but which is obviously meant to represent one of those enormous pillars of compacted meat found rotating in the vertical grills of Lebanese takeaways. The ball of his foot falls slightly short of the step and he is put off balance, but immediately rights himself with the support of the burnished, stainless steel bannister that divides the staircase in two, its surface reflecting the overhead fluorescent tubes which, temporarily strung up with wire, straggle along the ceiling like the spine of a prehistoric animal.

As he climbs the stairs he notices a surveillance camera staring at him from the ceiling, its tiny lens housed in a small, rectangular stainless steel box that gives it an old-fashioned, low-tech look, as if it were a toy, or broken, or completely fake, empty inside, no circuit boards, no transistors, no wiring leading to a busy control centre where, as in the series of posters advertising the effectiveness of the Tube security system, benevolent figures scan computer terminals and video screens.

In fact, had it not been concealed from view by the passing crowd, he would have noticed one of these surveillance posters on the wall directly opposite the SUN IN girl in the previous section of tunnel, its photograph depicting, in full colour, the three-quarter profile of a preppy young Englishman in a crisp white shirt and navy tie, his blue eyes ostensibly gazing out into the tunnel, but in reality fixed on an out-of-shot computer screen that casts a green glow onto his face, his delicate fingers poised over a keyboard, perhaps ready to send a command to one of the surveillance cameras, his smile, which would have been archaic had it not been retouched, directed not only at the tubular microphone that extends from his headphones to his lips, but also seemingly at the SUN IN girl, who smiles back at him, her vapid good looks perfectly complementing his.

For a reason he isn't quite sure of, the man in the trench coat finds the presence of the surveillance camera annoying. The arrogant way it hangs from the ceiling, its smug aloofness, makes him want to scream abuse into the lens, to make obscene gestures at it. He suddenly feels as if everything is conspiring to humiliate him. Not only does he have to put up with a public transport system that is expensive, inefficient and dangerous, but the management has the audacity to record these pathetic journeys as well; he is convinced that the security people must sit around in front of their terminals, coffee in hand, laughing uproariously as everyone scampers about, ignorant of the delays that only they know are occurring.

Full of indignation that he is being spied on, he climbs to the top of the stairs, but fails to notice an old woman approaching him, leaning heavily on an aluminium walking stick. He stops dead in his tracks, only a few centimetres away from her. Positioned on the lower step, he finds himself staring into her puckered mouth, which opens and closes with laboured breathing. She wears a lime-green suit made from a synthetic fabric, judging from the way the light shines on the broad shoulder pads and wide lapels of her jacket. Her bony hand rests on the railing, trembling, its skin white and pasty in contrast to the lurid green of her jacket sleeve and the gleaming lines swirling over the burnished metal. Her bleary eyes tinged with anxiety, she stares at some point that coincides with his face, her head lolling forward like a marionette's.

The young man mumbles an apology and, cautiously glancing to his side, begins to skirt around her but, as he steps to the left, accidentally knocks into the person coming from behind, a black woman in a smoke grey overcoat with braided hair pulled back into a long plait. She turns her face towards him, scowling. At the same time he feels something hard and smooth through his shoe. He pauses, lifts his foot and thrusts it onto the next step, for a moment nearly losing balance and bumping the woman again. He glances down and sees the distinctive shape of an empty Lucozade bottle rolling back and forth on the step. The woman with the braided hair snorts in irritation, then quickens her pace and disappears into the crowd.

The sight of the Lucozade bottle makes him realise his mouth is dry. As if to confirm this observation he runs his tongue over his teeth and gums and is satisfied to discover a slightly thickened layer of saliva, the tip of his tongue then poking into the large cavity left by the absence of a quarter of one of his top molars, top left row, third from the back, which had come dislodged many years ago when he was eating, of all things, a Cornetto, the piece of tooth, which must have only been waiting for a final nudge, falling off just after he had munched into the ice-cream's crunchy top layer of nuts and chocolate, the sudden shock of cold causing him to suddenly swallow the entire contents of his mouth, tooth fragment and all. Running his tongue over his sticky gums and teeth, he decides to quench his thirst with a bottle of Lucozade, which he will buy at the first available opportunity. He strides past the old woman into the next section of tunnel with a renewed sense of purpose, relieved that he has at last found an achievable objective.

Four

After I finish university I decide to make some money so I can travel overseas. I go down to the CES and am interviewed by a restrained but friendly woman with short dark hair and big earrings. Once the paperwork is over, she directs me to the maze of noticeboards that fills half the office. Inside the maze I find several other job seekers (that was what she called me at the end of the interview– a job seeker). I check the headings at the top of each board. TRADES AND TECHNICAL, even though it's full to bursting with rows of neat computer-printed job descriptions, has no takers. Neither does PROCESS WORK or CLERICAL. The MISCELLANEOUS board is completely empty, a large barren rectangle of the same grass-green carpet that covers the floor. All the action seems to be at HOSPITALITY, where there's a small crowd. I hover around, waiting for a chance to get a closer look, wondering if my face is wearing the same expression of nervous expectancy as my fellow job seekers, who all seem to be about my age. Two of the guys are even wearing exactly the same jeans as me. This I find truly disconcerting. I'm relieved when they move onto other boards without noting down any of the reference numbers. It has taken me exactly five minutes to see them as nothing more than competition.

I look over the jobs for waiters and, using the pen and reference slips provided, write down the number of the job with the highest hourly rate. The reception clerk takes the slip of paper, finds the appropriate phone number, and tells the voice on the end of the line that she has a well-presented young man interested in a waitering position. She scribbles down the relevant details, briefly asking me if this afternoon is okay. No waiting, no fuss, everyone polite, everything neat and organised. Out on the footpath I examine the appointment slip. The sun shines so brightly off the paper that it takes a few moments for me to read:

Referred to: Steve. Pancake Manor, Charlotte St.
Designation: Duty Manager
Time: 4 p.m.

A suit of armour with a sword strapped to its side stands at the rear of the restaurant's foyer. As I pass it I resist the temptation to rap my knuckles against its breastplate. I enter the main dining room, a spacious, high-ceilinged area where the medieval theme is further developed in the form of long rustic tables of dark polished wood and heraldic devices hung from the supporting beams. In the middle of the room, penned off by four extra-long tables, is an enormous chessboard neatly stacked with ornate pieces. Judging from the vaulted ceiling, the building must have been a church. Light filters in from the round windows set high in the walls. There are only a few customers scattered around the booths and smaller tables.

I look around for the closest thing to an authority figure, and see a young woman perched at a kind of high, narrow pulpit positioned at the front of the restaurant. She has short blond hair, a case of acne that she is only barely managing to control, and wears a red T-shirt that features, printed in black, the Pancake Manor logo, the head of a smiling medieval lady lifting a fork to her mouth. The young woman fiddles with a state-of-the-art electronic cash register mounted to the top of the pulpit. She feeds a card into the machine and punches a few buttons; the printer responds with a shrill, screeching noise that fills the dining hall. She glances over in my direction and breaks into a fixed smile. Can I help you?' she half-shouts over the screeching machine. 'Yes,' I shout back. 'I've got an appointment with Steve.' The printer stops halfway through my sentence and the word Steve echoes around the hall as if I'm calling someone. Some customers look up at me. I feel like an idiot and my hands start to sweat.

'Did the CES send you?' asks a voice from behind. I turn around. Standing in front of me is a woman in an enormous pink pinafore, an equally enormous pink bow fastened to the top of her head. Long blond curls spill over her shoulders. In one hand she holds a lollipop the size of a traffic sign, its milky white surface covered in a yellow swirl. The skirt of the pinafore come to just above the knees, revealing blue and white striped stockings. 'Did the CES send you?' she repeats. 'Yes,' I answer. 'They gave me an appointment for four o'clock.' She looks me over with a practised eye. 'I'm Mandy, Head Duty Manager. Come with me.' Her boots clatter across the wooden floorboards as I follow her over to a small door in the back corner of the restaurant. She pulls a packet of Marlboro out of the pouch in her skirt, lights one up and takes a deep drag. 'Go downstairs and introduce yourself to Steve,' she tells me briskly, smoke drifting out of her nostrils. 'I'll be down once I've got out of this Alice outfit.'

Crossed over the top of the doorway are two spears, tufts of white fur wrapped around the base of their blades. I go down a short flight of stairs, the sound of The Eagles getting louder as I reach the bottom, and enter a medium-sized office with a low ceiling. My attention is immediately taken up by one of the walls, which is completely covered by a photograph of a row of trees, their leaves full of the light cast by the sun setting behind them. Shafts of golden light fan out from between the tree trunks and across a luminous stretch of grass, which is cut off by the bottom of the office wall.

Standing beside a large desk of glazed pine is a tall, lean man dressed in blue denim everything: denim jeans, short-sleeved denim shirt, even a denim tie. Clipped to his shirt pocket is a tag that says Steve, Duty Manager. He has blond shoulder-length hair and a sandy moustache. The shadows of freckles haunt his tanned arms. The phone pressed to his ear, he listens intently, all the while staring at the setting sun. He gives me a quick glance and resumes staring at the poster. I suddenly realise that I've been holding the appointment slip in my hand for the last hour, and that it's now damp with sweat. I hope he doesn't ask for it. I notice he's wearing tan cowboy boots with decorative topstitching. I hate cowboy boots, especially tan cowboy boots, and especially ones with topstitching. An irrational fear overcomes me. Perhaps they only employ blond people here. The girl at the cash register was blond. Mandy is blond. Steve is blond. My hair is brown. Perhaps they don't like brown-haired people. Perhaps they only interview brown-haired people because they can't tell the CES: blond people only, thank you.

Steve replaces the receiver with a click. He gives me a good long stare and says: 'I'm Steve.' He has clear blue eyes and a smooth, high forehead that for some reason reminds me of a choirboy. 'Did the CES send you?' he asks. If I hear that question one more time I'll scream. Determined to keep my cool, I say what has now become the ritual yes. 'Can I see your appointment slip please?' I hand him the damp piece of paper. He reads it and places it on the desk, then motions at me to sit down. I sink into one of those low chairs with a frame of moulded chrome tubing, the seat and back nothing more than sections of slack leather. He takes his place behind the desk in a large, padded office chair and I stare up at him, waiting for the interview to begin. I cross my legs out of nervousness and my body sways sideways, the chair like an unstable rope bridge. 'Hotel California' goes into its dying phase, a lengthy, strident guitar solo. I notice his tie clip, a miniaturised version of the smiling Pancake Manor woman. We sit there for a few moments, silent, taking in the music, two friends in a pub who have run out of things to say to each other. I hate these kinds of silences. I always want to fill them, crack a stupid joke, burst out laughing, anything. Steve shuffles some papers on the desk, now avoiding eye contact. I get the feeling he may even be more nervous than me.

The phone rings. Within seconds the receiver is in Steve's hand. After a few seconds he hangs up with a 'yeah': it's clear he's not much of a talker. He rifles about in a desk drawer and hands me some papers. 'Fill this application form in. Mandy can't make it for fifteen minutes or so. I'll be back then.' He stands up and lopes out of the room, forgetting to offer me a pen.

I flick through the application form, put it down, then, in search of pen, go and bounce about in Steve's big comfy office chair for a few moments. Now that I'm alone in the room, the wall covered in the row of trees becomes overwhelming; I look down at the floor, half expecting the shafts of golden light cast by the sun to also fan out across the polished floorboards. I return to my unstable chair and begin to fill out the forms. The first questions are predictable enough: name, age, date of birth, education, experience, previous employers. Things get more difficult with hobbies: I put swimming (I haven't stepped into a pool since the grade four swimming carnival), and add, just for good measure, squash (well once, anyway). The next question, however, is a real stickler.

NAME AN ACHIEVEMENT OF WHICH YOU ARE PROUD

_____
_____
_____
_____
_____

An achievement of which I'm proud? How about that memorable grade four swimming carnival where I couldn't even beat Greg Snelling, a fat sausage boy with stumpy little legs and glasses. Or perhaps they would like to hear about the grade nine debating finals, when, mid-speech (and it was a brilliant speech – we couldn't lose!) I was struck dumb by the ninety-second warning bell and led my team to an inglorious defeat. Then there are the achievements of my brief adult life: above average first year uni marks, high competence in watching TV, and a genuine, although as yet undeveloped, talent for daydreaming. I skip on to the next question.

DO YOU THINK THE WORLD OWES YOU A LIVING?

_____

_____

_____

_____

_____

_____

What sort of question is this? All for a job at the Pancake Manor? Are these people insane? And six lines, they want six whole lines, two more lines than they wanted for achievements. Why couldn't they just have a closed yes/no response, a simple tick and it's all over. But no, they want a *reason*, a reasonable reason. In six lines.

All I want is the money, not a job. I want to travel. To be in a big silver bird hurtling towards foreign climes. Okay, I'll put up with a lot to get what I want. I'll put up with rude customers, abusive chefs, impatient cashiers. I'll wipe down the tables and smile and be charming all the while. Okay. No problem. But I'm not going to give them the satisfaction of answering this bullshit question.

The whining guitar solo of 'Hotel California' fades into oblivion, only to be replaced by the even more whining voice of Neil Young: 'The Needle and the Damage Done.' I stand up, more confused than ever. I step over to get a closer look at the reproduction of the forest and start counting leaves. My mind races with all sorts of responses to their stupid question.

DO YOU THINK THE WORLD OWES YOU A LIVING? (possibility A)
The Soviet Union's Constitution ensures the right to work, the right to rest and leisure, the right to health protection, the right to maintenance in old age and sickness, the right to housing, the right to education and the right to enjoy cultural benefits. Why should the irrational, arbitrary nature of supply and demand (equilibrium? nonsense!) and private property decide who works and who doesn't? From each according to his abilities, to each according to his needs.

DO YOU THINK THE WORLD OWES YOU A LIVING? (possibility B)
Governments should recognise their responsibilities and assist in providing the opportunity of employment for all who want to work. The market, while ensuring a high standard of living, can't alone guarantee jobs for all. Cooperation between Government, Trade Unions and Employers' Associations, the creation of training schemes, reorientation programs, the gearing of education to life skills and workforce preparation, all this can result in a fairer, more inclusive job market.

DO YOU THINK THE WORLD OWES YOU A LIVING? (possibility C)
Full employment is desirable but can't be guaranteed. Employers, in order to operate without unnecessary constraints, have the right to keep their labour needs sensitive to market needs. In an ever-expanding and diversifying economy, employees must be both flexible and adaptable, ready to accept job changes, and willing to retrain in new areas. Short-term unemployment may be inevitable. More entrenched forms are regrettable but at times unavoidable in the current economic climate.

DO YOU THINK THE WORLD OWES YOU A LIVING? (possibility D)
Drop all the small 'l' pinko bullshit. Dole bludgers don't want to work. If I didn't have a job, I'd ring up some factory boss, ask him if there was someone who wasn't pulling their weight, and say I'd work twice as hard for $50 less. Government handouts aren't helping. Who wants to work when you can get paid for doing nothing? Young people can go straight on the dole after leaving school. That's not

going to help them find work. They've got to learn to get off their arses and look after Number One. If everyone did that, there wouldn't be any unemployment.

DO YOU THINK THE WORLD OWES YOU A LIVING? (possibility E)
Work is allocated by means of a random order in a system whose functioning no one really understands. Accidentally being born to parents who happen to have access to capital will possibly lead to some job or other if the person in question has the right attitudes, abilities and, of course, lucky breaks. When all these elements are present and fall in the right configuration, the likely outcome will be, best-case scenario, a regular fat pay cheque, prestige, and the right to not work too hard.

The phone rings again, breaking my train of thought. I let it ring until it stops. I go back over to the desk, telling myself that I have to be practical, that I have to compromise, that's it's me who'll lose out in the end, not them. I decide that filling in the achievements section won't cause too much pain. I sit down, take pen to hand, and am about to write (my fifty metres freestyle victory at the grade four swimming carnival), when I hear the sound of footsteps on the stairs.

Steve comes into the room, followed by a woman with dark curly hair. She's dressed in a blue skirt and red blouse, the right pocket embroidered with the Pancake Manor logo. It takes me a moment to realise that it's Mandy. In case I need confirmation she is wearing, clipped to her left pocket, the same identification tag as Steve. I stand up and try, unsuccessfully, not to gawk at her. Noticing my bewilderment, she explains her outfit. 'I've just come from a Pancake Party. I host it as Alice in Wonderland.' Then she adds, more to Steve than to me: 'That wig is a killer in summer.' The pleasantries over, she gets a chair and seats herself next to Steve, who has already taken up his place behind the desk. She asks for my application form. Her face remains impassive as she reads through it. She passes it to Steve and looks up at me.

'So why have you left uni?'

Just as I'm about to answer, the opening riff from 'Satisfaction' fills the room— *do do, do do do, do do do do do, do do, do do do; do do do do, do.* Mandy frowns. Steve reaches under the desk and, with the click of a button, the music stops. It must be a compilation tape of his favourite songs.

I cross my legs and fold my arms, which sends me swaying sideways again. I suddenly remember something I heard about body language in interviews: don't fold your legs or cross your arms, it makes you look as if you're under attack. I unfold my arms, but can't bring myself to do likewise with my legs. Mandy and Steve sit there staring at me. I'm taking too long to answer. The mood in the room becomes decidedly serious.

'I haven't left uni,' I answer, hoping my nervousness doesn't show. 'I'm just taking a year off.'

Mandy nods. Approval? Confirmation of what she was already thinking? Steve just stares at me, unblinking. He hands the questionnaire back to Mandy. She asks:

'You say you've had a few months experience waitering. Where?'

I'm ready for this one.

'In my uncle's cafe. Out west.'

Dubious looks. Rightly so, it's an out and out lie. Steve takes up the reins.

'Why do you want to work here?'

A chant goes off in my head: because you pay more, because you pay more, because you pay more.

'The place has a great atmosphere,' I reply. I get nods from both Mandy and Steve this time. I unfold my legs and lean forward slightly.

'Did you do any drama at high school or at uni?' Mandy asks. 'We need pirates for the kids' pancake parties.'

'We did some drama. A bit. At high school.'

Mandy waits for me to elaborate. I don't. She looks disappointed. She picks up the questionnaire again and leafs through it.

'You haven't answered the last two questions,' she says with an air of slight accusation. Steve drums his fingers on the desktop. Crawler.

'I...I...didn't know what to say.'

'Forget about the achievements,' Mandy says, getting out her packet of Marlboro. 'I'd never be able to answer that either. It's a stupid question. I'll get it taken off the questionnaire. Steve, remember to get it taken off. All it ever does is spook people.' She lights a cigarette and proceeds to smoke it. 'But the last, question, I think the last question is important. So what do you think?'

'What was the last question again?' I ask. Mandy repeats it.

'Do you think the world owes you a living?'

The way she asks transforms the question. It's no longer an intrusive, impersonal command on a questionnaire. There's something very personal in her tone of voice. Something hard and nasty that bespeaks an old grudge, a bad past experience.

'Well, I think that, you know, you've got to, you've got to do what you've got to do...'

Silence. Steve's blank expression seems to soak up my words without leaving a trace. Mandy's face is a hard mask that bounces them straight back at me. Not good enough. Try again.

'...that, well, you know, you've got to...well...'

It occurs to me that they actually want to give me the job. I haven't said anything particularly brilliant, but then I haven't said anything wrong either. I'm young, I'm healthy, I'm well presented. I've got pirate potential. All I have to do is say the right thing one more time. They hate this whole interview process as much as I do.

All my life I've wanted to please people with power over me. Put an authority figure in front of me, and all I want to do is please them. I want to please Steve and Mandy, but especially Mandy, because she's more demanding. With a resolve that surprises me I say:

'You've got to get out there and get what you want. What you need. It's not going to walk up to you or fall in your lap. It's up to you to go out there and get it.'

It's as if someone else is talking.

I can tell Mandy and Steve nearly want to weep with relief.

Mandy stubs her cigarette out in an ashtray. She turns to Steve.

'Will we give him a go?'

Steve nods.

'Check the rosters and start him on two six-hour shifts, afternoons. If he's any good he can have some night shifts after two weeks.'

Steve nods again. Mandy stands, comes over and shakes my hand. I stare at the Pancake Manor logo, but quickly turn my eyes away, afraid she'll think I'm staring at her breast. 'Welcome to Pancakes,' she says with a smile, and leaves the room.

Steve immediately puts the tape on again, bringing Mick Jagger's jaded lament back into the room.

'Dress regulations: blue jeans, not too old, black shoes, sandshoes are okay as long as they're new. And a Pancake T-shirt, which we supply.'

He rifles in the top drawer and produces yet more forms.

'Fill these out at home. What size T-shirt do you take?'

'Mens.' I stand and step over to the forest. I look at the sun, feeling elated and completely hollow at the same time.

'Come back on Friday at four for a two-hour training session. You'll get your T-shirt then. That's all for now. See you on Friday.'

With the forms clasped in my hand I go back upstairs and cross the main dining room. The restaurant is fuller now, one of the long tables that surround the chess board filled with what looks like a group of public servants. Two of them are having a game, one of the players, a man in cheap grey suit, pushing the white queen, half his size, to a new position. Overlooking the dining hall, like a guard in an observation tower, is the girl in the cash pulpit. I pass closer to her. The cash register is an IBM. On its side are Visa, Master, Diners Club and Bankcard stickers. Her fingers are poised at the keyboard as if she was about to play cocktail music. She smiles down at me as I approach.

'I got the job,' I tell her. I have no idea why I want to impress her, but I do.

'Well good for you,' she says with genuine warmth. 'Well good for you.'

Five

The Lucozade bottle rolls back and forth, caught in a dip in the step, until it is kicked forward by a passenger on their way down to the platform, the thin glass clinking loudly but refusing to shatter as it tumbles down the stairs. It bounces off the bottom step, jumps over the Ribena tetrapak and, narrowly missing the puddle of blackcurrant juice, lands on its side and rolls across the floor towards a little girl in red overalls, her wavy blond hair brushing against the collar of her blue anorak as she trots along as quickly as she can, struggling to keep up with her mother who, dressed in a black leather jacket, matching ski pants and stilettos, is walking faster than normal, impatient to get out of the congested station.

The little girl's blue eyes widen with delight as she watches the bottle roll towards her, magically avoiding the feet of one passenger after the next, wiping from memory her mother's refusal of half an hour ago to buy her a Milky Way on their way to the station. The idea that no one else is aware of the bottle gives her delight all the thrill of an illicit secret. As the bottle rolls closer and closer, still managing to avoid passenger after passenger, she feels the same sense of suspense as in a cartoon she had seen that morning where, on a section of spaghetti freeway shot from aerial perspective, the camera slowly zooms down onto a tiny speck (a baby) as it makes its way in a straight line through the gaps in an endless wave of blurred rectangles (cars), the blaring of horns and the cursing of drivers distant but still clear at this height, the same scene then shot from an angle perpendicular to the curb through the space between the cars' wheels, body and road surface, these boundaries forming a transitory frame of differing sizes as one car succeeds another (this process accompanied by a standard studio 'whoosh!' and a blur of colour), a frame through which the baby smiles, its crudely drawn chin covered in dribble, its chubby little arms playfully outstretched to the audience.

At the sight of a woman hurrying down the staircase the little girl's blue eyes widen even more, something about the relative speeds of the woman and bottle telling her that its miraculous journey is about to come to an end. The woman, in her late thirties, with a *Dallas* hairstyle and a mouth that looks as if it had been surgically fixed into a whingeing sneer, is wearing a faded blue denim jacket with tin silver stars pinned to the lapels, a soiled purple T-shirt through which the shape of her nipples can be seen, and a pair of worn, dirty lemon-yellow tracksuit pants. She is extremely fat, most of this weight having collected around her middle, leaving her arms and legs rather thin. Rolls of fat swell against the waistband of her tracksuit pants as she stomps down the stairs in a pair of filthy black trainers with what were once white stripes, the impact of her heavy steps making her excess flesh quiver and ripple against the stretched fabric, these undulating forms flecked with tiny balls of pilled polycotton fibres.

Cast into the rubber soles of her trainers are the words Blade Runners in italic, the serifs of the B and R extended to make it look as if the words have been freeze-framed while moving at a great speed, this impression contradicted by the feeling of absolute stasis given by the rubber and the crude mould in which they have been set. At the bottom of the stairs she steps into the puddle of blackcurrant juice. As she crosses the tunnel the words BLADE RUNNERS are printed in reverse onto the yellow tiles in a sugary solution of street grime, fruit juice, preservatives and processed flavours, which immediately evaporates into the stale air, leaving only an invisible residue.

The little girl suddenly stops, rooted to the spot as she watches the woman hurry forward, her every step closing the gap between her and the Lucozade bottle. Her mother, whose only concern is to get on with her shopping as quickly as possible, hauls at her daughter's arm and curtly tells her to come on. The little girl, more indignant than hurt by her mother's mildly aggressive behaviour, stands her ground, her mouth opening in a kind of gleeful terror as the fat woman gains ground on the bottle with such speed that it looks like she is pursuing it.

The woman's foot descends towards the spinning label, a blend of glittering red-orange and yellow streaks that makes the word Lucozade illegible. The label itself has never touched the dirty floor; two slightly raised strips of glass flanking it take all the punishment, in this way protecting the royal coat of arms printed there, used exclusively by companies that have secured a long-term supply contract with a member of the aristocracy, in this case the Queen herself. This protection is put to an abrupt end by the filthy sole of the woman's right trainer which, bearing her full weight, comes down directly onto the tiny, glittering example of heraldry, smothering it in a layer of grime and fruit juice.

For a split second the woman freezes in mid-step, as do the coat of arms (HONI SOIT QUI MAL Y PENSE : DIEU ET MON DROIT), the bar code (5013 4021), two sequences of letters and numbers whose purpose isn't stated (LH8/21 and C11DLN), the KEEP BRITAIN TIDY logo, the company name and address (SMITHKLINE BEECHAM CONSUMER BRANDS BRENTFORD MIDDX, UK), and a small table for the health conscious:

> NUTRITIONAL INFORMATION   per 100ml
> Energy..309kJ/72cal
> Carbohydrates (as monosaccharide)..............19.3g
> Protein and fat...Negligible

There is also a more comprehensive list, no doubt there by law:

> LUCOZADE SPARKLING GLUCOSE DRINK
> INGREDIENTS: CARBONATED WATER,
> GLUCOSE SYRUP (22.4%w/w), CITRIC ACID,
> LACTIC ACID, PRESERVATIVES (SODIUM
> BENZOATE, SODIUM METABISULPHITE),
> FLAVOURINGS (INCL. CAFFEINE), VITAMIN
> C, COLOUR (SUNSET YELLOW)

and, finally, the brand name and slogans:

> LUCOZADE
> THE SPARKLING GLUCOSE DRINK
> REPLACES LOST ENERGY

Standing there, utterly still, caught in a moment of perfect equilibrium before she either loses or regains balance, the woman glances down and, with the help of the polka dot pattern of raised glass circles that decorates its neck, recognises the distinctive shape of the bottle sticking out from under her foot. The Lucozade TV commercial, set in a gym, flashes through her mind, all gleaming chrome precision-lit against a crisp dark background, where a black athlete, having just finished a punishing workout – pumping iron, straining muscles, spraying showers of sparkling slow-motion sweat against an aural backdrop of clanging steel, grunts of exertion and synthesised piston bursts – is in desperate need of replenishment. Enter a bottle of Lucozade Isotonic Sport (a sister product), which he puts to his lips and tilts back, sucking out the amber liquid with gravity-defying force, his whole body a vacuum that operates on Lucozade rather than air, his Adam's apple, covered in beads of moisture, bobbing up and down in his muscular throat in syncopated rhythm with the diminishing level of liquid that sloshes around violently as it is consumed, his lips, mouth, trachea and stomach now coated with residues of caffeine, lactic acid, metabisulphite, glucose syrup and carbonated water. Having finished his drink he lowers the bottle from his face, sweeps the back of his hand over his rejuvenated lips and, smiling a coy, warm smile, falls into a posture of athletic repose, nonchalantly flexing those biceps and pectorals built up with the aid of regular carbonated glucose hits.

Her gaze locked onto the mixture of pink and yellow light reflecting off the cusps of the raised glass circles on the bottleneck, the sort of colours found in the semi-translucent icing of cup cakes, the woman thinks about how much she hates Lucozade. For her it is not sunset yellow or amber at all, but the urine of a seriously ill person, a sample produced with great difficulty and embarrassment behind a curtain in a doctor's surgery, needed for the testing of the presence of a disease, an unwanted pregnancy, a malignant growth. The first and last time she tried Lucozade was on a very hot day when she was extremely thirsty. The drink, unrefrigerated for whatever reason, frothed up in her mouth like an oven cleaner, transforming from a liquid into a scummy, synthetic foam with a sickening bitter-sweet taste. Furthermore, she can't imagine why she would need a drink especially designed for athletes, considering she never does sport of any kind and can hardly bring herself to walk more that fifty yards. When she does have to do a lot of walking, she does so under protest, marking out a lane in the middle of wherever she is and crashing into people if necessary to show that she is not moving for anybody. Whenever she wants an energy fix she goes for Mars Bars, Kit-Kats, Twixts, Twiglets, Marathons, M & Ms, Milky Ways, Picnics, Bounties, Crunchies, Phileas

Fogg Corn Chips, His Nibbs Crisps, Mentos, Summer Rolls, Milka Swiss Chocolate bars, Hershey Bars, Milky Bars, Milo Bars, Cadbury Fruit'n'Nuts, Brazil Nuts, Yogi Bears, Violet Crumbles, Fry's Five Fruits, Fruit Pastilles, Aeros (peppermint or orange), Toblerones, Weston Wagon Wheels, or anything else sitting in the massive trays of the newsstands to be found in the ticket halls or concourses of almost any station.

The little girl's mother, surprised at her daughter's uncharacteristically stubborn refusal to budge, looks around to see what she is gawping at, and is astonished by the sight of a rather badly dressed, overweight woman pivoting on a drink bottle. In an unconscious gesture she puts her hands on her daughter's shoulders, unable to tear her eyes away from the crucial moment that will determine whether the woman in the yellow tracksuit pants either falls or regains her balance.

Teetering for an instant, she starts to fall, her mouth stretching into an even more pronounced sneer than usual, as if her lips were being pushed against a plate of glass, this sneer crystallising into an expression of pure hatred as her head jerks back.

At this moment a train arrives on the Piccadilly line platform, flooding the tunnel and enveloping the falling woman in its complex roar, the frenetic hammering of metal hitting metal – the carriage's suspension mechanism, the impact of the wheels on the tracks – bouncing off the undulations of the flesh pink walls. As the train slows down, the dying surge of the engine comes to the fore and merges with the hammering metal, only slightly less frenetic, into a bellowing cushion of electromechanical noise into which the woman falls backwards, her right leg flailing forward, her left shoulder pitching back.

A short distance away the Lucozade bottle, kicked by a passerby, revolves on the spot, the gritty surface of the yellow stone scratching its thin glass and slowing its circuits. The woman's body twists as it falls, her breasts simultaneously spilling towards her left shoulder, their movement made visible by the changing volumes of the T-shirt fabric and the position of her nipples. Her head tilts further back and the sneer of hatred now directed at the ceiling is tinged with fear. Points of fluorescent light float across her eyes, across the surface of her crooked teeth, across the garish silver sheriff stars, their lower tips flaring bright as she falls lower and lower. Her fingers splay in confusion, not sure what they will have to do next: grab, support, or cushion.

The train continues to pull into the platform, the hammering of the suspension mechanism slowing to a rhythmic clacking, the shriek of the engine falling in pitch until it is an insistent moan. Now well on her way to the floor, the walls rushing past her in a pink blur, she grimaces and expels a puff of breath to form the sound 'Fu...', her sneer momentarily extinguished, all its hatred pouring into this syllable.

A man walking directly behind her, warned by this cry, quickens his pace in an attempt to swerve around her, but doesn't step far enough to the left and hits her elbow with the strip of metal that divides the two halves of his heavy black briefcase. The pain of the blow shoots up her arm. Her mouth opens wide, round and tense, registering the blow. In blind rage her face twists round after him, a fresh spasm of pain stabbing her neck.

Apart from the slow rhythmic clacking and low moan of the engine, the dragging of metal as the brakes are applied also resounds throughout the tunnel, a grinding of teeth against teeth, a war of attrition between brake pads, wheels and track. Piston bursts sound under the carriages up and down the train.

Her left hip hits the yellow tiles first, the layer of fat there pounded between her hip bone and the compacted stone. Her breasts jolt diagonally across her torso and her *Dallas* hair formations swarm across her red contorted face. Her elbow takes the second blow; dozens of capillaries are crushed under the surface of its thin chaffed skin as it strikes the yellow stone.

The clacking and moaning of the train dies abruptly, leaving a low, steady hum against which the automatic doors rumble open, the heavy sheets of grey metal sliding to in a series of clangs and jolts.

She lies on her back for a moment, then sits up, all the while staring ahead, looking for the man with the briefcase who has now disappeared. 'Fuckin' black bastard! she shouts furiously. Puddles of light fill the film of tears that has spread across her face. 'Fuckin' black bastard! You fuckin' black bastard!' she shouts again, her face flushing. Hot tears continue to flow into the puddles of light on her face. Salt particles seep into the corners of her mouth. Her left hip and elbow throb painfully.

The carriage doors rumble closed, the background hum surges into an hysterical whine as the train picks up speed, this whine at first smothering the rhythmic metallic clacking, then dominated by it as it transforms once again into a frenetic hammering, the battle between the two roaring fields of noise cut off by the close-fitting black tunnel that devours the train, leaving a short-lived echo and the squealing vibration of tracks in its wake.

The passengers flow all around her. They either ignore her, sights set firmly on the next task of the day, unwilling to waste precious brain-space on some incompetent, or give her the sort of look reserved for zoo animals of no particular novelty, ones that have to be given some attention so that people feel they have got their money's worth. The little girl's mother, however, feeling somehow responsible for the woman's dilemma, or perhaps guilty for not having intervened in any way, goes over and bends a concerned face towards her. Before she can say anything the fallen woman turns and, her face red with anger, bellows 'Fuck off! Why don't you just fuck off!' into her face. With a mixture of astonishment and revulsion, the little girl's mother feels a light spray of saliva settle onto her cheeks and lips, her daughter on the verge of tears at the shock of the fallen woman's vicious outburst. Grabbing her daughter's hand, the mother quickly leaves, her face set into a mask of suffering patience that gives the impression she is used to being abused when offering help to strangers.

The fallen woman sits there, rubbing her elbow through the grimy violet fabric of her T-shirt. She closes her eyes, squeezing out the last of her tears, then suddenly opens them again and scans the floor for the object that caused her fall. She spots the empty Lucozade bottle behind her, lying near the crushed Ribena tetrapak. Her hip throbbing, she rises and goes over to pick up the bottle, grasping it in her hand like a trophy. She turns around and walks over to the threshold of the pink tunnel where she stops and, raising her arm with a snarl, throws the bottle as hard as she can at the far wall of the platform tunnel, taking no notice of the passengers pouring into the Thameslink from the recently departed train.

Meanwhile, at the foot of the stairs, the dribble of blackcurrant juice from the Ribena tetrapak stops, a final droplet prevented from escaping by the ragged edges of plastic coated aluminium around the straw hole. A thin film of juice remains stretched across the hole for a moment, then bursts, immediately absorbed back into the remaining liquid lapping at the bottom of the perforation. As she goes to mount the stairs the little girl's mother steps on the tetrapak, her spiked heel stabbing it with such force that a small shower of juice is sent into the air. Pale violet droplets cling to the yellowish white of her exposed heel. Warmed by her skin, they evaporate immediately.

Six

Mr Parker is standing in his favourite spot, a broad expanse of the blackboard behind him, a portrait of the Queen above him. The huge window next to my seat is open, the colour of the sky so intense that you could reach out and rub off a fingerful of its blue pigment. Mr Parker starts to write something on the board, the white chalk sliding and clacking in the quiet of the classroom. I can read the syllable COMM, but the rest is hidden by his stout body. The Queen gazes down at us through her pane of dusty glass. She was once black and white, but over the years has turned the same green as the blackboard.

Adrian Richards, the boy who sits next to me, thinks we should call the blackboard the greenboard. We both have Olympic Stripe exercise books; my stripes are orange, purple and navy, his lemon yellow, gold and light blue. He takes his pad from the desk, rests it on his knees so that Mr Parker can't see, and silently pulls out the middle page. He smirks at me, the fringe of his straight brown hair brushing his blue eyes. Then he starts scoring the fold in the paper with the nails of his thumb and forefinger over and over again.

Mr Parker turns round, his tanned face full of the same benevolent authority as a detective from *Homicide*. Some white chalk has rubbed off onto his narrow black tie, pushed forward by his generous belly. Hands held behind his back, he takes a few thoughtful paces and reveals the words COMMUNIST CHINA. It's time for our history lesson. Last week we did France, the week before that Indonesia, the week before that Brazil. He rubs his chalky fingers through his greying fringe, slick with California Poppy. When the sun fills the classroom in the morning, the smell of hair oil turns the front rows into a barbershop. He starts talking with an enthusiasm he seems to have only for this subject, taking up the story at some point he likes rather than at the beginning.

'At the moment something is happening in China called the Cultural Revolution. Children your age are not allowed to believe in God, Santa Claus or fairytales. They are not allowed to listen to pop music, like the Beatles, for example. They do not have Coca Cola there. They are not allowed to see Western films, such as James Bond. They do not have afternoon television shows like *Batman* or *F Troop* or *Skippy*. They say that it is a fantasy world, an escapist world, that is a world people escape into because they don't want to think about the real world, about their real lives. Also, there is no advertising. They think that advertising is bad for people's minds as well, that it is a form of social control. They do not understand the idea of freedom of choice, that businesses need to tell people about their products so that they can choose to buy the one they need the most. So you can imagine how boring their cities and towns and magazines must look, without advertising to make them look a little brighter.'

We are never expected to raise our hands and ask questions about what he says, his eyes don't scan the room searching for bewildered expressions or bored fidgeting as they do in other lessons. He just looks into middle distance and talks, enjoying himself. Meanwhile, Adrian has finished tearing the paper in half. He puts one of the halves back in his pad, and starts to fold the other into quarters. He undoes it, then scores a small section of both folds at the centre of the paper. In action he is quick but careful. His humour is spontaneous but precise. He has an opinion on everything and watches *Monty Python*, which no one else has ever heard of because no one else is allowed to stay up so late. He's smiling hugely at the Olympic pad paper, at some secret joke. I shove him in the arm with my elbow.

'The government's reason for banning all these things is that it thinks they are bad for the minds of the people. It thinks that these parts of Western culture will contaminate the minds of the people, and make them lose their belief in communism. But that is the official reason, and shouldn't be taken too seriously. The real reason is more that they don't want their own people to see how we live in the West. If Chinese people knew about the high standard of living in Western countries – and Australia has one of the highest standards of living in the world – then perhaps they would realise that there is something wrong with their society.

'In China one of the most important parts of the Cultural Revolution is treating the leader of the country, Mao Tse Tung, like a God. This may seem strange in a country where they don't believe in God, but it is the case. Chairman Mao is the father of the whole country, and represents power. Everyone with responsibility is in a way a small Chairman Mao, and people try to imitate him at all levels of government. People sing songs about how much they love him. The house he was born in has been turned into a museum and many schools are ordered to arrange bus trips so that the children can see it. All schools have portraits of Chairman Mao in the classrooms, and most people have portraits of him in their houses. Many of them don't want to, but they have to because others might accuse them of being Western spies if they didn't, and they could be taken away by the police and put in jail or shot. This type of behaviour is called the cult of the leader, and happens in all communist countries, especially in the Soviet Union, which was the first country to become communist, in 1917. What it is important to know is that the leader is a dictator, and that he doesn't deserve the love of the people. He was not voted into office; the people did not choose him. He chose himself. He is little more than a bully who controls the army and terrorises the people.'

Adrian pokes his finger through the scores in the centre of the paper. He carefully extends the tears a little then, resting the paper on his leg, folds back the flaps to form a diamond-shaped opening. He takes his pencil and draws short heavy lines, like grass, all around the hole. Glancing up to check that Mr Parker is not looking, he covers his finger with saliva and rubs it onto the flaps, repeating this operation until they are shiny. He begins to roll his eyes and snorts with suppressed laughter. I elbow him again, in the ribs this time. He ignores me. His hand trembling, he takes the paper off his knee and places it on his groin. He cups his hand over the paper and his genitals and starts to slide the paper up and down over the grey fabric of his shorts. It makes a sound similar to the rustling gum tree outside the window. He glances over at me, his eyes half-closed in mock bliss, then down at his hand, which he rubs vigorously up and down the shiny plastic-looking material. He works his groin into his hand, moving his hips slightly. The skin round his knuckles reddens. I glance down at his thighs, his lean white flesh spreading over the varnished wood of the seat, the subtle marbling of blue arteries under his skin. From time to time he checks to see if Mr Parker is looking in our direction.

'Life for children of your age in China is very different. They are encouraged to think about "reality". Reality in this case means a mixture of practical things and Communist Party thinking. For example, they still have music and games there of course, but they are likely to sing about making more tractors, or digging up more potatoes, or playing a game that gets them ready for their future jobs in old-fashioned factories. They are forced to join communist organisations for young people where youth leaders organise their activities to the last detail. In this way, the minds of young people are kept on what the Communist Party wants them to think.

'One of the most important ways in which the Communist Party brainwashes the people is through the slogan. A slogan is a short sentence, or it can just be a few words, that sums up a very important idea. In many parts of China people have to learn the slogan of the month in their school, factory, or office, and try to put into practice what this slogan says. For example, while a child your age works at midnight in the rice fields, trying to meet the deadline for his village's quota, he may take strength from a slogan like 'hard work makes you work harder' or some such thing. Many of these slogans come from *The Little Red Book*, written by Chairman Mao, which is full of short sayings that can easily be turned into slogans. This book is free, and there are millions of them all over China. Many people learn its contents by heart.

'Recently our new government "recognised" this communist government, one of the first countries to do so. This means that we sent them a letter saying that we agree that they really do have a country. Before this, we only recognised a small country next to them as China, which is called Formosa. From now on we will have full diplomatic relations with China. This means that we can send diplomats there. These are men and women who represent Australians and the Australian Government overseas. And the Chinese Government will be able to send diplomats here.'

With a final tug Adrian stops rubbing. He looks over at me again, grinning and smirking. He lifts his hand, the paper stuck to it, and peels it off. The pencil marks have smudged and the flaps curled and frayed. He looks at it with a disgusted expression. He gives me a lewd smile then, leaning over, drops it on my groin. I look at him. His face is hard with challenge and curiosity.

'This is very important, because it means that we will have closer relations with one of our biggest Asian neighbours from now on. Even though we are very different, we can benefit a lot from doing business with them. There are nearly one billion people there. A billion is a thousand million. If we can sell them some of our wheat, or coal, or wool, we can make a lot of money, and become even richer than we are now. We could also sell them technology, so that they could become more modern, and make a better life for their people. But many people don't want to sell them too much technology in case they become too modern and too powerful, and try to dominate us.'

I cup my hands over the paper. It feels damp. I begin to rub up and down. Adrian is nearly gagging in his effort not to laugh, staring at the floor, then at me, his face swollen with energy. The more I rub them, the more my genitals seem to shrink. I want to stop, but Adrian's contorted face somehow stops me. My fingers clench tighter. I stare at the sticker on the back of my pad: THIS IS THE YEAR FOR OLYMPIC STUDY GEAR 'COS OLYMPIC STUDY STRIPES...ARE HERE! All at the same time it feels as if I'm rubbing some insensitive piece of flesh, or pushing my genitals back into my body, or as if someone else were doing it. Suddenly I realise Mr Parker has finished talking. I stop rubbing and look up. He is standing motionless in his favourite spot. The fingers of both his hands are spread and joined at the tips. He slowly shakes them up and down at chest level, sometimes scratching his slight double chin with his thumbs. I give the paper back to Adrian. He flattens it out on his knee, grabs his pencil, then writes something on it. Unable to keep back his laughter any longer he splutters out a shapeless yelp.

Mr Parker looks over towards us. Adrian pulls himself together.

'Class,' he says in a gentle voice, his eyes fixed on the powder-blue sky, 'could you please get out your copies of *Jonathan Livingston Seagull.*'

Adrian passes the paper to me. Around the diamond-shaped opening he's scrawled 'Fuck You! Fuck Me! Fuck You!', the vertical strokes of the exclamation marks no different from the short strokes of grass, the full stops nearly stabbing through the paper.

Seven

The Lucozade bottle flies towards an enormous advertising poster pasted to the tunnel wall, one of a series that stretches the entire length of the platform, this variable series repeated in nearly every Tube station throughout the city. Restless passengers stand at the edge of the platform and read the advertisements, some of them engrossed in the ones with long passages of text that resemble magazine articles, though many times magnified.

Standing at the edge of the platform is a young woman in a black leather jacket and an untucked blue-green sweatshirt. She is slightly knock-kneed, and the stripes of her white tights meet in a row of chevrons that point down to the ground. One or two millimetres of the tips of her black leather Doc Marten shoes protrude over the platform edge. As she waits for the next train her thin fingers toy with the green plastic beads woven into the tip of a single fine braid of her long blond hair. Her mouth hangs slightly open; she is suffering from a dazed, disoriented feeling caused by a futile search in John Lewis for a new pair of Walkman earphone covers. Her visit to the huge Oxford Street department store had begun resolutely enough with the home entertainment department as her destination but, in no time at all, turned into series of guilty little detours (women's wear, cosmetics) until, led more by association than by need or want, her trajectory became more and more irrelevant to achieving her goal, taking in visits to white goods (the flat already has a fridge and washing machine), travel goods (she isn't going anywhere), the book section (she can't afford to buy books), finally ending sometime later in a seemingly endless circuit of escalator rides with no specific destination whatsoever.

It is only now that she is waiting on the Tube platform and wants to listen to some music that she remembers the earphones, which she normally would be using, but which are now coiled in the top pocket of her jacket, their tiny holes clogged with fragments of ear wax and hair that have been accumulating there since she started wearing them without their coverings. It revolts her, the fact that her body has slowly been transferring itself to something made of plastic, that something so inanimate could become so personal. A few moments ago, when she had put them on, she felt as if she were slipping into a bed filthy with her own oils and dead cells, the mock choirboy voices of the Pet Shop Boys, one of her favourite bands, only partially penetrating the screen of plastic holes caked with her body effluent and that of her boyfriend, who listens to her tapes as well.

Her shoulders slowly hunching forward, her knees and thighs pressing closer and closer together as she adjusts her balance, causing some of the chevrons on her tights to go out of alignment, she examines the series of huge posters in front of her, to her left a single, enormous eye with a rainbow vanishing into it, to her right a group of rock stars live on stage, the lead singer clutching the shaft of the microphone in one hand, the cord in the other, his sweat-soaked hair frozen in a riot of curls as he throws his head back. The woman's green eyes come to rest on the advertisement directly in front of her, which is made up purely of type. Just as she is about to read it, she feels a wave of fatigue start to build in her body. A tingle of slow warmth blurs her vision; the sensation is not entirely unpleasant and, had she been anywhere else, at home on the couch or in a warm tub for example, it would have been positively luxurious. Here on the crowded Tube platform, however, it is an imposition that only serves to make her body feel ten times heavier. She tightens her knees further and straightens her shoulders, these simple movements seeming to cost her an enormous amount of effort. She becomes aware of the taste of something like stale milk in her mouth, as if she had woken up after going to bed without having brushed her teeth. She frowns in confusion; she can't remember having eaten anything that would leave such an aftertaste. She immediately starts to make a list of everything she has eaten that day – two pieces of toast with margarine, coffee – when her train of thought is interrupted by a faint pounding in her head, accompanied by the sudden need to take a deep breath. Her jaws quiver as she tries to stifle an oncoming yawn. Her eyes watering, she reads:

Thure.
Noable
inly
inments.

Annoyed by the meaningless words, she screws her eyes shut in the hope of being able to focus properly. Against her will, her shoulders begin to slouch forward again. Small tears, too small to fall, seep into her eyelashes, immediately going cold. She feels her sinuses swell, and sniffles.

While her eyes are shut the Lucozade bottle (thrown by the woman in the filthy tracksuit who, the moment the bottle has left her hand, turns on her heel and stomps up the steps towards the exit, even though she had originally been on her way down to the platform to catch the next Tube) sails over her head and hits the capital T of the headline in front of her. By this time the bottle has lost most of its momentum and, due to the angle of impact and the cushioning layers of posters glued behind the one she has been looking at, hardly makes a noise. The bottle also strikes the space between the V and E of the poster glued underneath, these letters part of the title of an advertisement for a horror film.

The advertisement is made up of an illustration of a drowning man being attacked by rats in a sewer. Only the top part of his head is visible; his contorted face, cut off at the chin by sewer effluent, juts up out of the water triple life-size, garishly lit as if by a spotlight. His screaming mouth is stretched into the shape of an arch and, into its blackness, white water rushes under his bared teeth. The background darkness is pierced by the eyes of rats rendered by slanting pairs of short grey brush strokes that could also be read as birds flying over a dark sea. The illustrator has made the man's mouth, which occupies the middle ground, the vanishing point of the composition's perspective, and the rushing water follows lines that disappear into it. His bulging white eyes stare down, only slivers of his pupils visible, at a group of huge rats swimming in an arc towards him, the closest rats only centimetres away from his face.

The young woman in the black leather jacket opens her eyes and tries to concentrate on the headline. Her jaws start to tremble again, this time much more violently. Her lungs clutch for air, and she takes in a series of short, intense breathes, her face creasing and puckering as if she were being forced to swallow something disgusting. Two large tears well into her eyes and run down her cheeks, reminding her of a small packet of tissues crushed into the outside pocket of her leather jacket. She retrieves a crumpled tissue, and, with what seems to be an enormous effort, lifts it to her face and wipes away the tears, the cheap paper, an insipid lime green, rough against her cheeks, every swipe against her skin accompanied by an image of microscopic tufts of green lint clogging up her pores. She sniffles and blows her nose. The pounding in her head increases, reducing the words of the headline to

heuftt
waival
nwelek
instlam.

She closes her eyes again, her feeling of tiredness giving way to intense irritability. If she were able to see the poster stuck behind the one she so much wants to read, she would be staring directly into the man's screaming mouth filling up with water. And if the lines of perspective used to render the streams of water were extended to include her in the composition, she would be standing two metres or so away from the centre of the action (perhaps on a slime-covered ledge instead of the Tube station platform) watching the group of rats race towards the man's screaming mouth, their leathery tails thrashing as they are swept along by the current, their pointed heads jutting out of the water, their pink ears reverberating with the gurgling shrieks issuing from his muck-filled lungs.

One rat, larger than the others, rests on a small piece of rotting driftwood, allowing the current to pull it towards its meal with leisurely contempt. Its size, relaxed posture and arrogant tilt of snout suggest that it is the leader of the pack, and much too intelligent to do anything as demeaning as waste energy swimming towards such easy prey. Underneath its rear foot (the tips of its bone-like claws jutting one or two millimetres over the edge of the rotting wood), the name Carl Brooks has been painted in small letters on the turbid water.

If the drowning man were able to forget his dilemma for a moment – forget the fact that in a second or so the rats with their sharp teeth will be burrowing into his cheeks, or else beginning their feast in his mouth, their hind claws desperate for purchase on his teeth and tongue so that they are better able to ferociously gnaw at the inside walls, chew into the roof of his mouth and through his brain, finally thrusting their blood soaked snouts out of his ears and eyes – if he were able to forget all this and look past his feral aggressors towards the poster's extreme foreground, he would see, floating above the stinking bilge, in crisp white sans serif letters against the sewer darkness, the long list of film credits in reverse:

QUATRAIN FILMS PRESENT A SAMUEL MORRIS PRODUCTION A PAUL SANDERS FILM ADRIEN DELORENZO'S DOCKYARD SHAFT CHRISTOPHER WILLIAMS LIYA KLEIS TAAHA KAY AND MARK ROSE AS THE INFILTRATOR MUSIC BY JOY SHAHAR AND GARFIELD GREVES COSTUMES BY PAULINE POISELLA DIRECTOR OF PHOTOGRAPHY HARVEY VANIN PRODUCTION BEN DIXON VISUAL CONSULTANT MELTON IBIYEMI VISUAL EFFECTS ADVISOR MAX BEYDEREMAN FILM EDITORS AMY PROBST JIM MORRISSEY ASSOCIATE PRODUCERS KAREN SMITHSON AND DAVID KARJANEN EXECUTIVE PRODUCERS JEROME WYNN AND MICHAEL HERMAN SCREENPLAY BY MURRAY MILLER III BASED ON THE SHORT STORY 'DOCKYARD SHAFT' BY ADRIEN DELORENZO PRODUCED BY ALEX H. CORDING AND PAUL SANDERS DIRECTED BY PAUL SANDERS PRISM RECORDING DOLBY STEREO IN SELECTED THEATRES AVAILABLE IN PAPERBACK FROM NEW GRANADA LIBRARY RELEASED BY QUATRAIN FILMS (UK) ©1990 QUATRAIN FILM DISTRIBUTORS, INC.

The young woman begins to yawn again. Millimetre by millimetre her jaws force their way apart, her lungs gulping down the warm dirty tunnel air in time with her quivering jaws in a sort of jerking counterpoint. This time, as the air flows in, she feels an exquisite sense of satisfaction in her aching lungs, quite different to her previous feeling of disgust. Cold air from the tunnel blows against her cheek and she hears the not so distant clatter of an approaching train. Barely able to focus, her mouth opening wider and wider, she stares down towards the tips of her shoes, which need a little polish, and beyond to the space between the train track and curved tunnel wall where, if it weren't hidden by the track, she would have seen the Lucozade bottle and, one metre away, also huddled against the track, a small mouse quivering in terror at the oncoming train. Small pains crease the corners of her mouth as the yawn reaches its climax. The ache in her lungs sharpens to a fine, stinging point then subsides, her blood enriched with oxygen (whatever oxygen the tunnel might contain) on its way to her brain. She feels a surge of energy deep beneath her lethargy.

The clatter of the train is much louder now, and the cold air comes in more substantial gusts, chilly against her neck. As if in response to the cold she explores the stale taste in her mouth and runs her tongue over her front teeth, making the strip of flesh between the top lip and nose bulge out as its sweeps across, dislodging small particles of the Dunkin' Delicious chocolate syrup and hundreds and thousands doughnut caught between her teeth. Yes she remembers now, she had stopped off at a Dunkin' Delicious somewhere near Charing Cross Station. Once more she frowns in confusion. How had she got to Charing Cross Station? Why had she bought a Dunkin' Delicious doughnut, given that she despises fast food on principal, and can proudly say she has never eaten at McDonald's or Wendy's. Her tongue curls around her back molar, top left, where there is a conglomerate of hundreds and thousands, dough and syrup wedged between her tooth and cheek. She pokes the doughnut remnant with her tongue, the sugar sweet against its tip, then swallows it. The clatter of the train draws nearer. Although it seems to take a monumental effort, she manages to drag herself two steps back from the platform edge. She raises her head from where it has again begun to sink towards her chest and looks at the headline one more time. Her vision is much clearer now. The tracks start to vibrate and squeal, these sounds smothered by the roar of the train as it bursts into the tunnel. The train abruptly slows down, and as it approaches, rattling towards her like an antiquated toy, she catches a glimpse of the small sign bolted near the top, where the word HEATHROW can be seen, flanked by a graphic of a small stick airplane, its vertical position suggesting that it is zooming up into the sky.

She turns back to the poster and, a split second before it is blocked off from view by the train, succeeds in reading the headline.

The future.
Now available
in weekly
instalments.

A series of windows packed with bodies glides by her, aquarium tanks full of purposeful, accurate people, preserved in a cloud of amber light. A wall of pale grey, shimmering with fine black dust, squeals to a halt centimetres from her nose. She inhales the smell of dust and metal and winces as the carriage brakes squeal in her ears. In response to the awful, piercing sound she tries to imagine she is wearing her earphones, that she is immersed in a sea of her favourite music, perhaps some Bryan Ferry or Led Zeppelin or Tracy Chapman (or, best of all, some Pet Shop Boys), all of whose tapes she has tucked away in the inside pocket of her leather jacket. The squealing stops and a low humming sound issues from under the train. Impatiently waiting for the carriage to open, she avoids the faces of passengers staring at her through the dirty glass window, one person's face circled by the Tube logo as if it were caught in a gun sight, their eyes hidden from view by the circle's crossbar, which seems to serve the same function as the crudely drawn black rectangles in violent detective or hardcore porn magazines that ostensibly wish to preserve the anonymity of the victim or model. She concentrates instead on the strips of black rubber that seal the doors, staring intently at them, willing them to separate. They open a split second later and, despite her fatigue, she gives herself a self-satisfied smile, as if it was indeed she who had made them open. As the doors part she catches sight of a cluster of rivets embedded in the window frame, their tiny black holes filled with grit, their metal cusps glowing dull silver as they drift by in the murky light.

Eight

It's lunchtime. I'm standing in the college canteen halfway down the queue that stretches along the serving counter. On the other side of the hot food bar serving ladies with doughy arms pile food onto plates. I'm very hungry. The hot corn niblets look good. So does the lasagne. Behind me is a very large, imposing Coke machine. I'm going to buy a Coke there afterwards, and not from the counter, because the Cokes in the machine are colder.

One of my students, Grit, walks into the canteen. I smile at her as she joins the end of the queue. She smiles back with her green eyes and slightly crooked front teeth. She has long blond hair. Some of it has been braided and threaded with rows of tiny bright plastic beads. She usually wears ripped jeans, but today she has a pair of tights on.

I get chicken, chips and a green salad. I feel a Coke just in case, but it's too warm. I pay, and find a table where there's plenty of room and no students from my class. A couple of minutes later she's sitting next to me, silently rearranging her orange juice, vegetarian lasagne and apple crumble with hot custard. We start on our food. Yes, it's one of those miracle canteens that make delicious, wholesome and generously subsidised meals.

And the serving ladies give big helpings: mountains of chips, large juicy chicken thighs, slabs of lasagne. You can buy a main meal, a drink and a dessert for £1.50. An unbelievable £1.50. We look at each other, smiling, chewing. I realise that I've forgotten to get a Coke from the machine.

I ask her about Marxism.

'Oh, Marxism...' she replies through mouthfuls of lasagne, '...we learned many things. For all my life we learned many things, we studied Marx, Lenin.'

'And Stalin?'

'No, not Stalin so much.'

'And what did you learn? In general?'

'Oh, many things. So many things I can't remember.'

Do you mind if I ask?'

'No, of course not. I like to talk of these things. But the words are complicated. So much technical words. I would have to translate all in my head.'

'Did they tell you that capitalism was evil, exploitative, out of date, always in crisis?'

'What means exploitative?'

'To give and get nothing in return.'

'Yes, yes.'

'And did they tell you that in a communist state the workers would not be alienated from their labour?'

'What means alienated?'

'To not be alienated? To feel like you work for yourself and society. That your work develops you, is part of you, not part of the factory, not only for the bosses.'

'Yes, more or less this.'

'And did they tell you that history with a big "H" was moving to one future, one future only, the free association of workers in pure communism?'

'Yes, yes.'

'And that the state would wither away?'

'What means whither?'

'Die, fade, not exist any more.'

'Yes, yes.'

'And that this wasn't just theory, not only ideas, but fact, science?'

'Yes, yes. Scientific Socialism.'

'And did they tell you that the goal of the West was the destruction of communism?'

'Yes, of course.'

'That we in the West are brainwashed, wasteful, living stupid, mindless, hedonistic lives at other people's expense?'

'What means hedonistic?'

'Hedonistic? To do things only for pleasure. Physical pleasure especially.'

'Is this such a bad thing?'

'No, I don't suppose it is.'

We pause and concentrate on our food. It's now that I notice one of my other afternoon students, Ibrahim, a Kurdish refugee in his mid-twenties prone to wearing second-hand paisley shirts, sitting next to Grit. From his half-finished meal it's obvious that he's been there for a while. He tries to establish eye contact with us and cocks his ears in active participation. I avoid looking at him. Maybe if I pretend he isn't there he'll go away.

Grit laughs quietly to herself.

'But you know, the music, oh the music, it was so terrible, no good music at all. Nobody could sing about nothing. Only silly songs, stupid songs, songs about love, always very bad love songs. And the style, oh it was so bad. They copy and copy the West, or they try. It was really ridiculous. Concerts organised by the communist youth organisations. You can't think how ridiculous they are. No alcohol. To be home at eleven o'clock. Everything organised. And now all these bands are gone. We can buy anything we want now, it is not more forbidden. But now the life is not so exciting, of course. Before it was so difficult to get even a Rolling Stones album. It was an exciting project to do this! Now, if you can have money, you can have everything you want. But London, London is so great. I can do what I want. I can go where I want. I can hear all the music I want.'

She scoops up a forkful of lasagne, which she's been cutting into small sections throughout her speech. I catch myself looking at her food, which is one of my bad habits: staring at other people eat while I'm eating. Still trying to dodge eye contact with Ibrahim, I ask her:

'Is this your first time out of the DDR?'

'Yes, yes, this is my first travel. We are the first generation to travel out of the DDR. Even to go to other communist bloc countries was nearly impossible. Can you imagine this! You can't know how terrible it is not to be travelling. Now we can go and live anywhere in Europe. I want to see Italy. To see Venice.'

She returns to her lasagne, eyes fixed on Venice. For a second I see Dirk Bogarde lying on his deck chair in the sun, a dribble of dye streaking his forehead.

Ibrahim takes the pause after the word Venice to be his signal to join in the conversation.

'Oh, oh, this interests me. This subject what you talk interests me. Can I talk with you?' And not waiting for an answer, he fixes his eyes on me and asks:

'You think it no good place?'

'I've never been to Venice.'

'No, not that place. East Germany.' It's hard to ignore him. He's so sociable, so friendly. There he is, a fellow human being who wants to break bread, communicate. What can you do?

'I don't know, I've never been there,' I reply, making a half-hearted attempt to hide my annoyance at his intrusion. 'Ask Grit, she's the East German.'

'But there is no more East Germany,' Grit protests, 'I am German.'

'You think it no good place?'

'It's not so easy to say it was good or bad...' We wait for

her to continue, but she trails off and looks away. Ibrahim is undeterred. Ever polite and affable, he asks me:

'You read *Communist Manifesto*?'

And he produces a slim, battered paperback from under the table and offers it to me for inspection. He seems very keen for me to look through it.

It's a Progress Publishers edition of *The Communist Manifesto* that he's picked up second hand for 50 pence, its acid-filled pages slowly eating themselves away. The margins of every page have been filled with cramped Kurdish words, written in many different coloured inks and sizes. Red, blue, green, brown and violet lines crisscross the yellowing paper and blotchy text. Some pages have been worked over so much that they give the impression of being flow charts of Ibrahim's reading process: there are red lines that dash from a hastily scrawled Kurdish word to a tight circle around the appropriate English one; blue lines wander about, tapering off in front of no word in particular. I'm quietly astonished by the dozens of hours he must have put into this. Most students apprentice themselves to the English of Talking Heads or The Smiths. I close the book. He's waiting for my opinion.

'You've done a lot of hard work reading this,' I tell him.

'You read it before?'

'Yes, I've read it.' I pass it back to him, and, putting it in his bag, he asks with the expression of someone desperate to meet like minds:

'You think it is good?'

'Yes, it is good. Or *was* good. Maybe not so good for today.'

'World is proletariat and capitalists... Capitalists have all things, workers no things... workers must fight with capitalists to be free... this is true now.'

'This may have been true one hundred and fifty years ago. I don't think it's so true now.'

He looks disappointed.

'Of course true now.'

'So, tell me, where is the working class now?'

'In all country.'

'No, I mean what people are working class. We can't say this man is working class, that man is a capitalist so easily any more. Things aren't so clear now.'

'I am not agree with you.'

'Are you working class?'

'I am worker with middle-class habits.'

'And your shirt, is that a middle-class shirt or a worker's shirt?'

'And your shirt?'

'I want to know about your shirt.'

'Shirt not important, why we talk about shirts!' Ibrahim says in exasperation.

'Working class! What is working class?' I counter, also getting annoyed. 'Marx says in *The Communist Manifesto* that the workers have no property, which was true at the time. But now many "workers" buy a house. They have property.'

'But it is no good having property. In communist country no person have property.'

'Does this make people happy? People were not happy with this situation in East Germany.'

'East Germany was no communist. There is no communist country. Maybe Cuba.'

'Yes, maybe Cuba. But Cuba has been having big problems since the Soviets stopped their support. Can it survive? Can it go on in this way?'

'Maybe yes, maybe no. But US want finish Cuba. You think it good Cuba have problems?'

'What I like isn't important.'

'Oh, you are politician. Conservative politician.'

'No, I am not conservative. I said nothing conservative. And you?'

'I am Marxist.'

'Yes, yes, well, maybe you are, and maybe you aren't.

Anyway, I don't agree with your way of looking at things. For you the world is so simple. Everyone is either for you or against you. If I don't agree with everything you say, I'm conservative. Like Christians. Everyone who's not Christian is a devil. It's all the same. Do you believe in God?'

'No.'

'Yes you do. Your God is Karl Marx.'

Grit laughs. I look over at her. Sweet complicity. Ibrahim sees that it's two against one, and resumes his assault.

'So what you believe?'

'What I believe is not important. What do I *see*? That's more to the point.'

'So what you see?'

'I see most countries developing market economies.'

'Market economy no good. Rich people, poor people. No...justice.'

'That's true.'

'So?'

'But I can see nothing else. Only the market. I'm a product of the market. Maybe the market can be good. As long as it's held in control by a strong democratic government.'

'Mixed economy.'

'Yes, mixed economy.'

I glance over at Grit to see what affect my advocacy of mixed economies has had on her. As far as I can tell, so far, so good.

'Oh, you are conservative, so conservative!' Ibrahim shakes his head and grins, as if he's finally trapped me. The word conservative really annoys me. I can't have him thinking I'm conservative. I can't have her thinking I'm conservative. I can't have myself thinking I'm conservative.

'So I'm a conservative, you're a revolutionary, and that's that. Tell me, what will you do when you've won the revolution.'

'Everyone will be equal.'

'You'll *make* everyone equal? What if not everyone wants to be equal?'

'This is stupid thinking. We must be equal.'

At the word equal, Grit says:

'In my country they said everyone is equal. This was not so. They wanted to make everyone the same. The same is not the same as equal.'

We fall silent. Ibrahim picks up his bag and gets ready to go.

'So, you *see* market. What you *believe*?'

'Believe. Believe. What is there to believe? I do. I do things. It's important to do things. Doing is more important than anything else. I need to get on the Tube so I put money in a ticket machine and then go through the electric gates. There's a Coke machine. I put money in it and drink the Coke. That's all there is to it.' I suddenly realise how thirsty I am. He rises, smiles again, and pats me on the shoulder.

'Okay. Goodbye Mr Coca Cola.'

'Goodbye Mr Revolutionary. See you in class.'

Just as he reaches the door I shout after him:

'Oh, wait, there is one thing I can think of that I believe in.'

'What thing?'

I take hold of my piece of chicken by the leg and wave it at him.

'Subsidised chicken.'

He leaves, a smug look on his face.

I turn back to Grit, who's clasping between her thumb and forefinger the end of a row of beaded hair, her green eyes fixed on the spray of blond strands forming the tip. She's no longer smiling. In fact, she looks a little annoyed.

'Oh, you two, you are so silly. You pretend to joke but really you think you are so serious. Serious men who think they can talk about serious things. I speak to Ibrahim before. I like him, he is nice, but he always wants to talk with me for politics. It is very boring. I didn't leave the DDR to be talking to every left person for communism. He thinks he will save the world. And you...' she lets go of her braid and looks me in the eyes '...you pretend to be an insect.' She mimics me: '"I put money in the Coke machine and I drink the Coke and that is all." You are so, so...what is a word for a person who is thinking he is more important than he is?'

'Deluded?'

'No, not that word.'

'Egotistical?'

'Yes, yes, egoist. You are so egotist. Do you really think anyone cares what you believe? I am from an experience that did not work. For me it is not necessary to any more believe anything. It was not necessary for me to believe anything before, why should I start now? Anyway, the most important thing for me now is to stay away from Germany. I want to stay here. To study.'

'Study what?'

'Oh, I am not so sure. I have many ideas. I have thought of this for a long time. I want to apply to university, and they must get my application papers soon. I am not sure which subject to study. I have two I like, but I can't decide which.'

'What are they?'

'I don't like to say. I feel if I will talk about it, I will make a decision, and I am not so sure yet.'

'If it's down to a choice of two, why don't you toss for it?'

'Toss for it?'

'Throw a coin. Every day thousands of people make the most important decisions in their lives this way.'

She laughs.

'It is a very good idea, but no, I don't want to.'

I take a coin from my pocket.

'Look, you don't have to tell me what the subjects are. Heads for one, tails for the other. Okay?' She hesitates for a second, then says:

'Okay.'

'Now, decide.' For a second her amused expression vanishes and she gazes into the future, into the great bureaucratic maze that is the future.

'Ready?'

'Ready.'

I toss the coin. It lands in the palm of my hand and I quickly cover it.

'Are you sure you've decided?'

'Yes, yes, I am sure. Now show me, show me please.'

I uncover the coin. Grit looks relieved.

'So, what will you study?'

'It will not be psychology; the other side was psychology. No, it will be economy. I will study economy.'

In the silence that follows we both sit staring into my outstretched palm, at the tiny copper image of a youthful Queen Elizabeth II, who in turn stares, cool and dignified, at a purplish fragment of chicken thigh that has managed to fix itself to the top half of my thumb.

Nine

Just as the young woman with blond hair is being swept by the crowd into the standing section behind the carriage doors (or shoved rather, as her slowness and lack of coordination has made her fellow passengers impatient, resulting in her being pushed from all sides, this sudden aggression from people who had been, a few seconds before, so passive, jolting her out of her torpor and replacing her sleepy, semi-dazed expression with an indignant scowl), the Lucozade bottle, now positioned directly beneath her and lying flush with the one of the metal train tracks, starts to vibrate from the force of the train's idling engine.

The mouse, hiding in terror behind the Lucozade bottle, waits for the train to leave. It has been unlucky today; not only has it been caught in the no man's land between the tracks, but the entrance to its usual resting place, a crack at the bottom of the platform wall, has been blocked off also, both of these events first time occurrences. Its heart beats rapidly, like some electrical appliance running on too high a current, its large black eyes motionless, in contrast to its whiskers, which tremble in time with the vibration of the enormous machine surrounding it. Despite the deep roar coming from the train's engine, the mouse hears most clearly the even rattle of the

Lucozade bottle against the metal track, the pitch of the rattling sound becoming higher and higher as the carriages creak into motion, clatter overhead and thunder out of the station.

The mouse is pregnant. Her swollen belly drags against the grimy floor of the tunnel, the fur there, once yellowish, now clogged with grease and dirt. Over the past week it has been hard to find food, and she is ravenous. The cleaners have been more efficient lately (part of a management purge), and have swept away most of the scraps of hamburgers, chips and other snacks thrown down the night before by people in various stages of drunkenness and, as if this weren't bad enough, today the trains have been running to an even more erratic schedule than usual, disrupting her routine and making it difficult to forage. Pregnant, forced to eat more than twice her normal amount and growing weaker as the food supply diminishes, she has become more and more desperate, taking the risks demanded by the six strips of flesh growing inside her, such as going out into open areas during the crowded daytime.

In this particular instance, what has made her stay out on the tracks during the arrival of the train is the smell coming from the Lucozade bottle. A few moments earlier, en route back to her nest under the platform, she was diverted by a strong smell that, previously, she had only encountered in the tiniest quantities: an odour sharp and bitter, yet sweet and tangy. Her desire to taste whatever produced it was so overwhelming that she risked going out between the tracks, even though a train was approaching.

The train having left, she rests on her front paws and eagerly licks at the outer rim of the bottle, her tiny pink tongue and moist nostrils following the thread of the screw top, the corner of its grooves covered with dried Lucozade deposits that sting her taste buds with the pleasure of their sharp, bright chemicals. She then starts on the inside, her attention centred on her greedy tongue, which leads her further and further into the bottle until her whiskers bend right back, until her body is wedged up to the shoulders into the mouth of the bottle, her tongue straining forward, aching at the root, the tip darting back and forth from her grimacing mouth to the surface of the glass like an organic piston, licking up ever diminishing quantities of Lucozade, the perimeter of the bittersweet layer ever receding as she pushes herself in deeper and deeper, until she is in danger of squeezing her entire body into the bottle, only at this point stopping and backing out, slowly, painfully, on the way giving the glass lip a few desperate nibbles to see if it can't be eaten.

Once she has withdrawn she sits there, her body quivering from hunger and exhaustion. A sudden gust of cold wind blows through the tunnel, signalling the approach of another train, bringing with it the smell of food from towards the middle of the station, this time real food, meat, vegetables and bread which, once she has had a few more seconds to analyse the smell, seems to be in some state of decay, which hardly seems possible considering the new cleaning regime instigated by the management in recent weeks. Disregarding the dangers of staying out in the open space between the tracks, the mouse leaves the safety of the Lucozade bottle, and keeping as close as she can to the inside of the train track, drags her swollen belly over the metal pins that fix the rails to the damp concrete towards the powerful smell up ahead.

The source of the smell, a fresh starburst of vomit, is much closer than she had thought, only two or three metres away in fact. She comes to the edge of the drying pool, spread over the area between the tracks in layers corresponding to the order of mouthfuls vomited, the edge farthest from the centre obviously belonging to the first, most copious mouthful, the successive mouthfuls impacting on the first, causing it to spread out further and further until it forms this outer limit she now sniffs at excitedly. In a frenzy of hunger the pregnant mouse attacks the first substantial lump she finds, a chunk of mushroom covered in breadcrumbs soaked with red wine, breathing in the yeasty smell that all but effaces the normal Tube odours.

The vomit was produced earlier in the afternoon by a young man who, having received a promotion at the advertising agency he works for, offers to take his colleagues out to lunch at a wine bar near King's Cross station, where he insists on buying three bottles of *Fleuris* at £17.50 a throw, much to the disappointment of his mates, who would have preferred to have gone to a pub and drink lager instead. The waiter arrives and the young man decides on a starter of mushrooms deep-fried in breadcrumbs which he swallows rather than chews, and some of which the ravenous mouse now bites into small pieces with her incisors, digging into the rubbery mushroom flesh that seems to have been hardened by the process of deep-frying and digestion rather than softened, swallowing the pieces her teeth have shredded with a frenzy that suggests she is afraid it will snatched away from her at any second.

The pregnant mouse progresses further into the starburst, her body sliding easily over the puddle of mucous and gastric juices, the pieces of mushroom a welcome change from the plastic coatings of colour-coded wires she had tried to eat a few minutes earlier (the green and yellow had been the softest), and which are still passing through her stomach. Over the past week she has eaten pieces of a vinyl overcoat, the top of a capital letter 'I' from the front page of a tabloid newspaper, the bottom of a styrofoam cup, the left rear fin of McDonald's promotional toy Batmobile pen-holder (made in China), a piece of brick, part of the computerised strip of a weekly travelcard, approximately five millimetres of a tangle of cassette tape (a recording of *Les Misérables*), and some of the moist, black insides of a smashed Duracell battery, none of which gave her any nourishment, their only positive aspect being that they yielded to her gnawing, to her raging hunger.

She reaches the second perimeter of the vomit, which is filled with smaller, softer pieces of matter, some of which have nearly broken down into liquids. These consist mainly of meat, bread, tomato and onions, redolent of red wine, and which are covered by a whitish layer that, when first vomited, was froth, but has now separated into scum floating on a cloudy fluid, the larger chunks jutting out of this milky sea like the tips of icebergs.

After thirty minutes of waiting the young man and his mates have still not received their main meals, their orders probably forgotten. All of them at this stage being fairly drunk, the young man suggests that he and a friend go to a nearby take away and order Donner Kebabs to be consumed in the wine bar as a sign of their dissatisfaction with the appalling service. Everyone agrees that this is a fabulous idea. The young man and his friend reappear fifteen minutes later with the kebabs, cylinders of white unleavened bread filled with meat, tomato, lettuce, onions and chilli sauce. A few moments later the waiter returns. His arms loaded with their elegant meals, he stands staring in surprise at this group of customers laughing, talking and tilting their heads sideways in order to take bigger and bigger bites out of their Kebabs, similar to the mouse who tilts her head so as to gobble down at ever greater speed the remains of the vertically grilled processed meat and pita bread.

The mouse's reason for speed is not so much her extreme hunger, which subsides more with every bite she takes, but rather her fear of an approaching train, which can't be more than a minute away. She also senses she is being watched by some of the people waiting on the train platform. In fact, quite a few people have been watching this spectacle of a mouse feeding on a pool of vomit in the build-up to rush hour from the beginning, some of them taking it in with the same curiosity they would read one of the large advertisements pasted to the tunnel wall, others immediately turning away (but glancing back from time to time), disgusted enough by the whole shabby, degrading mass-transit ritual they are forced to undergo everyday in order to survive in that city, as if having to prove to it that they deserve to live there, as if they must seek its permission to stay, without having to endure the added humiliation of watching some Tube mouse, some travesty of the animal world, so scrawny, so bedraggled, in short, such a pathetic specimen, feed off the puke of one of their number, someone obviously so uncivilised that he or she (most probably he, some ill-bred lager lout or football hooligan) sees it fit to spill their guts in public. The mouse, her whiskers sodden with whitish liquid (the bread?) glances up at these hovering grey shapes, uncertain whether to leave or keep feeding until the train comes. She decides on the latter and makes her way to the centre of the starburst, where she comes across a pool of caramelised liquid which has already started to dry, its skin a mass of small bubbles that have burst and set in the alternating currents of hot and cold air.

The waiter, a man in his mid-forties, quickly recovers from his astonishment and orders the arrogant young men to either dispose of their kebabs immediately, or pay up and leave. The young man, now very drunk, takes on the role as spokesman for the group and informs the waiter that he has been recently promoted, that he is enjoying himself with his kebab, his colleagues and his *Fleuris*, for which, incidentally, he has paid a rather inflated price, and that if the waiter doesn't like it then he can stick it. The headwaiter nods and disappears with the meals. The young man's friends smirk and cackle and continue their little party, which is growing more raucous by the minute and attracting the disapproval of the busy wine bar. The waiter returns (his arms, now free of plates, are revealed to be well-muscled), grabs the young man by the shoulders, pulls him off his stool and frog-marches him to the door. On the threshold he frisks him, pulls his wallet from the appropriate pocket and takes out a few notes before throwing him out onto the street. The entire restaurant watches in silence. The smirks have vanished from the faces of his friends who, too frightened of the waiter's furious expression to do otherwise, pay for their meals and join their now brooding friend outside.

On the way back to the Tube station they succeed in cheering themselves up, and their raucous mood is fully re-established by the time they reach the platform. However, the recently promoted young man suddenly feels ill, and before anyone can stop him, is bending over the platform retching. Staring into the murky space between the tracks, strands of his long black brilliantined fringe stabbing his eyes, his thin fingers clutch harder and harder at the cold non-slip stones of the platform's edge as his stomach muscles violently spasm on themselves. He moans and vomits. His friends find this terribly amusing and urge him on. The first mouthful he expels is greeted by loud handclaps and hoots of delight. He turns around muttering you bastards, you bastards, flecks of regurgitated food on his chin and on the lapels of his dark blue gabardine Topman suit and silk Tie Rack tie bought for him by his mother, with whom he still lives. One of his friends looks over the platform and, turning to his friends, holds his fingers over his nose in the shape of a peg before bursting into guffaws. The young man throws up again, this time to louder cheers and clapping. By the third vomit – the remains of a Mars Bar he had eaten at tea break – his friends have tired of their game and decide to find him disgusting, looking at each other and the surrounding crowd with affected scorn for their gross colleague. They haul him up from his knees and drag him back from the edge of the platform. Leaning against the wall, his legs splayed out in front of him, the trousers of his cheap suit riding up ridiculously high, exposing his white sports socks and bony, hairy ankles, he stares at his worn Doc Marten brogues, the protruding tips of their vulcanised soles streaked with the contents of his stomach, some of the perforated holes in the leather now filled with bits of food. You bastards, he mutters over and over again. You bastards.

After trying a single mouthful of the caramelised liquid whose heavy, creamy consistency blocks her nostrils and makes her whiskers stick together, the pregnant mouse decides to leave. The gusts of cold wind that have been coming down the tunnel have merged into a breeze that quickly gathers strength. The metal rails start to vibrate, giving off a high-pitched noise that sets the Lucozade bottle vibrating again. When the mouse hears the first distant rattles of the train she tries to move but, tired out after the intense feeding session and weighed down by the food and her young, discovers she hardly has the energy. She redoubles her efforts, but her tiny paws slip in the vomit, her belly stuck to the concrete. The rattle of tracks, now deafening, makes her ears quiver, and she stares up at the headlights of the train, still some distance away, her paws feebly thrashing in pool of sour liquid and macerated food particles.

Borne by the wind, an aluminium foil packet floats out of the black mouth of the tunnel towards her. Light from the overhead fluorescents reflects off the packet as it does slow, deliberate cartwheels in the air. It lands in between the tracks and skids to a halt in the pool of vomit, the wind pushing it up against the stranded mouse. The packet gapes open in front of her. With her remaining strength she pitches forward, the front half of her body disappearing into the packet's silver interior, into the remnants of corn chips and other ingredients which, stated on the back of the packet in a small box, are:

> Pure Vegetable Oil, Cheese Powder, Salt, Dried Onion, Yeast Extract, Dried Garlic, Natural Flavouring, Spices and Spice Extract.

Printed to the left of this box is a letter, which says:

My Dear Aunt Agatha,

We have now been in California for three days.
Yesterday, we travelled along the coast by train,
towards the San Francisco Bay.

To occupy ourselves on our journey, we indulged
in a spot of poker until the early hours.

We played with these strange betting chips that

are apparently a valuable delicacy in California.

These corn chips are rolled from a flour paste and well seasoned with spices and garlic. The recipe contains a particularly strong cheese, not unlike one I encountered in Switzerland.

Unfortunately, Passepartout became a trifle peckish half-way through the evening and quietly feasted on our supply.

Needless to say, we lost the game and could not meet our debts. Our fellow gamblers did not take kindly to this and mercilessly threw us from the train.

As I write you this letter, dear Aunt, I am having a cactus thorn removed from a rather unfortunate place. Enclosed you will find some of the temptingly delicious Californian Corn Chips.

Dare I suggest you take them with you to your fortnightly whist drive evening.

Your affectionate
and respectful nephew,

Phileas Fogg.

The mouse, confused and unable to see, scrabbles with her free hind legs, splashing through the vomit in the direction of the oncoming train. On the underside of the packet, scraping along the ground, is an engraving-style illustration of a steam train rendered in exaggerated perspective, its old-fashioned head lamp and wedge-shaped mudguard hugely distorted, as is its funnel-shaped chimney, which belches clouds of white smoke that recede in size along with the carriages, these two lines vanishing into a horizon of tiny desert cliffs and rock formations. The illustrator, for all his or her skill in the use of foreshortening and subject matter (receding smoke, jet of steam from blowing of whistle etc.) has not succeeded in giving the impression that the train is moving: rather, the surfeit of detail, especially in the rendering of the wheels and exposed machinery of the engine, makes the train look utterly still, stalled in the middle of the cornfield through which it is meant to be passing, the billowing smoke issuing from the funnel, motionless, frozen against the pale blue sky. To the right of the locomotive, standing in a clearing amongst fat ears of corn (printed a shiny amber colour), two men with sideburns that flow into bushy moustaches wave cheerfully at the passing train. The man in the extreme foreground, wearing a frock coat and brandishing a top hat, must be Phileas Fogg. The other man, small suitcase in hand, wearing a hacking jacket and waving a more modest hat, could be none other than his companion, Passepartout.

Ten

The purple curtains glide open and the film screen fills with a luminous, deep grey-blue. The white silhouette of a seagull in flight dominates the right of the screen; the left is reserved for the credits, which fade in and out to the time of the opening music, a solemn beat of percussion accompanied by distant violins.

I'm the only person in the theatre. I glance down at my arm: the grey-blue light has turned my skin grey. The purples and reds of the interior, so bright before the lights were dimmed, have turned grey as well. The colour seems to be the colour of my headache, a shapeless pain that has been slowly filling my head since I left home. As the credits continue, the rising volume of the music makes the theatre seem more and more empty. I feel uneasy, somehow responsible for filling up the space, the rows of vacant seats all pointed at the screen. I'm a little nervous because I'm still not used to going to the movies by myself. When I was younger I always went with my big brother and sister, when I was older, only with my brother, now finally alone. It was only after the first few times I went alone that I realised they were missing.

In my lap is a large box of Jaffas, the type you can only buy at the candy bars of cinemas. I tear open the box, and put two in my mouth. I suck on them as gently as possible, allowing their bright orange colouring to dissolve in my mouth. The flood of sweetness makes my head throb; the shapeless grey pain seems to flash with the bright orange. If I cut myself, perhaps I'd bleed Fanta.

The credits end and the screen floods with light: we're flying above the clouds, veils of brilliant gold and white that are sucked out of the bottom of the screen as the camera passes rapidly over them. The soundtrack now consists of a single trumpet that seems to come from the vast emptiness of the sky itself. Then the words

To the real
Jonathan Livingston Seagull
who lives within us all

appear, slowly dissolving into the clouds as the trumpet falls silent.

My saliva has weakened the Jaffa shells to the point where they break easily. I crush them with a little pressure from my molars; the bittersweet taste of warm chocolate is a welcome change from the sickly orange shells. I put another two into my mouth and try to concentrate on the film, but can't. I shut my eyes. As soon as they're closed I feel a presence, the presence of someone near. I open my eyes and jerk my head to the left. No one is there, only empty rows of seats. I remember my brother always used to sit two seats away whenever we went to the movies. I look around the theatre. Light from the screen bounces off its purple walls. My head throbbing, I turn back to the screen; it demands my attention, refuses to let me think about anything else. I want to go home but can't move. The guilt of not being able to fill the emptiness crushes me to my chair. At this moment there's nowhere else in the world I belong more than in this acrylic seat, in the middle of the right-hand row halfway down Cinema Three, basement, Greater Union Cinemas multiplex. I should leave: my headache will only get worse and the rest of my day will be ruined. But if I go, I'll have to leave the cool of the theatre. Outside the midday heat will be melting the bitumen, shrivelling plants, making metal too hot to touch. It's better to be here, alone, hiding in the air conditioned darkness.

I feel a heavy surging in my ears, bordering on pain. I close my eyes and concentrate on the soundtrack. I can hear distant birds; their squawking grows louder and louder until it's as if they are bearing down on me. I become afraid again and the feeling that someone is near returns. The bird cries suddenly stop and I open my eyes again.

The screen is still full of sun-drenched clouds. A lone white bird flies over them: it's Jonathan Livingston Seagull, soaring through a perfect blue sky. The slow, rhythmic music starts up again. We watch him as he's shot from various angles and distances, gliding, flapping, swooping. Then, filling this inhuman perfection, a deep male voice sings:

Lost

this word suspended there, profound, solemn, full of hope, the lone seagull flying through a space echoing with its emotion. The singer continues his song, a simple hymn addressed to the bird on the screen, the lyrics describing a world of painted skies, distant shores, the wings of dreams. After a few minutes, the song finally climaxes on a single word sung in a manner even more monumental than the first:

B-E-E-E-E

this word addressed to both seagull and audience, an audience of one, an audience of me, and I feel the terrible responsibility of that word. I respond to that deep male voice, all-seeing, all-powerful. I respond to that awful command, in spite of my headache, even though I don't have perfect white feathers and am not flying around at 1,000 feet or however high seagulls fly. I respond even though I'm not sure what I'm supposed to respond to, what I'm supposed to BE.

I do my best to concentrate on the film. I've read the book, and try to link it to what's happening on the screen. Throughout the song it becomes clear that Jonathan Livingston Seagull is not just flying around aimlessly, but is in fact trying to perfect a fast dive. He climbs higher and swoops down, climbs again, dives again. Finally, he builds up to his biggest dive. He soars up and then free falls, holding his wings as still as he can. He soon starts to lose control. The camera takes his point of view as he plummets, and the screen is filled by an aerial shot of the sea and sky spinning round and round. Jonathan crashes into the sea, resurfacing a few seconds later looking bedraggled and defeated. Flying off with pained, laboured flaps to the accompaniment of the mournful trumpet, he asks himself why, why can't he flap his wings fast enough? Are seagulls doomed to never fly faster than 62 miles an hour? After a moment's reflection his thoughts become more hopeful, and with a kind of suppressed rapture he muses about high he could really fly, what the world would look like from way up in the sky.

The pounding and surging of my headache starts up again. I put two more Jaffas into my mouth, and this time crunch them up immediately. For a moment I imagine I can smell Jonathan's brine-soaked wings, and when I touch one of the Jaffas I see his round eye, huge and expressionless. I run my tongue over my front teeth, trying to dislodge some of the Jaffa fragments that have stuck there. I start to tremble slightly. I want to leave. The film is stupid. I hate the theatre: the empty seats look like headstones, the headstones of a perfectly maintained graveyard where purple carpet grows instead of grass, where the exit signs flanking the screen lead into the inferno of shopping arcades above. I close my eyes. My head pounds harder and I go into a sort of daze filled with seagull squawks and seagull voices and the roar of surf.

My eyes open onto a helicopter shot of an enormous rubbish tip, flocks of gulls swarming over like sheets of heavy rain. They scavenge through the hills of rubbish: rotting sheets of cardboard, rusted cans, doorless refrigerators. From the split bags of garbage the seagulls pick out shreds of grey muck that must be food, it can't be anything else, judging from the way they gobble it down or at times fight over it. A battered yellow bulldozer ploughs its way through the trash, making new furrows for the gulls to forage in.

The camera cuts to Jonathan standing on top of the now stationary bulldozer, gazing out over the hills of waste at the survival ritual of his flock. He watches two gulls fight over a large piece of food. As the camera closes in, their yellow beaks and vacant eyes are blown up to huge proportions; they streak across the screen as the attacking seagull tries to wrest a stringy grey clump from the beak of its opponent. Again and again the beak of the attacking seagull rams into the head of the seagull with the food, until its head feathers are stained with blood. Finally the defender drops the food and they lock beaks. The camera leaves them at this point and returns to Jonathan, who flies off in disappointment and disgust.

The theatre has become very cold. The elastic band of my shorts digs into the small of my back, but I don't even try to do adjust it: it's as if I'm stuck to the seat. The pounding in my head gives way to a hammering that seemed to be aimed at one spot: the front of my head, to the right. I grip the arm rests and a wave of goose-pimples rises on the back of my thighs. I can't understand why I've come. To watch seagulls act? To watch them peck each other to death? Suddenly I want to shout out aloud, shout at them in their own brutal language. I start to open my mouth. I take in a deep breath of the chilly air. I'll shriek, I'll give seagull shrieks. I feel powerful, strong, as strong as the deep male voice that accused me of not knowing what to be.

Just as I part my lips I feel my row of seats shift, a dipping movement that lasts only a second. To the left. The movement came from the left. I glance over. Four or five seats away there's a man, his head turned towards the screen as if he'd been sitting there for hours. His legs are crossed. Not crossed in the way a man crosses his legs, with the calf muscle on his thigh, but twined around one another, like a woman. I look closer. He's exactly four seats away, exactly four headstones away. The only way to the centre aisle, the only way out of the cinema, is past him: the other side of the row finishes in a wall. I try to concentrate on the film, to forget about him. I tell myself there's no need to be afraid. I stare at the screen, but see nothing; the man's presence bleeds into every corner of the deserted purple theatre. I blink rapidly, and my eyes fill with patches of light reflected off the screen, bright chemical fields of blue, gold and white, Technicolor-VistaVision-Eastman-Kodak-Agfa fields that are clouds and sky, yes they are clouds and sky for Jonathan to fly in.

Why should this man worry me? He's only come to see the film. But why is he sitting so close? I decide to leave. When I've finished my Jaffas, I'll leave. I rummage in the box and find there are still quite a few left, too many. I put a handful into my mouth and crunch them up. The flood of chocolate makes me feel sick: it has the texture of clay. I swallow the nauseating mass quickly, to get it over and done with. After a few moments the nausea recedes. I glance over at the lone man. He's sitting there, watching the film, taking no notice of me. The sight of Jonathan wheeling through the sky, as well as my decision to leave once I've finished my Jaffas, calms me down. Little by little my fingers unclench the armrests.

I watch the film in a kind of daze, following the story more from my memory of the book rather than what's happening on the screen. Jonathan perseveres at his diving experiments. His biggest problem is keeping control at high speeds. After yet another only partially successful dive, he scolds himself for his lack of nerve, for being afraid, for resigning himself to a life of merely gliding around when he knows, in his bones, that he is capable of so much more. He dives again, once again losing control and crashing into the cold slab of wrinkled green, much more violently than before. A few seconds later he resurfaces and climbs onto a piece of floating debris, the base of a wooden crate. He shakes his bloodied head and waterlogged feathers, a tiny broken creature bobbing up and down on the open, featureless sea. The plaintive orchestra starts up again. His voice heavy with resignation, he tells himself that he must live with who and what he is, that he will be a seagull like any other seagull. His head slumps onto the wet plank of wood. The screen fades black.

After a few seconds of blackness the scene continues, this time at night. Jonathan, a shining speck, floats on the sea of dark blue and purple. As the camera bears down on him the sound of violins, high-pitched and sustained, emerges out of the roar of distant spray, out of this chord emerging the deep, rich voice of the male singer. Once again he's singing *B-E-E-E-E-E*, his urgent tones stretching over the full length of the sea. The singer pauses for breath and starts again at a higher, more desperate pitch, which the orchestra matches; he's singing not only to the elements, but also to Jonathan, who, the object of a long zoom, now appears in close-up, still bobbing up and down on his piece of broken crate. Bedraggled as ever, he stirs as if from a deep sleep. His beady eyes focus and he defiantly whispers to himself that his quest is not to end here, that he wasn't born to drown in the ocean. A revelation hits him. He has a choice: to die an ignoble death, or to force himself to fly. His voice starts to surge with joy as he tells himself to look deep within, to confront what burns in his heart, to kindle that flame and to achieve what he knows he can achieve if only he dares to try. In a surge of strings, horns and cymbals, he takes off into the night sky, the singer's voice soaring around him as he makes his triumphant ascent.

Out of the corner of my eye I look over at the man. He sits calmly, absorbed in the film. On his wrist I can see a large gold watch glinting with the light that bounces off the screen. I turn my head a little, even the tiniest movement making me terrified that I may capture his attention. I look at him as closely as I can. His hair is short at the back and longer on top, just like mine. It's dark and neatly combed, like mine. I turn my head a little more, to get a better look at his face. It's impossible to see properly because of the angle he's sitting at. I turn my head further and squint. I can't be sure, but his skin seems pale. Just like mine. He seems to be smiling to himself, smiling to himself in the dark. I try to figure out how old he is. He's much older than me, perhaps twenty. For a second I imagine he's my future self. Suddenly he moves his leg a little. Startled, I turn back to the film.

Reborn, Jonathan wastes no time getting back to his diving experiments. At first he flies about aimlessly, thinking aloud, talking to himself until he hits upon the secret: dive on the wing tips only, like a falcon. He climbs into the dark blue sky and, tucking his wings in close to his body, goes into a graceful dive, levelling out over the foaming white cliff of a crashing wave. He's overjoyed. After all the self-doubt he's finally proven to himself that his instincts were right; there is a world beyond the world of the rubbish tip, beyond the struggle for survival. He practises all night, perfecting his discovery, increasing the speed and distance of the dive.

By dawn he's mastered not only a basic fast dive, but many other manoeuvres as well: loops, corkscrews, figure eights. Full of enthusiasm for the new world he's seen, he decides to demonstrate his findings to the flock. They are, as usual, scavenging for food at the rubbish tip, waiting for the bulldozer to unearth fresh reserves of garbage, fighting the battle of survival that has become their way of life. At a safe distance, Jonathan starts his demonstration. Many gulls interrupt their feeding and form a small crowd that watches him wheel and dive with extraordinary skill. Spurred on by the flock's attention, and eager to show off his most prized manoeuvre, Jonathan decides to perform his fast dive. He climbs high into the air, tucks his wings in like a falcon, and plummets through the sky. The flock watches in amazement. But their amazement turns to horror when he loses control, ploughing straight through them and causing a flurry of panic as hundreds of surprised gulls scramble to get out of harm's way.

I feel my seat move again. I glance over at the man. He has leaned forward in his seat. His fingers drum lightly on the armrest, making his watch move and flash gold rims of light. His legs are now uncrossed, the one nearest me rapidly jiggling up and down in exactly the same way mine does when I'm nervous or bored. I stare into my Jaffa box. Still too many to get through, way too many. I'll stay until the end of the scene, just until the end of the scene. Then I'll leave. I'll get up quietly, as if I'm going to the toilet, and before he even notices I'll be past him. I'll even say a polite 'excuse me' as I go by. He'll be so surprised he won't do a thing.

Immediately after Jonathan's demonstration, the flock assembles on the nearby shore and cliffs. Jonathan arrives, sure that the meeting has been called to congratulate him on his discoveries. He takes his place in the middle of the shore, eagerly waiting to be rewarded for his achievements. But one after another the gulls turn their heads away; it takes him some moments to realise that the flock is shunning him. He's stunned by their reaction. The elders, perched here and there on the cliffs, look sternly down at him. A cold, hostile silence reigns. Standing on the highest crag is the chief elder, his white feathers immaculate against the blue sky. Slowly, menacingly, he stretches and flaps his huge wings, the low camera angle adding to the grandeur of this gesture. Breaking the silence, the elder announces in an ominous, echoing voice that he, Jonathan Livingston Seagull, has been called before them today to be judged in the sight of his flock …

I look over at the man. He is looking directly at me. His face floats in the semi-darkness. I can see it clearly now. Yes, he's definitely smiling, a calm, glowing smile. Briefly, our eyes meet. Confused, I lean forward, rest my forehead on the hard, slightly greasy acrylic of the chair in front of me, and stare at the darkness between my feet. My shirt tail rides up as I lean forward, exposing the small of my back to the cold air. I feel my skin shining in the darkness. My seat dips suddenly. The elder's voice echoes, cruel, ignorant, in the darkness between my feet as he lays his charges against Jonathan, as he condemns him for reckless flying, for setting himself apart from the flock that has nurtured him, for turning his back on its traditions...

The seat next to me creaks. I press my forehead more tightly against the seat, my eyes screwed shut, plates of black and dark red cracking and shifting over one another. The small of my back is very cold: coldness seeps into the imprint of elastic left by my shorts. I feel the touch of his fingertips, warm and dry, on those faintly aching marks. I freeze. Realising he won't meet any resistance, the man slowly rubs his warm dry hand over my back, lifting my shirt higher as he caresses my side, my chest, tracing a line down my spine before moving downward, gently downward, inching under the elastic of my shorts. I move forward to get away, but this only encourages him. His hand works its way under the elastic of my underpants. My buttocks clench.

All the while the elder continues to condemn Jonathan. He condemns Jonathan's refusal to live as his flock lives, to fly as it flies, to believe as its believes. In a harsh voice the elder reminds Jonathan of the seagull creed, that life is the unknown and the unknowable, that seagulls are put into this world to survive anyway they can, as long as they can...

My seat rocks as the man moves closer. We are shoulder to shoulder. He pauses. I can feel the tense muscle of his arm. He leans over and his hand touches the Jaffa box on my lap. It stops, confused. He puts his hand in and whispers: Can I have one?' A moment later I hear a muffled crunching sound. The hand returns, takes another Jaffa. He puts it to my lips, and asks politely: 'Would you like one?' His breath is sweet. My lips part as he pushes it in with his finger.

Finally, it's time for the elder to lay down his sentence. He rears his wings as he pronounces that, from this moment on, Jonathan will never again see his flock, never again have the protection of his flock, is forever banished, made *outcast*, this last word echoing against the cliffs with a terrible finality.

The man lowers his hand and searches for the front of my pants. His other hand, which had stopped for a moment, continues to inch down. The two hands will not stop until they meet. He pulls the front of my shirt up, his thumb brushing against my navel. The two hands will not stop until they find the centre of my body. I open my eyes and stand up abruptly, the Jaffas spilling out, the screen a harsh blur as I push past him. For a second his hands get caught in my shorts. I struggle to free myself, my shorts pulling halfway down my buttocks. I slip on some Jaffas and fall, my hip hitting his knee, my face and nose knocking heavily against the carpeted floor. I get up and, momentarily dazed, stare at the screen, which now seems like a giant backlit postcard stuck to the front of the room. Two seagulls, Jonathan's parents, are staring back at me, questioning themselves in agonised tones, asking themselves over and over, why, Jonathan, why?

I run up the central aisle, pulling up my shorts. The screen, now dark, now bright, makes the empty seats flash purple. Before I push open the exit door, I look back to see if I'm being followed. The man sits there, the back of his head motionless in the empty cinema.

I lock myself in the toilet and, falling to my knees, hug the cold white porcelain bowl. My headache returns, pounding so heavily that the beige tiles of the cubicle seem to warp in time with the waves of pain, with my heartbeat. I lie there stunned, motionless in the harsh fluorescent light and smell of disinfectant. I notice blood smeared across the bowl, down the front of my shirt. It's coming from my nose, and for the first time I feel the clogging heat in my nostrils. I hang my head over the bowl and watch the drops hit the water, streaking it red, then pink. I am not bleeding Fanta, but Cherry Cheer. My stomach starts to heave. I grip the rim of the toilet bowl and, elbows in the air like wings, vomit up mouthfuls of a thick brown-orange liquid flecked with white, each spasm accompanied by the splash of water and a short, harsh, inhuman cry. I squawk and vomit, the taste of my stomach in my mouth, and take one hand away from the rim of the toilet bowl, shoving it down the back of my shorts to clasp the centre of my body.

Eleven

Once the train stops, the mouse, able to collect her wits in the comparative silence, backs out of the Phileas Fogg packet and heads toward the base of the platform where she finds an escape hole unfamiliar to her but which, in her panic, she nevertheless uses. Feeling calmer in the darkness of the gap between the brickwork and concrete she runs along quickly, further encouraged by a faint current of air blowing against her whiskers. Almost immediately, however, the tunnel narrows and, unable to stop in time, she finds herself stuck, her belly wedged between two jutting bricks. She scrabbles with her hind legs and tries to push herself through to the other side, each tiny increment of progress accompanied by shooting pains in her belly.

Directly above her a tall elderly woman arrives on the platform from the Thameslink tunnel. Her arms are weighed down by two large carrier bags full of groceries, the words Marks and Spencer printed in blue on the white plastic. She is smartly dressed in a fitted mauve trench coat, the belt pulled tight around her waist accentuating her lean build and upright posture. Slightly out of breath from having hurried through the tunnel at the sound of the approaching train, she comes to a sudden stop when confronted with the sight of dozens of people squeezing themselves into the already overflowing carriages.

An overweight businessman in a grey overcoat, determined not to miss the train, pushes roughly past her. She watches him go up to the carriage doorway and pause for a second in front of the people crowding between the doors. He turns around and, suddenly throwing his arms over his head, bends backwards as if he were doing a limbo dance. He grabs the hand rail above the doors inside the carriage, pushes his shoulders into the tangle of bodies wedged there and tries to haul himself in, provoking cries of protest from the other passengers. The all clear whistle blows and the doors begin to roll shut, even though the businessman has not managed to get his whole body into the carriage. At the sound of the whistle he pulls harder on the overhead bar and wriggles back against the unyielding wall of people in a kind of frenzy, the stiff collar of his white shirt partially disappearing under his double chin as his head tilts forward, his eyes darting from one side to the other as he tries to avoid the doors which, in spite of his best efforts, close on his hips. With a muted clanging that echoes up and down the length of the platform, the doors of each carriage come to an abrupt halt. The elderly woman winces, certain that he must have been hurt. The expression on the businessman's face, however, shows frustration and annoyance rather than pain. The doors roll half open and he once more pitches back with his shoulders, more violently than before, his entire body exerting pressure on the compacted wall of people, slowly squeezing itself in, his head tilting further forward and spreading his double chin over his collar until only two tiny white triangles of fabric remain visible. The doors start to close again, the sheets of grey metal rolling into place slowly, cautiously, only millimetres away from his face, their black rubber strips this time closing on a piece of his overcoat, which protrudes from the now sealed carriage like a fin. The all clear whistle blows again and the elderly woman watches the dark grey triangle of material, possibly a wool and mohair blend, drift by as the train departs.

She glances up at the overhead signal board, which says HEATHROW..........5mins, and sighs at the dim prospect of manoeuvring her shopping safely home through the crowd which has rapidly begun to build again. She is standing just outside the Thameslink tunnel entrance, and every third or fourth passenger arriving on the platform knocks her bag of groceries, making it strike against her thigh. She realises she has no chance of getting onto a train if she stays there so, hitting people as if by accident with her carrier bags (an act of revenge she feels is beneath her, but which she quite enjoys), she pushes her way to the edge of the platform and takes up a much coveted position in the long line that forms the border of the crowd, on her left a man with an enormous backpack, on her right a middle-aged woman, the line of people assembled there like some frayed edge of material, a miraculous force binding it, preventing it from being pushed onto the tracks by the crowd that surges behind it as rush hour progresses.

The elderly woman craves a cigarette. On her way to the Tube station she had started one but, misjudging the remaining distance to the entrance, had been forced to throw it away after only a few puffs. If it weren't for the shopping bags, which are becoming heavier and heavier, the tips of her fingers beginning to tingle as the circulation is cut off, she is sure that she would reach into her inner coat pocket and get out a Marlboro, risking public scorn, the shriek of fire detectors, a disastrous fireball, anything to satisfy the nagging in her chest, fuelled largely by the stressful task of having to get home through this crush of people. She can taste the tobacco in her mouth (as well as the residues of the aerosol breath freshener she uses after every cigarette), and for a split second has the sensation she is smoking; she feels her pale lipstick sticky on the soft, light brown filter, the tensing of her mouth as she draws in a cloud of bitter smoke (the air feeding the burning red tip already full of chemicals and

95

pollutants breathed again and again by the tens of thousands of passengers passing though the Underground network), the tightening of her throat as the particles glide down into her lungs where they swirl through a system of tunnels and passages that crisscross and branch out into cavities already rich with nicotine, the swirling motion reversed as she exhales, as she blows the grey blue smoke out through her nostrils, particles catching in the hairs on her top lip which have not yet become so thick that they can't be successfully hidden with face powder. She looks up again at the signal board which, to her surprise, still says HEATHROW..........5mins, even though at least one minute must surely have passed since she arrived.

Following her example (and the example of dozens of others), the young man standing next to her swivels to the right in order to look at the signal board, accidentally hitting her on the hip with his backpack. The backpack is a quality item made up of sections of tough plastic fabric manufactured in Singapore and assembled in Hong Kong. It was once a bright red with blue hood and side pockets, but the colours have been dulled by the layers of grime from numerous countries, as suggested by the international stickers and bag tags covering it. Attached to his body by thick padded straps (which dig into his shoulders) and a loosely fastened waist belt, it seems impossibly dense, much too heavy for even a young man of medium build to carry, stuffed as it is to bursting with clothes, books, maps, tapes and personal sundries, a damp, unpleasant-smelling towel peeping out from under the hood, a dirty pair of trainers dangling from the hood straps by their laces and which at this moment are pressing against the stomach of the short Asian woman standing behind him, much to her disgust. His backpack towers over his head as if it were a person and not a piece of luggage, propped up there like a young woman on the shoulders of her beefy boyfriend at a seventies rock concert.

The elderly woman, feeling the impact of something hard in the backpack, turns her head and glares at him. He is young, probably no older than twenty, with scruffy, short blond hair and a two-week growth that he may be trying to pass off as a beard. He could only be a tourist, one of those lone wolf Australians or Canadians or Americans on his three-month to three-year adventure in the youth hostels of Europe and Asia. The elderly woman continues to glare at him, but the young man, his attention fixed on the signal board, doesn't notice. She gives up, wondering how anyone could be inconsiderate enough to come into a public transport system at rush hour with such an enormous piece of luggage when people like herself were trying to get home and cook a decent meal for their family. In her purse is the receipt for the groceries she has just bought:

MARKS AND SPENCER
OXFORD STREET
VAT NO. 232 1288 92

4 BUTTER CROISS	0.73
/// GROUND ST	2.45
10 OZ DBL CREAM	0.95
CANADIAN HONEY	0.89
SML SHRY TRIFLE	0.49
SMOKED HAM 10	0.99
MULTI TIROLA	1.09
CORN FED CHK	3.01
HOUMOUS 10OZ	0.95
BRITISH STREAKY	0.99
PL DEVON SCONES	0.63
ENGLISH BUTTER	0.69
PLAIN SWISS MOU	0.65
STD-BRIE	0.84
STRAWBERRY CONS	0.89
JAFFA ORANGE	1.19
BROCCOLI	0.99
17 ITEMS TOTAL	18.42

CARD: AMERICAN EXPRESS
16.37 2905 24714 033

MAJOR REDUCTIONS
HOMEWARE
2ND FLOOR.

The groceries were bought with her husband's American Express card, the third from the top of the many credit cards stowed away in the neat compartments of her purse, the first being Diners Club, then Barclay Card, American Express Card, MasterCard, Harrods Card, Natwest ATM card (their forge-proof holograms pleasantly flashing rainbow colours when exposed to any bright light source), followed by a City of Westminster library membership card and finally a British Telecom Phonecard valued at £5 with only 50 pence credit remaining.

The backpacker too has an American Express product: in a denim pouch strapped around his belly under his jeans is a vinyl wallet containing a single American Express traveller's cheque, the last of five thousand dollars' worth that started in denominations of five hundred and worked down to five, the cheques originally sorted into bundles by counting machines back in the far off days of prosperity, shrink-wrapped in plastic like straws or prerecorded cassette tapes, and spent one by one on various items in Italy (coins in the light box for Michelangelo's Moses, pizza), Greece (taxi fares due to public transport strikes, souvlakia), Germany (fruitless and expensive pursuit of American girl, tough-skinned sausages with mustard and sauerkraut), Belgium (fruitless and expensive pursuit of Belgian girl, lonely drunken night in nightclub dancing to The Cure, Talking Heads and Madonna), Holland (on-the-spot fine for fare evasion on streetcar, chips with mayonnaise) and finally Paris, France (three *cafés-au-lait* a day, *crêpes*, rip-off hotel) from where the young man has come just this morning by ferry via Calais to Dover, British Rail to Victoria, and then Victoria to King's Cross by bus in order to catch a fleeting glimpse of London, which he can't afford to see before he flies home to Australia later that evening from Heathrow.

The young man is furious at himself for having squandered all his money on the Continent. London, a city that has fascinated him all his life, and which he had scheduled for the end of his trip with the intention of saving the best for last, will be no more than the public transport system and the airport departure lounge. He also feels ill from the Kentucky Fried Chicken he ate an hour ago en route to King's Cross (the first substantial meal he has eaten in three days), consisting of two pieces of chicken (wing and leg), a tub of coleslaw, a sesame seed bun, a small serving of chips, and a coke, a meal he had developed a mad craving for to the point of dreaming about on the ferry crossing and which, due to the poor quality of chicken and the over-recycling of the fat in the deep-friers, completely failed to live up to expectations. As if to add insult to injury, he feels his arms slowly going numb. He desperately wants to take off his pack, but both his position and the density of the crowd make it impossible. A combination of nausea, the growing pain in his shoulders, and the dialogue of recrimination at his lack of money-sense running through his mind send him into a sort of trance; it would only take a small push from the woman behind him to topple him onto the tracks below. A flicker of light on the signal board, the changing of 5mins to 3mins, brings him to his senses. He straightens his drooping posture and hitches up his backpack, which frees the Asian woman of his trainers, but hits the elderly woman on the hip again.

The elderly woman draws a sharp breath in response to the pain. This time determined to catch his eye and show her indignation, she turns and gives him a wrathful stare. She is on the verge of making a remark, but his blank, self-absorbed expression (perhaps he is on drugs) renders her speechless. The pain in her hands is getting worse, the sections of thin white plastic stretching into narrow strings that seem to cut into her flesh; she is certain that her fingertips must be turning blue. She glimpses the signal board and on seeing the 3mins displayed there immediately resolves not to let the situation affect her; following the advice given to her during a stress management workshop, she concentrates on pleasant images, the first being the bottle of Rochas perfume *Lumière* she also bought that day but which she paid for in cash, not wanting the purchase of yet another fragrance to appear on her husband's credit card statement.

The bottle lies in the left carrier bag on the breast of the shrink-wrapped corn-fed poussin (flown in from France yesterday afternoon), only a sheet of cling film separating its luxuriously yellow skin (so different to the greyish cast of Tesco, Safeway and Gateway chickens) from the deep purple surface of the *Lumière* bottle which, when held up to the light, reflects a spectrum of colours, like a soap bubble, or a patch of oil on water, or an expensive camera lens. The elderly woman breathes deeply, searching for traces of *Lumière*, but seems only to smell stale tobacco. She breathes deeply again, this time able to detect the perfume's fragrant odour drifting up from where it has spread over her skin, from the fingerfuls she daubed behind her ears, on her wrists (now straining with effort), on her neck and a little on her chest, for old times' sake, just for a laugh, a droplet trickling down between her breasts whose nipples sport long curly hairs that she refuses to remove despite the protests of her husband, but which he insists on pulling out whenever she is not looking in some deluded attempt to make her look younger. The alcohol solution, which makes up the bulk of the perfume, has long since dissolved, and the scent, chemical simulations of flowers blended and marketed to suggest light, has penetrated deeply into her skin, into its wrinkles, its pores, where, warmed, it forms a delightful cloud wafting around her, a barrier that protects her from the stale air of the Tube station, of London, of the whole of south east England.

The young man can hardly stand his load any longer; his

shoulders are burning, the small of his back is aching, the inability to move in this dense crowd has made even standing unbearable, the weight of not only his backpack but his whole body centred on his heels, which feel as if they were being crushed through the rubber soles of his trainers and into the concrete. In desperation he looks up at the signal board, which refuses to change from 3mins, even though more time must have passed.

To take his mind off his discomfort he imagines ways of getting enough money to stay in London for at least two days. He would need no more than, say, £30. There had to be hundreds, perhaps thousands of pounds stowed away in the purses, wallets, pockets and moneybelts all around him. How could he get some of it? Pickpocketing? During his brief transit through Victoria he remembers having seen a poster warning people of pickpockets, or the idea may have come to him from Carol Reed's *Oliver*, one of his favourite films when he was a child and whose real purpose (hidden at the time) may have been to plant the image of the Artful Dodger in his head, provide him with a role model that would later help him survive in the kind of tight spot he now finds himself in, penniless in an indifferent foreign country. He could do it here, or in the train when it came, or at Heathrow, this last option being the best due to the open spaces, the number of people eager to get rid of their last few pounds, but also the worst due to the heavy security and, above all, the fact that he would have spent his whole journey out there thinking about it, which would ruin his nerve. No, such an idea had to be acted on as soon as it was conceived: the most important part was spontaneity.

He glances to his left to examine his potential victims, a tallish man in his early thirties, clean-shaven, hound's-tooth jacket; he would have a wallet stuffed full of cash. He glances to his right: a woman in a mauve trench coat with heavy make-up, neat grey hair and a kindly face resembling, remotely, his mother's, who he might be seeing in a day or so. Pickpocket her? It was obscene! How could he rob his own mother? He could just ask her for the money, she would understand. She could only say no, and he wouldn't later regret that he hadn't tried. He turns his head and looks at her. She is staring straight ahead, calm, patient, approachable. Suddenly his heart begins to beat wildly: yes, he will do it, he will ask, it is beyond his control now. Words turn over in his head: Excuse me, you might be able to help me... Excuse me, but I need... Excuse me, I have a terrible problem... He turns to the woman, a pleading look on his face.

The elderly woman, however, has problems of her own, and is no longer paying attention to anything except the large poster pasted onto the tunnel wall opposite. The poster consists mainly of a flat field of blue which, once looked at for more than a few seconds, disorients her, this effect created by the way the colour seems to occupy the fore-, middle- and backgrounds simultaneously. In the middle of this blue field is a compass enlarged to human size, a precision instrument of burnished stainless steel with small cogs for fine adjustments. The left leg of the compass stabs the lower middle of the picture plane with its sharp metal pin, while in the right leg a bright yellow pencil traces a square, still unfinished, the yellow line luminous in the blue field, as if the pencil tip had scraped away the chalky blue background to expose a layer of incandescent mineral. Both compass and square are positioned at a peculiar angle that makes them appear to lean out of the poster and hang over the train tracks. Below the main image there is band of white with the following words:

STOP SMOKING AND REDUCE
THE RISK OF LUNG CANCER
Surgeon's Commission for Cancer Research.

The compass, suggesting a surgical instrument, the yellow line, so much like an incision, the acidic yellow square where a circle should be, the dizzying blue field that makes her feel as if she were falling forward, and especially the words 'risk of lung cancer', these elements, accumulating one by one as the woman's gaze takes in the picture, slowly fill her with fear, a stealthy, step-by-step fear that sends her heart beating faster and makes her conscious of a tightening in her chest. After thirty years of smoking she dreads to think what her lungs must look like (X-rays with shadowy patches legible only to doctors but which represent bitter treacle-like deposits, enormous upside down pieces of broccoli, aerial shots of the Brazilian jungle, mangrove swamps dying from chemical waste, storm clouds floating in a bird cage, the smoke of a burning oil tanker, ruined military installations choked with volcanic ash) and remembers an anti-smoking campaign featuring Yul Brynner, himself dying of lung cancer, his voice once so full, so commanding, reduced to a mere whisper of itself, but making up in gravity for what it has lost in strength as he says: 'Whatever you do, just don't smoke.'

The woman turns her head to look at the signal board, and is met by the young man's stare, a frantic, supplicating stare that she can't break away from, his face, in an instant, having become shockingly intimate, no longer a generic face in the sea of faces to be avoided, but something with eyes, a nose, lips, hair, a configuration of human features filled with urgency that is demanding something of her.

The young man, who is about to address the woman and is in the process of forming the 'ex' of excuse me, his mouth dry, his heart hammering in his chest, is caught off guard by the woman's sudden attention and reacts by hitching up his backpack, striking her once more on the hip with the heavy object packed there, a hardback copy of James Joyce's *Ulysses*, the compact Bodley Head edition of 1960 he had bought for 300 francs at Shakespeare and Co. a month before in Paris, and on the last page of which he has pencilled the following unknown words: quixotic, shibboleths, chilblain, corantoed, phillic, nisi, appellative, nomenclature, kudos, annals, maugre, mogrims, rhabdomancry, anadromous, galoptious, cormac, houched, albeit, viands, prehensile, trapster, trews, vespertine. This time the impact of the book is enough to cause the woman to open her mouth (and, later, together with the preceding two strikes, cause her hip to bruise), though not sufficient to make her cry out in pain.

The elderly woman and backpacker stare at each other, mouths half open. In a nervous reaction the young man, his arms tingling, seemingly weightless, squeezes his fingers against his thumbs and stares into the elderly woman's stunned face, noticing for the first time how her thick flesh-coloured powder soaks up the fluorescent light, charging her face with a glow that reminds him of television faces saturated with colour. He squeezes his fingers tighter and tighter, grinding the layers of chicken fat, salt, the residues of the Colonel's eleven herbs and spices, and the black ink from the headline of the discarded tabloid newspaper he read on the bus, GIVE 'IM ONE!, deeper into the concentric loops of his finger- and thumbprints, pressing the ten surfaces of grooved skin together as if to weld them into a single entity, to transform them into smooth, featureless knobs of flesh at the end of his arms, an undifferentiated mass like the one the crowd has become, its normal flow having been momentarily stopped, the delay in trains interrupting its normal process of self-division and dispersal into smaller units and causing it to slowly implode, to congeal.

Hundreds of passengers watch the time on the electronic signal board change from 3mins to 5mins. Neither the elderly woman nor the backpacker notices.

Twelve

The only round shapes in the office seem to be the clock, which says 8.30, and the arrangement of desks in the middle of the floor. Everything else is right angles: the aluminium-framed windows looking onto the city centre nineteen floors below; the green vinyl floor tiles, their grid pattern mirrored in the ceiling of white plastic squares; the forms and folders spilling over the desktops. The fluorescent lights are on, even though sunlight is streaming into the office. Why are they on? There are some things about the public service I will never understand.

I sit at my desk in the circular configuration, paused between inactivity and the day's work. None of the others has arrived yet, except Chris, the supervisor, who also sits motionless, his elbows on his desk, a streak of light under the long greasy hair swept over his bald spot. His legs, with their long, pilling grey socks and battered loafers, stick out from under the desk. Between his elbows is the flexi-sheet folder.

The morning routine is simple. You arrive, anywhere between 8.00 and 9.30. You go up to the folder where your flexi-sheet nestles in between the flexi-sheets of the other Assessment Clerks. You enter your time of arrival in the time of arrival column. As you sign on you say hi or g'day to Chris, the act of speaking always coinciding with the time of writing. Then you sit down at your desk and start on your batch, a large pile of forms sent from the Data Processing Operator room. If the batches haven't arrived you stare expectantly at the door of the DPO room, always closed.

There are six Assessment Clerks, including myself. Last week Chris arranged our desks into a circle in accordance with new management guidelines. Briefly stated, greater attempts were to be made by section heads to create a sense of community amongst staff. Of all the strategies suggested in this circular letter, which included lunchtime 'sharing' sessions and consciousness-raising workshops, moving the furniture seemed the easiest option. Chris' desk is outside the circle. Wise move, Chris, wise move.

At 8.35 Paul, a young Fijian guy, arrives. He has the neatness that only mothers can give to sons fresh in the workforce. He says g'day to Chris, signs on and sits down at the desk opposite mine, looking clean-cut in his white polo shirt and short black hair. We smile at each other. Paul always looks as if he's smiling. You only notice he isn't when he gives you a real smile, a warm friendly grin. I try to respond in kind, but can never manage more than a watery grimace. Once I went to the toilets and practised smiling like Paul in the mirror. I looked like a used car salesman.

At 8.45 Allen arrives. He crosses the floor, the expression on his face either one of grim resignation or vague terror at the prospect of spending eight hours in the office. He's about thirty and always dresses in what looks like a school uniform: light-blue shirts and grey trousers. Allen never says hi or g'day to Chris; he nods instead, nods and signs. Chris nods back. Allen takes his place at the desk to my right and turns on his electric stapler, which lets out a low humming sound. The batches still haven't arrived. Allen looks annoyed, the standard annoyance of someone who wants to show they're better than the inefficiency surrounding them. Career public servants, they're all the same. Thank God this is only a summer holiday job. I get the morning paper out of my bag and read a paragraph of every article.

At nine o'clock Wayne and Greg swagger in, talking loudly at each other as if there were no one else there, the words 'fuck' and 'shit' and 'cunt' repeated over and over again in the few seconds it takes to cross the floor and sign on, Greg with a pack of Winfield rolled into the sleeve of his Crystal Cylinders T-shirt, Wayne a fag hanging out of his mouth. Wayne wears polyester shirts with stand-up collars that ride too high and goes roo shooting on the weekend. Greg, pudgy and prematurely balding, does nothing in particular on the weekend and is somewhat more urbane than Wayne, his swearing level dropping radically when his mate is not around. Both are in their late twenties and share a flat. You can feel Allen's face tighten at the sight of Wayne and Greg, you can feel an electrical charge of panic go through his skin at the sound of their voices first thing in the morning. Wayne and Greg take their places at their desks and comment to each other on the absence of those fucking cunts of batches. Allen tries to avoid eye contact with Greg, directly opposite him, as well as the smoke from Wayne's cigarette. Paul sits there placidly. He never looks uncomfortable.

At 9.40, ten minutes after the official flexi-deadline, Ted arrives. Wayne and Greg fall silent and smirk at each other as he limps over to Chris' desk, his club foot enclosed in a shoe of heavy black leather. He's a giant, well over six feet, swarthy and heavy-boned, and would appear even bigger if it weren't for a stoop that verges on a hunchback. He has huge staring eyes, one of them bleary and bloodshot, the other clear but apparently paralysed. His nose is large and hooked with hair coming out of his nostrils. He's been working for the Department of Finance for seven years and is a local legend, renowned for his ugliness and stupidity. He is the rock Wayne and Greg sharpen their fangs on. Office life would be inconceivable without Ted.

As Ted leafs through the flexi-sheets Chris straightens himself up and, trying to sound patient, says: 'Ted, you're late again.' Ted finds his flexi-sheet and slowly fills it in. Chris swivels the pad around and checks the entry. 'It's nine-*forty* Ted, not nine-thirty, nine-*forty*. Change it and initial it. Right. Now go to your desk and get to work.' Chris directs this last comment not only to Ted, but to all of us. 'And no bullshit from you two while I'm gone,' he adds, walking across the office and throwing a warning glance at Greg and Wayne. He disappears into the DPO room, no doubt to chase up the batches. A few moments later, Luke, the Clerical Assistant, appears, pushing a trolley stacked with bundles of forms tied with purple string. CAs, the lowest of the low. He drops them onto our desks and disappears into the DPO room.

So here we all are, one big happy family in a big happy circle, paused between inactivity and a day's hard yakka, immersed in a pool of fluorescent-enriched sunlight, or sun-enriched fluorescence, waiting, inexplicably waiting in the positions allotted to us between the floor and ceiling grids. Dazzling dust motes fall through the light, settling on our shoulders, our hair, the tips of our ears.

Wayne turns on his stapler and feeds in a piece of scrap card, stapling the same spot over and over, the burst of sound, as the staples are driven home, like the shots of an air rifle.

Chris' warning fresh in our ears, we get to work. The procedure is as follows: you untie the batch and take an application form, verifying that the accompanying cheque has the same name, address and claim amount as those entered on the application form. Cheques with errors must be put aside for reprocessing. Mistakes occur frequently, due to the high volume and speed of applications processed. Once the Assessment Clerk is satisfied the details are correct, s/he tears off the cheque receipt at the bottom of the form, staples it to the back of the top left hand corner of the cheque, then places the two pieces of paper in the window envelope provided, ensuring that the name and address of the applicant are clearly displayed through the window for effective posting. If part of the address can't be seen through the window, it must be put aside for reprocessing. Each AC must find at least ten errors per day. If ACs consistently find fewer than ten errors per day, their performance is reviewed by the Section Head. Each batch should contain two hundred and fifty forms. Each form should take between thirty and forty-five seconds to process. Each AC should process at least three batches per day.

Paul and I have been doing it for two weeks, Allen for four months, Wayne and Greg, on and off, for four years. Ted is sent down here when other sections have had enough of him. As we work the office fills with the rustle of paper, the sound of tearing, the metallic burst of staplers. Scan, rip, staple, fold, scan, rip, staple, fold, Arthur McKinley, Karen MacRow, Siobhan McQuirter, Ronald McDonald. When I close my eyes at night I hear the staplers and see the succession of names. It's like being forced to read the phone book for eight hours a day. It's only for another nine weeks, I tell myself, only another nine weeks till uni starts. From time to time I pause, dizzy with boredom, and stare at the fake wood laminate desktop, whose streaks are like some flowing stream of brownish liquid that has been freeze-framed. I am surrounded by plastic: green vinyl tiles, brown vinyl seats, white plastic ceiling tiles, surrounded by rigid and flexible polymers, chains of atoms fused together and cut into rectangles and stuck onto every available space, a patchwork of textures and colours imitating everything from skin to marble and inserted between my body and the world.

I look up and watch the others. Paul is methodical, anxious to find errors. Ted wrestles with the sticky tape; he's ripped one of the cheque receipts while tearing it off. Greg furiously tries to keep up with Wayne, who, as usual, has started his mid-morning race with Allen. The staplers set up a continuous volley of shots as Wayne and Allen rip, staple and fold as fast as they can, ignoring the main reason for their job: checking. The rhythm between them becomes a kind of frenzy. For five minutes or so there's a tug of war until they plateau out, neither of them going faster than the other, at which point it becomes a question of who will cave in first. And there is no doubt who will: the pattern is always the same. Wayne always makes some kind of mistake. Today he makes the most common one; he tears a cheque receipt in half, just like Ted, which you can tell he doesn't like at all. He just doesn't have Allen's light touch. No one does. He scowls at Ted and grabs the sticky tape. Just to ram home who's boss, Allen keeps up speed for another few forms, then slacks off and concentrates on finding mistakes, careful to keep up the quota of ten errors per day.

Swearing under his breath Wayne fixes the receipt, then leans back in his chair, at the same time taking a packet of Winfield from his top pocket. He lights up and, his glance flickering between Allen and Ted, draws so hard on his cigarette that he finishes it in a few drags. He screws the butt into the ashtray and, looking at Allen, asks Greg: 'Did you watch last night's movie?' 'Which one?' Greg says with a stupid grin. '*The Hunchback of Notre Dame.*' They start laughing. Wayne turns to Allen. 'What about you, Allen. D'ya see it?' Allen pulls out a dud cheque and puts it in the reject pile. 'I didn't watch TV last night.' 'Well, too bad for you...' Wayne says, leaning back in his chair with leisurely contempt, '...cos Ted here acted real fuckin' well. He was fuckin' brilliant. Weren't ya Ted?'

Ted looks up and fixes his bloodshot eye on Wayne, his other eye staring into space. 'I don't know what you're talking about,' he finally says in a soft, slurred voice. Even though he is trying to appear indifferent, even though he must have heard the same kind of taunt all his life, you can tell he's upset. 'Yeah Allen...' continues Wayne, '... ya shoulda fuckin' seen it. Ted did a...' Allen doesn't let him finish. 'Don't you ever get sick of your stupid jokes? Can't you just leave him alone?' Wayne grins at Greg. 'What a stupid poofter,' he says, lighting up another Winfield and turning to Allen. 'You are such a fuckin' poofter. That lumpa shit's not worth stickin' up for. Look at the stupid cunt. He's a fuckin' monster. Why d'ya stick up for him?' Greg throws in his five cents worth. 'Pieces of shit always stick together.' Wayne guffaws in approval, then says: 'But Allen, if ya like sticking up for Ted so much, why don't ya stick it up him?' Wayne jerks his hips up and down.

This impromptu Tom Jones performance is interrupted by the arrival of Nerrida, head of the DPO section and second in command after Chris. She has permed blond curls and a matching suntan, and today is wearing a short pink skirt with a bright blue lycra top, one shoulder cut away in an Amazon look. After a quick examination of the progress we have made with the batches – during which Wayne and Greg do their own examination of her left breast, most of which is exposed – she tells us to get a move on: our slowness is creating a bottleneck. She reminds Wayne to be careful with the checking.

'Ya know Nerrida,' starts Wayne in a friendly drawl, 'I wouldn't fuck you with a dog's dick.'

Nerrida goes red with anger.

'And I wouldn't fuck anyone whose brain was smaller than his dick,' she snaps back, turning on heel and storming off, her bouncing skirt hem followed by Wayne and Greg's ogling eyes.

We work in silence for the rest of the morning.

At twelve o'clock Paul and I go on our lunch break. Neither of us takes longer than half an hour. Arrive early, short lunch, leave at four. I call it stress management, Paul must have his own reasons. We sign off under Chris' watchful eye, who's returned to oversee the flexi-sheets. At first I hated filling in those mean little squares, barely large enough for the numbers you have to put in them, but after two weeks I've learnt to enjoy it, seeing the folder not so much as a surveillance tool but as an energy map, yet another grid on which I can plot myself. When no one else is around I sometimes flick through the sheets, studying the handwriting, the different coloured pens, the patterns of attendance, telling myself that the flexi-sheets aren't really keep-the-bastards-honest documents, but a series of corrals into which thousands of numbers need to be herded, numbers that otherwise would wander meaninglessly across huge fields of time.

Paul and I catch the lift to the canteen, where I buy a coffee milk, a chicken schnitzel sandwich and a carton of chips. Paul brings his lunch from home, so only ever buys an orange juice Popper. We go back up to the nineteenth floor and eat our lunch in a small tea room no one else uses. Hunched over the low fake wood table, we concentrate on our food, me munching on my sandwich and chips (help yourself Paul), him tucking into his cold samosas (no, no, not for me thanks), his Popper sputtering empty after a few sucks on the tiny straw.

Paul asks me what Christmas presents I'm buying. It being mid-November, I tell him I don't really know; it's early days yet. He launches into a long list of relatives – both near and distant – he has to buy gifts for, and asks me for suggestions about what he should get his kid sister. He produces a picture of her from his wallet: immaculate long black hair, stunning smile, frumpy dress. A family portrait number: mother runs the show in that house. I ask him what kind of music she likes. Heavy metal, he answers, heavy metal. Judas Priest, Def Leopard, Black Sabbath. All their friends in the Presbyterian Youth Fellowship like it too, but their parents don't, no, they don't like it at all. I suggest cosmetics and jewellery, but these ideas are met with an anxious look: he's intimidated by that sort of stuff. On second thoughts, she's probably not allowed to wear make-up. You'll think of something, I say with a laugh, don't worry about it so much. His anxious look is replaced with the usual smile. Thank God for that. It makes me nervous when Paul looks unhappy.

I finish my lunch and ask Paul the time. Five minutes to go. I venture a conversation about work.

'Well, Wayne and Greg gave Ted a mauling today, didn't they?'

Paul's face shows complete incomprehension.

'You know,' I add, trying to jog his memory, 'those sadistic hunchback jokes.'

Paul starts to pack up his lunch things.

'I don't take much notice of the others,' he replies. 'I'm finding it really hard to find the mistakes. I've only found three today. How about you?'

'Two.' It's a lie. I haven't found any. I still can't believe he didn't notice today's little squabble.

'We'd better get back,' Paul says, glancing at his watch.

I tell him I'll be there soon. I dawdle for a minute or so, tearing open my coffee milk carton and crushing all my rubbish into it before sealing it shut again. There, I've done my bit for the environment. So. Well. Really should get back. I'd rather stick pins in my eyes. Anything, Mr Wolf, anything, but don't throw me into the briar patch. I look around the tea room: the same green vinyl and fake wood laminate. On the sink there are some abandoned tea cups, dirty in the way that only public service tea cups can be, fit to be props in some post-apocalypse movie set. I look at the colour of the chair seats, a light brown vinyl that reminds me of artificial limbs. As I go down the corridor, busy offices to my left and right, I glance at the people sitting on these fleshy vinyl rectangles, polymer skins stretched over white foam muscles and held in place with staples. Yes, this place is getting to me. Only another nine weeks. Minus one day.

Before I return to work, I drop into the men's room to wash the chicken and chip fat off my fingers. In such a totally planned building, the men's room smacks of improvisation; it's so small that it's impossible to enter without slamming the main door into the cubicle wall, and it's impossible to enter the cubicle without slamming its door against the toilet. The urinal is so close to the sink that it's a health hazard. I turn on the tap and squeeze soap from the dispenser bolted to the wall. As I wash my hands, I watch drops of pink goo drip to the floor, where they add to the puddle that I realise I'm standing in. I scrub the grease off my fingers, slightly nauseated by the stink of the soap. I practise my Paul smile in the mirror a few times, but it's too close to tell if I'm making any improvement.

Behind me I hear the sudden roar of the toilet flushing. The cubicle door swings open and, reflected in the mirror, I watch Wayne squeeze himself through the narrow opening until he is right beside me. He stands completely still and stares into the mirror, the sleeve of his shirt brushing against mine. Startled, I mumble that I won't be a second, my voice apologetic, as if washing my hands in his presence was some sort of crime. I glance at his face in the mirror. He is staring at himself. 'Yeah, yeah, no worries,' he says to his reflection, his voice offhand, but surprisingly gentle. I move over to the hanging towel, glad to put an end to our body contact. He moves over to the sink, pressing up against me again. 'Four fuckin' years in the army, four fuckin' years in this shithole,' he tells the mirror as he turns on the tap. His muscled shoulder digs into me as he soaps. 'Four fuckin' years,' he repeats under his breath. 'Yeah,' I finally answer as I dry my hands, hating the sound of my crawler's voice. 'Four years is a long time.' He turns to me, his expression a self-deprecating sneer. I can see his teeth, slightly crooked and stained with nicotine. I look down at the floor, unable to meet his gaze. A horrible, frigid pause fills the tiny room, ended only by the squeak of the tap as Wayne twists it shut.

I try not to bolt out of the room but make a complete hash of it, pulling the main door open with such force that it nearly knocks the partition off its mountings.

When I get back to the office I'm met by loud disco music coming through the DPO door which, for the first time since I've been there, has been left open. I watch through the door. Four or five long rows of women are standing behind clean white computer terminals, bringing their arms up over their heads and joining their fingertips in time to the fat beat booming out of the ghetto-blaster on the front desk. Nerrida faces them, her tight blond curls wriggling as she raises her arms, presses her fingertips together and sways her head from side to side, all the time narrating her movements to the Data Processor Operators: 'Lift those arms, squeeze those fingers, tilt left, tilt right, tilt left, tilt right, that's it girls, lift those arms, squeeze those fingers...'

For the most part her troops, dressed in a variety of casual blouses and T-shirts, keep sloppy time with their leader. A few are as crisp and energetic as Nerrida, while others flap their arms half-heartedly. One woman, dressed in a lemon-yellow tracksuit, openly sneers at the whole stupid idea, perhaps especially at the song's ecstatic refrain, *Ce- li- brate good times, c'mon!* being chanted over the mix of bass and cheap Sony treble. Nerrida notices me watching, storms over and slams the door in my face.

I sign on (hi Chris!) and return to my desk, where Paul is hard at work on his batch. I smile at him and he smiles back in an action replay of 8.30 this morning. Not only is time standing still, it's going backwards. I start on my batch and immediately come across three foreign surnames whose spelling I couldn't possibly know: Chwah, Ciucikowski, Crikman. I look at the amount of each cheque, piddling sums of $12.78 and $6.34 and $4.23. I hope they spend their money wisely. Scan, rip, staple, fold. The next two big events in my life will be refilling the stapler and finishing the batch. Whatever I do, I mustn't look at the clock.

At one o'clock Allen returns carrying a clear plastic bag full of Christmas decorations in one hand, a wide roll of sticky tape in the other. He gets up on his desk and, obviously in a hurry to finish before Greg and Wayne get back, fixes thinning fronds of red, green and silver tinsel to the ceiling tiles. At the joins between lengths he hangs a shiny red ball. He jumps from desk to desk until he's constructed a glittering circle over our heads. With a final screech of tape he finishes, then sits down at his desk with a satisfied look. All three of us stare in silence at his creation, the strips of tinsel quivering like the whiskers of a neurotic pet, the scratched red balls gently swaying left to right, right to left. Distorted rectangles reflect off them, fish-eye miniatures of the office below. I can't wait to see what Wayne and Greg think.

Bang on the 2.30 flexi-deadline, Ted fronts up. Soon after, Nerrida briefly appears to complain to Chris about the slowness of the batch processing. At 2.45 Wayne and Greg arrive to an angry reception from Chris who, before leaving for a meeting, gets stuck into them seriously, threatening to lodge a formal complaint. Wayne and Greg give a standard keep-your-shirt-on aw-give-us-a-break response, but you can tell Chris has made his point, especially to Greg, who starts stapling away dutifully as soon as he sits down. Wayne, however, wants to show us he's unfazed. He leans back and, between drags on his cigarette, munches down his Mars Bar. Once it's finished he throws the wrapper into his ashtray then crushes his butt in it, for a second filling the air with the smell of burnt plastic. Then he looks up at the Christmas decorations. I look up as well. He asks in a practised growl:

'Who the fuck hung that shit up there?'

He answers his own question.

'Well it musta bin Allen, good ol' Allen, Ted's bum chum. Thanks Allen, thanks, cos now there's somethin' in the room uglier than Ted.' He laughs at his own joke. Everyone keeps working. Wayne doesn't like being ignored. 'So Ted, ya lumpa Lebo shit, you gonna give a thank you speech to ya bum chum here for makin' the place look so nice. Speech! Speech!' Wayne claps his hands and repeats the word over and over, glancing at Greg to join in. Greg, glad for an opportunity to show solidarity with Wayne, joins in the chorus, stapling a cheque a few times over in time with Wayne's clapping. Suddenly Wayne stops. So does Greg. They lounge back in their ergonomic chairs and stare at Ted, waiting for an answer. After a brief silence, Wayne leans forward and says:

'C'mon ya cross-eyed Lebo bastard, where's our speech?'

Ted rearranges some forms with his large hands, the rustle of paper filling the room. He stops. His shoulders sag forward. He sits there motionless, a mountain behind a desk. Finally he looks up. He fixes his good eye on Wayne.

'I'm not Lebanese. I'm Armenian. I'm not cross-eyed. I have a glass eye.' His speech is slow and clinging. His good eye has blurred over: with tears? What about his glass eye? Can a glass eye cry? There's something strange in the way he says it. I'm not Lebanese I'm Armenian, I'm not cross-eyed I have a glass eye. It's not a direct answer to Wayne's taunting. It's a mantra. It's an inscription in stone at the top of some gate. It's addressed to everyone on the planet and to no one but himself.

'I don't care what fuckin' wog country ya come from ya piece a Lebo pus. And if you don't make a speech I will, ya stupid cunt. Here's a speech for Ted. You are so fuckin' ugly I nearly don't come to work because I have to look at ya. You are so fuckin' ugly it makes me wanna spew. You are so fuckin' hairy ya get five o'clock shadow at nine in the fuckin' morning. You are so fuckin' ugly ya make Quasimodo look like Robert Redford.'

Wayne stops, lights up another cigarette and leans back in his chair. We all work in tense silence except Wayne, who stares at the decorations swaying above, especially the red balls.

'Hey you,' he suddenly says to me. My heart starts hammering in my chest and when I go to say something I find I've lost my breath. I look up at him.

'Get me one of those red things.' It's an order. No animosity. Just an order.

'What things?' I manage to say.

'One of those fuckin' red things, shithead,' he says, pointing above me. 'Now fuckin' well get it down, will ya?'

I climb up on my desk, peel back the tape, give the red ball to Wayne then sit down. Wayne cups it in his hand and looks into it as if he were trying to read the future. He goes over to Ted's desk. Ted stops working and stares down at the form in front of him. Wayne stands in front of him, his collar riding higher than ever like a perverse ruff, and holds the glittering red ball up to Ted's face.

'Here Ted, look into this...' he sneers, '...and see what normal people look like. C'mon Ted, all you gotta do is look into it, and you'll know what it's like to be normal.' He holds the decoration between his thumb and forefinger and crouches down in front of Ted's desk, bringing it closer to his downturned face. 'C'mon Ted, don't you wanna know what it's like?' he almost croons. He places the ball on the desk, right under Ted's gaze, and returns to his desk.

Ted looks up at him, his glass eye focussed on naked space, his other eye streaming with tears. Everyone stops working. I don't know where to look, where it will be safe to look. Ted starts to sniffle, then whimpers low, tortured sounds. Words? Moans? His uneven breathing slowly builds to wet gasps. It's monstrous. Each gasp sends a nauseating charge through me, an energy current I can feel surging through everyone in the circle of desks. We watch him disintegrate. I catch Paul's eye, then Allen's, then Greg's, catch their eye over and over again in a volley of confused glances. Ted covers his face with his hands and weeps for a good five minutes, sniffling, mewling, gasping. Eventually he falls silent. It's like watching someone drown. I stare at his covered face. Gold rings on his fingers. Never noticed them before.

The silence is broken by the sound of sliding paper; Paul has knocked some of his forms onto the floor. Scowling, he bends over to pick them up. Allen goes over to Ted and, putting his arm around his shoulder, around his stooped back, leads him away. A cup of tea. A biscuit. Some cold water on the face. There, there, all back to normal.

One by one, at uneven intervals, we start to rip, staple and fold, first Paul, then Greg, then me. Wayne sits there staring at the glittering red ball on Ted's desk, a thrill in his eyes, a fresh fag dangling from his lips, blue smoke charged with satisfied hate drifting up from his mouth, his nostrils, swirling around the red, blue and silver fronds of tinsel swaying above us in the air conditioned breeze.

Thirteen

A gust of wind blows into the elderly woman's face. She recognises its particular quality immediately, an angry burst of air that attacks from every direction at once, and that always comes a few seconds before the arrival of a train. She glances up at the signal board, which still says, as she had known it would, HEATHROW..........5mins, and gives a satisfied snort of contempt. In a futile attempt to spare her fingers, which are turning blue at the tips, she shifts the handles of her Marks and Spencer bags from the end finger joints to the middle ones, a process that gives minimum relief for only a few moments and promotes the stretching of the plastic handles so that they dig deeper into her flesh. The young backpacker, having had no more than an hour's experience of the London Underground, doesn't notice how the gust of wind contradicts the message on the electronic signal board; unlike the elderly woman, who has been riding the system since she was a toddler and who, if pressed, would perhaps remember how, as a child, she sat on the carriage seats in a frilly white dress, the backs of her chubby legs sticking to the leather upholstery no matter what the weather, her shiny black shoes hanging over the edge, jiggling up and down to the train's rhythm, all around her mouth a sweet film of dried ice cream that she licked whenever her mother, sitting beside her, was not looking, one of those ice creams she always had in the lovely summers of long ago when her body was still unformed, before it had undergone its many transformations, from adolescence to adulthood to middle age to the present day, during which she still uses the Tube system as she has done for over sixty years and whose idiosyncrasies she has, albeit unconsciously, internalised, from, generally speaking, the most efficient connections, the stations to avoid at rush hour, the lines that are slower, that have faulty lifts or escalators to, more specifically, the different passenger speeds and densities at different times of day, the particular types of carriage noises that echo throughout the tunnels, platforms and walkways, as well as the various patterns of airflow, which reveal just as much about the movement of trains as any platform attendant or timetable.

The young backpacker is unaware of these subtleties; he is more concerned with what is happening to his body. The burning in his shoulders is still present but, much to his alarm, the tingling in his arms at times vanishes, leaving gaps of sensation like the silences in a faulty tape recording. The absence of feeling becomes so complete that he imagines he has no arms at all, that they have disappeared, or fallen off. He starts to panic, irrationally, he knows, and tries to calm down by telling himself that he is suffering from fatigue, from stress, from intense disappointment at the premature end of his European trip. But the more he tries to calm himself, the stronger the image of his armless torso becomes; his arms may at this very moment be lying on the ground between the feet of the passengers, waiting to be trampled once the train arrives. Desperate to reassure himself that they are still there, but also aware that the notion of them having fallen off is ludicrous, he lowers his head to get a glimpse of them, but can't see for the bodies wedged in around him. He adopts another strategy, rolling his eyes downwards as far as possible, which at first makes him go cross-eyed, then, straining to focus, glances from left to right, from right to left, a fresh gust of wind blowing fine grit into the exposed whites of his eyes, his field of vision transformed into a murky blur of foreshortened shapes that makes him a little dizzy. Aware that it would only take a small push from behind to throw him onto the tracks, he looks up to steady his balance. He stares straight ahead at the poster with the enormous compass against a grey-blue field, but sees nothing, overcome as he is by a wave of self-pity. His jaw quivers, his eyes moisten; he vaguely realises that the last few days have reduced him to this pathetic state, pauperised, on the verge of hysteria, semi-hallucinating that he is an armless torso. He can't let the situation get to him, he tells himself. He must somehow rise above it. He must be strong.

Suddenly his fingers start to tingle, as if swarms of tiny insects – possibly dust mites, the kind shown magnified in carpet cleaning commercials – were crawling under his skin, this tingling giving way to a hot surge of pain that shoots up his arms and into his shoulders, a sensation that makes him want to cry out in relief at having solid evidence that his arms still exist. His mounting hysteria evaporates instantly; as if celebrating a victory he takes a small step back from the platform edge, pressing his backpack up against the short Asian woman, who also takes a half step back, this gradual reduction of space between waiting passengers a trend that has increased since the sharp gusts of wind began. The young man, able to move his arms again, finds to his surprise that his fingertips are still squeezed together. He releases them – or rather unsticks them, as the layer of newsprint and chicken fat have provided a binding medium that, along with sustained pressure, has made them join together – and wipes them against his thighs. Out of the corner of his eye he notices the signal board change from Heathrow..........5mins to ...TRAIN APPROACHING...

The gusts of wind follow one another in rapid succession, building into an erratic breeze, a mixture of warm and cold air that carries with it muffled sounds that seem, to the elderly woman, simultaneously distant and nearby, sounds that she finds difficult to distinguish, undoubtedly because they have many sources: vibrating metal, scuffing rubber and fabric, coughs, sneezes, snatches of voices, all of these sounds released into the semi-fetid air and mixed by the wind and erodes its fragile layer of face powder, opening up tracts of bare skin and exposing her pores to the clouds of grit whose residues will only become visible later, when she gets home, where it will appear as black smudges on the cotton wool balls she soaks in cleansing mousse and wipes over her face, the cool, fragrant cream applied liberally, its ingredients, plant oils and herb extracts, the direct inversion of and antidote to the negative effects (dryness, ageing) of the blend of fumes and abrasive particles that fills the tunnel air.

With a suddenness that suggests the approaching train is moving very quickly, the tracks vibrate, setting up a noise more high-pitched than usual, like the sound of rain on a corrugated iron roof that starts off as a lazy spatter, but quickly builds to a tinkling roar. The wind blows faster, for a few seconds almost violently, making the elderly woman's Marks and Spencer bags billow out, adding a small increment of weight that increases her pain. Preceded by a furious clattering, the train bursts into the station and roars along the platform so fast that it seems impossible for it to stop. The carriages, densely packed with standing passengers, pass only millimetres away from the faces of the waiting crowd. With an horrendous squealing that gives the elderly woman goose-pimples, the train abruptly stops, the doors of a carriage positioned right in front of her; she can see the overcoats press up against the dirty glass windows of the still unopened doors as they are pushed forward by passengers impatient to get out. Meanwhile, all around her, the arrival of the train has caused contradictory movements among the crowd on the platform. She and others closest to the doors attempt to take at least one step back, in order to allow the passengers to alight, while those further away push blindly forward, determined not to be deprived of a place on the train, in fact jealous that some people have been lucky enough to be standing in the magic spot that will enable them to get home and, perhaps later, even a seat. In spite of her attempts to step back, the elderly woman is pushed forward, until her forehead brushes against the glass of the carriage door, the layer of dirt there giving off a complex odour, like dirt soaked in urine and dried out over a long period, so that its smell is only faintly present, but no less disgusting for it.

Just as her forehead touches its grimy surface, she feels the impact of something hitting the door from the other side. She pushes back and is surprised to see a hand pressed up against the glass, its fingers splayed as if it were about to grab at her face, the way its skin spreads out, especially the fleshier parts of the palm, like the moist belly of a snail fused to a sheet of glass. The elderly woman stares into this surface, at the fractured patterns of dust superimposed over the distorted form of the hand, over the reddish purple lines creasing the muddy pink flesh, weak light catching on the swirling ridges of skin and allowing some of its lustre to penetrate the dirty glass; for a moment she forgets the presence of the surging crowd, the pain of the strips of plastic cutting into her palms, and gazes at the outstretched hand as if it were a sign to be read, something mysterious yet monumentally simple, like a cave painting or ritual object stumbled upon in a remote part of the world.

The hand belongs to a young Japanese woman who, seconds before, pitched forward when the train came to its sudden halt, and desperately tried to steady herself by thrusting her arm out for some support. After hitting the back of a man's shoulder, her hand has ended up against the glass, where she has left it so that when the doors finally open it will provide a lever that will enable both her and her husband, squashed up behind her, to get out of the stifling carriage more quickly.

The way her husband presses up against her, as well as the contortions of her own body in this confined space (requiring a certain patience, dexterity, and suppleness to avoid too much contact with the bodies surrounding her) remind her of the games of Twister she played as a teenager with her family and friends; for a moment she imagines that the carriage floor has been laid with the plastic Twister mat marked out with spaces to put her feet. These games afternoons, usually beginning with cards, or Ludo, or Chinese Checkers, were always well attended by her brothers' friends who, naturally, had no interest whatsoever in the games themselves, but were only waiting for the appearance of the Twister mat (which did not always happen, depending on her mood), and do their best to get as close to her as her protective brothers would allow. Always present at these afternoons in her parents living room – which, being only very small, would often feel as crowded as a rush hour train carriage – was her youngest brother's best friend, who she ignored for years because of his scrawniness but who, through his persistent courting of her, and the later development of both his physique and charm (the former of which she had the opportunity to examine in regular detail over three of four summers on the Twister mat) succeeded in becoming her husband and, years later, in winning a postgraduate scholarship to attend the London School of Economics, thus bringing her to London.

The Japanese woman, although she does not realise it, is pregnant. For two years she and her husband had been trying to have a child but, ironically, considering that for the first five years of their marriage they used every available means of contraception, she had not succeeded in conceiving, at least not until three days ago. Following a method prescribed by her doctor that determines likely times of conception according to the menstrual cycle and body temperature, she realised, just after lunch, that conditions were perfect, and called her husband to demand he come immediately home from university and perform his conjugal duty which, over the last two years, has grown increasingly ritualistic, starting with a lengthy sucking of his penis and testicles – a practice she is still not sure about and did only sporadically, to her husband's disappointment, in their first years of marriage, but which she now often performs in order to prolong his erection for as long as possible, in the belief that this will promote both a more copious amount of semen and a more forceful ejaculation, fellatio being a much more successful technique than prolonged intercourse, during which her husband was likely to ejaculate too early for her liking – followed by, once her vagina is well and truly moist, penetration itself, for which she adopts the missionary position, slowly accepting her husband's penis, waiting for him to work it in before raising back her legs until her knees press against his chest, well-developed from work-outs at the university gym (although he has started to put on weight around the hips and stomach), at the same time putting her hands to his buttocks, at first caressing them, then clenching them as she pulls him into her for maximum penetration, his buttocks hardening as he thrusts, her vagina open, spread, totally accepting of the organ that, for all its singularity of purpose, is nevertheless blind, submerged, potent but dumb. He arches back so that she can watch him, his powerful arms propping up his torso (this display of athletics, while pleasing in its own way, she finds rather irrelevant), then slumps forward until once again his chest is pressing against her raised knees, which in turn press onto her breasts, flattening her nipples. As they make love she continues to press him into her, trying to somehow connect the external mass of his body – lithe, dense, crisply redolent of skin and hair and soap – with the orgasm that is sweeping through her. His body tenses, his thrusts slow down; trembling, he pushes hard against her pubic bone and with a groan, ejaculates. Deep inside she feels his psh psh psh, the spasms at first clearly defined, his orgasm accompanied by a wave of goose-pimples on his buttocks that sends a shiver through her fingertips, his goose-flesh the outer form of what is, for her, the less specifically localised but even more powerful sensation sweeping through her body. She caresses his buttocks until his ejaculations slow and stop. He collapses onto her, his mouth wet and slack against her ear. She flexes the walls of her vagina around his soft penis before she gently pushes him aside. They lie there, a tangle of limbs, breathing in the centrally heated air of their flat, which has become, due to their exertions, too warm, but which is positively comfortable compared to the sweltering conditions inflicted upon them in the packed train carriage, where she is finding it more difficult to keep her arm extended, to keep this route to freedom open, as the passengers from further inside the carriages press towards the standing area in front of the stubbornly closed double doors, their compacting bodies threatening to crush her arm unless she withdraws it.

As passengers from the aisles and seated areas continue to surge towards the doors, the woman's husband is pushed up closer against her. Like his wife, he is used to dealing with crowded public transport systems – although the dirtiness of the London Underground has at times tested his patience – and does not feel particularly uncomfortable wedged in amongst so many people; in fact for the last few minutes he has hardly noticed his surrounds at all, engrossed as he is by an article on genetics and the labour market, the reverse side of the magazine that a neighbouring passenger, hidden from view by its pages, has persevered in reading despite the decreasing amount of space in the carriage. The owner of the magazine, obviously bored by the article, flicks on a few pages, the glossy paper dragging across the Japanese man's face. Not being able to finish the article irritates him nearly as much as the sheer rudeness of the magazine's owner, who must have noticed that her (it is a woman, judging from the long dark hair he had glimpsed as the page was being turned) magazine was brushing against the face of a fellow passenger, but who carries on as if nothing has happened, not even muttering an apology, in fact once again bumping his nose as she straightens the magazine with her fingers. Only a few centimetres from his face is a full-page black and white advertisement, which he starts to examine.

The top of the page is taken up by the headline **Concordia, The Resourceful Provider**, under which are three rows of miniaturised people, standing shoulder to shoulder, the overall effect created being one of lines of type with human figures instead of letters. Each tiny person has been deep-etched against the white background of the page, which makes them appear to be standing on a plane, but also, paradoxically, floating in space, as if they were assembled in an office that had been stripped first of its furniture, then of the floors and walls, then of the landscape itself, leaving only this white corporate void. Underneath them he reads:

> People – the crucial element in making a business work. Concordia has an abundance of them; a working population of 300,000 in an urban concentration of more than a million. With a proud history of exacting standards, and a major presence in vital industries that shape our daily lives.
>
> Concordia's dynamic, diversifying skill pool now includes digital media, aeronautic engineering, textiles manufacture, chemical processing and financial services, in addition to well-established pharmaceutical and fabrication operations.

He looks more carefully at the tiny figures, no more than two centimetres tall. The people chosen (actors? models?) form a selected cross-section of professions and trades, each represented by a small group of two or three standing together: men in suits, men in hard hats, women in long pleated skirts clutching ring-binders to their chests, women with vacuum cleaners or brooms, mixed sex groups in white laboratory coats or catering uniforms. Some of the groups, usually the semi-professionals and blue-collar workers, stand with their arms on each other's shoulders in rehearsed postures of spontaneity. Even though the page is so close to the Japanese man's face that he can distinguish the dots constituting the image, and which makes it hard to pick up any detail, it is still possible to see each and every miniaturised face smiling up at him from the white void, the expressions ranging from, at either extreme, determined half-smiles to muted ecstasy, the majority of expressions pitched somewhere in between, at a kind of compulsory optimism.

The bottom of the page is partially covered by two of the woman's fingers, which are tapered and slightly wrinkled. The Japanese man notices the fingers start to move and, correctly taking this as the signal that she is about to turn the page, shifts his head out of range. The magazine comes to settle on a page with the heading THE WORLD IN HEADLINES featuring news and predictions about the Middle East. Various countries are represented in mini-profiles: Egypt, Iran, Israel, Saudi Arabia and Iraq. He reads:

IRAQ
Population: 19 million
GDP: USD$38 billion (1989)
Foreign Debt: 57,000 (USD Millions)
HDI: 50/130 (1988)
• In all likelihood Saddam Hussein's
  dictatorship will collapse before the end of
  1991. The withdrawal of Iraqi forces from
  Kuwait may extend Saddam's rule for a short
  while, but American pressure is mounting to
  the point where his government will almost
  certainly lose power.
• The international community's patience is
  at breaking point. Politicians are fed up with
  Saddam's blustering and brinkmanship, and
  as sanctions erode and news of atrocities
  continue to come out of Kuwait, there will
  be pressure to...

The blast of a whistle penetrates the carriage from outside, and before he can finish reading the column the magazine vanishes, to be replaced by the face of its owner, whose eyes stare straight into his, the two of them a little startled, as if they had caught each other spying through a keyhole.

The double doors roll open, slowly, painfully, their movement impeded by the bodies crushing up against them. The Japanese woman lunges forward the second they begin to move, her left hand slipping between the black rubber strips, her right hand grabbing her husband's and dragging him forward, past two other passengers who are not quite as fast, and out onto the narrow strip at the edge of the platform only wide enough for her first step.

Blocking the Japanese woman's path are the elderly woman and the backpacker. Since the doors rolled open the backpacker has become little more than a tottering ruin kept standing by the various forces that buffet him from all sides. In fact, giving up his will to the crowd, allowing himself to become a limp rag, a spineless jelly fish is, in the circumstances, the most sensible line of action to take. All he has to do for the moment is stay upright: the crowd will do the rest. The elderly woman, on the other hand, more furious now than she has been for many years, is trying to maintain some sort of dignity, some sense of decorum, and not give in to either her anger or the monstrous herd instinct gripping the crowd; she attempts to step back to let the passengers out, as is only polite, but the wave of people pushing from behind stops her from doing so, crushing her up against the backpacker so that the two of them form a wedge slowly being forced nearer and nearer the open doors.

Once she sees the mass of people ready to pour into the carriage, the Japanese woman, her husband's arms clasped around her waist, checks the speed of her advance as best she can, given that she is also being swept forward by the passengers behind her. Nevertheless she pushes straight into the elderly woman and backpacker; their four bodies merge into a single entity, a conglomerate rock formed, not over hundreds of years, but in a split second. Locked together in this formation, they obstruct only the centre section of the double doors, allowing passengers to manoeuvre themselves in and out of the carriage through the space on either side, this flow of passengers within moments building into a steady stream that binds the four of them even closer together, and which prevents the elderly woman and the backpacker from skirting around the Japanese couple and boarding the train themselves.

The Japanese woman, taking recourse to a technique she has perfected over many years in the Tokyo Underground, swivels her left shoulder forward and works her way into the join between the two bodies blocking her path. The backpacker, whose balance is poor, lurches to the right. Having breached the barrier, the Japanese woman pushes forward, squeezing her body into the growing gap, pulling her husband along with her, their feet shuffling centimetre by centimetre over the non-slip concrete, oblivious to the fact that, as they advance, they are pushing against the elderly woman's Marks and Spencer bag and exerting a steady pressure that stretches the handles to near breaking point, while also causing the strips of plastic to cut deeper into her flesh. The pain in her hands, which has become agonising, as well as the fear of losing her shopping altogether, makes the elderly woman pitch back violently. The Japanese couple burst through the space, leaving the backpacker like a tower about to collapse, and work their way across the platform which has become, in only the last few seconds, less densely packed, other carriages, miraculously, having allowed a more efficient exchange of passengers.

The elderly woman, unable to endure the agony any longer, drops her bags onto the platform and rubs her hands together, feeling the grooves that the strips of plastic have dug into her palms and fingers. At the same time the all-clear whistle blows, followed by the closing of the doors. As the train, heavy, sluggish, clatters away from the platform, her bags slowly crumple upon themselves, the items falling over one another until they come to rest in a new configuration. She glances around to see if the backpacker is still there, but he is nowhere in sight.

Fourteen

The armchair I'm sitting in is so low that my knees are nearly level with my line of vision. Its maroon upholstery – the fabric of the armrests now smooth with the grease of a thousand elbows – sweats in the summer heat like the hide of some decrepit animal. Through the lumpy cushion I can feel the metal springs that have, over the years, forced their tips through the layers of cloth and stuffing, none of them having quite succeeded in piercing the armchair's skin. On my lap rests a stubby of beer, the lone survivor of my six-pack of Four X. I pick up the bottle and swig down the last warm, hopsy mouthful.

All around me Mark'n'Paul'n'Caitlin's party is in decline. The murky living room is now more full of empty beer cans and cigarette butts than people. Those remaining are either sitting on the massive couch, or on the floor with their heads in the laps of boy- or girlfriends, sprawled out in little tribes amidst rock magazines, creased paperbacks and empty Enzo's Pizza containers. Hardly anyone is talking. They sip their beers and smoke their Drum rollies and stare, self-possessed, at the floor, at the ceiling, at the 'What Now Chairman Mao' poster blu-tacked to the wall.

The hi-fi stacked next to me has that latest model look

that makes you want to rush out and trade everything in. The turntable, orange stroboscope flashing, finishes playing some early Miles Davis. I listen to the tone arm glide to its resting place with a gentle clunk, the Bose speakers, ultrasensitive, reporting its every movement.

In front of me Mark'n'Paul'n'Caitlin stand in a circle, Mark'n'Paul on Carlsberg, Caitlin on Jim Beam and Coke, passing a joint, talking to each other as they have been talking all night, although I can't imagine what they could have to say that's so interesting, considering they live together. Still, I shouldn't complain, because after all I'm just a hanger-on, an art school acquaintance Caitlin invited to make up the numbers just in case, an afterthought who doesn't have the good manners to leave when he's being ignored. But I feel brave tonight and have decided to stay on, even though I'm unprotected by a gaggle of like-minds, even though I've just run out of beer. I'll leave when I want to leave, and I won't let anyone or anything pressure me. I order myself to be relaxed, friendly, accessible.

When Paul hears the sharp click of the turntable turn itself off he takes a quick puff of the joint, passes it and his drink to Caitlin, and comes over to where the records are stacked around the hi-fi. He squats in front of me and sets his fingers running over the covers' top edges, deftly tilting them forward, his narrow blue eyes intent on the records. He has fine blond hair, high cheekbones, a lantern jaw, and is wearing a white sleeveless T-shirt that shows off his well-developed biceps. I watch him select a record, whisk it out of its cover and flip it onto the turntable. As he rises his gaze meets mine. I smile at him, knowing full well that he'll snub me. He doesn't disappoint, returning a suitably distant look, the smile on my face freezing into a silly grimace as he clunks away in his Beatle boots and tight black jeans and studded belt – a self-consciously cute blond – back to close the circuit of Mark'n'Paul'n'Caitlin.

He gets his drink back from Caitlin. Tonight she's wearing

an orange garbage bag cut as high as a miniskirt. She's stood in the same spot just about all evening, the party naturally centring on her. The prickles of her bleached blond hair soak up the yellow light of the bare bulb, no more than forty watts, and her red lipstick glows dully as she talks and talks to Mark'n'Paul, to Paul'n'Mark, energising the circuit of Mark'n'Paul'n'Caitlin.

The last time I saw them was a few weeks ago at Caitlin's college performance, based on Munch's painting *The Scream* and titled *The Scream II*, in the spirit of the recently released *Superman* sequel. Mark'n'Paul in attendance, she appeared in an ill-fitting bald headpiece wearing a green garbage bag sticky-taped to her much admired body. Clutching her head, elbows sketching crazy circles, ellipses, and zigzags, she screamed her way through the audience of twenty-five or so who, grazing on carrot sticks and sipping cask wine, listened to her voice range from a sonorous moan to short, fierce shrieks. ('Very painterly,' a painting lecturer later remarked in his written report, 'like the short, fierce brush strokes of her intimate abstract works.') Sycophant that I am, I complimented her on her performance. Three days later she rang to invite me to this party, during which she's cold-shouldered me in every way possible, beginning with a forced smile when I arrived, later progressing to the refusal of eye contact, finally adopting the crudest but most effective strategy in the book: acting as if I didn't exist.

Forced to the periphery, I stare at the all powerful centre. For something to do I play telescope with my empty beer bottle, putting its rim to my eye and staring at the light bulb: an amber glow in dark brown glass. I notice that Paul has forgotten to put the record on, so I lean over and press the play button. Seconds later the strumming of an acoustic guitar fades into the room. An English voice, plaintive and wan, sings as if from some vast distance. It's major Major Tom, lost somewhere in the stellar void, establishing contact with Ground Control. There he is, my old favourite, David Bowie. As an adolescent I worshipped him, bought all his albums, poster books, biographies, watched hours of Saturday morning rock television to catch a glimpse of him. Major Tom repeats his request, the words split into two separate vocals dubbed over one another, his voice strained and emotional in the left channel, lugubrious in the right. A few people sing along, automatically half-mouthing the words as they lie there amongst the domestic debris, some of them beginning to fall asleep. In the right channel David begins a deadpan countdown, which is taken up by two or three people: Lift off! a woman shouts in time with David, mimicking him in a twee English accent. Her friends burst out laughing. I haven't seen them so animated all evening. Caitlin, however, doesn't find it so amusing; she stands there with her arms crossed, contempt stamped on her face.

I glance over at the label revolving on the turntable, the same orange as Caitlin's dress, my eyes swivelling as they follow the letters RCA. I must have listened to these songs thousands of times; they are coded into my brain cells just as they are into the grooves of vinyl. The turntable is so close I can hear the vibrations coming directly off the record. I imagine the stylus which, inclined at an angle of forty-five degrees, vibrates as it's knocked to and fro by the tiny indentations pressed into the record's glossy black vinyl; at the moment David's voice is swarming up one of these chips of sharpened mineral. 'Space Oddity'. David is the hippy astral waif, the orphan astronaut in a pink lurex jumpsuit. He's been turned down by just about every record company in Britain. He's been a mod, a Teddy Boy, a Beatle clone. He's fucked Hermione Farthingale, Lindsay Kemp, Natasha Cornilof, Mary Finnigan, who makes him scrambled eggs at midnight. He becomes a Buddhist, does an ad for an ice cream called Luv. He screws Mercury talent scout Calvin Mark Lee, a gorgeous Chinese-American from 'Frisco', and scores a record deal. He marries Angie, career rock wife. David wants to be famous. He's sung about, will sing about, anything: fairies, folk festivals, shoplifting, the ill-starred paths of love and insanity, especially insanity, because insanity sells and sells and sells. David records 'Space Oddity'. June 20, 1969. Neil Armstrong walks on the moon; on earth the BBC plays 'Space Oddity', one of the shrewdest marketing tie-ins in music history. David's performance fee shoots up to £125 a night. He and Angie buy antiques, cross-dress, have threesomes at Haddon Hall, Beckenham. David is on the road to immortality: he's shouted into a microphone at London's Trident Studios, and years later his voice is replayed here, in Brisbane, at Mark'n'Paul'n'Caitlin's party on a mild summer's night, all around me invisible David Bowie particles fusing with beer, cigarette and marijuana fumes, festering in the living room of a wooden house as shabby as the armchair I'm sitting in. Sweat has started to seep through my shirt to the upholstery; its prickles rub against my skin. I seem to be sinking deeper into the armchair every second. If I don't get up soon, I may be swallowed whole, vanishing into some perverse Narnia, a world under the cushion, full of toenail clippings, biro lids and torn sections of the TV guide.

I'm about to haul myself out when Caitlin's voice cuts through the air.

'I want to *dance*, but not to this Bowie shit!' she shrieks in her best *Scream II* tones.

Paul pulls a face and folds his arms, a gesture he probably realises shows off his biceps to best advantage. He looks to Mark for support then, no doubt used to these screaming matches, shouts:

'But *you've* been deciding the music all night. Let someone else have a go, for chrissake!'

Miffed, Caitlin storms out of the room. Mark'n'Paul exchange a smirk of complicity and stand there, rocking on their heels in time to the music. But, a few moments later, perhaps worried he's offended her, or perhaps just in need of another drink, Paul leaves the room as well.

To my surprise Mark comes over and sits on the edge of my armchair, the remains of a joint between his fingers. Ever hopeful for human contact, and perhaps a drag of something intoxicating, I smile at him; he glances back at me with what may or may not be a half smile, but which is definitely a sign of acknowledgement. He's the straight man of the trio, dressed in blue jeans and a red-checked flannel shirt which, together with his red hair and freckles, make him look like a mid-Western farmer's son. He sits there as if he were waiting for a bus.

'So, what are you up to these days,' I ask him, careful not to show too much interest.

In a casual voice he replies:

'I've taken a year off psych to work on *Excrement Sex*.'

I pause, waiting for him to explain *Excrement Sex*. After a few seconds of silence I ask:

'So, what's *Excrement Sex*?'

'It's a musical I'm working on with Paul,' he answers, slightly surprised that I don't seem to know. 'It's going really well. We've been rehearsing the music all month.'

He breaks off again, waiting for the next question. I oblige.

'Any plans on performing it?'

'Yeah, we're trying to go to next year's Adelaide Fringe Festival, and getting a development grant from the Australia Council.'

He breaks off again. Is the only way to communicate with these people to interview them? I change the subject, asking him who all the records belong to; there are hundreds of them stacked in red plastic containers around the arm chair and hi-fi. They're all Paul's, he tells me, all 462 of them, at last count. Paul spends up to five or six hours a day sitting in his armchair listening to music. Mark has taken his out and put them in his room so people won't scratch them. I ask him if Caitlin has any. She used to, but she sold them; she thinks listening to records is passive. She's not into passive activity. She's into energy, releasing your energy. 'That's what's so great about Caitlin,' he tells me devoutly, squinting as he puffs on his joint. 'She's active, not passive.'

Meanwhile, Caitlin has returned from the kitchen and is

dancing by herself, obviously having decided that her need to release her energy is greater than her loathing of David Bowie. Throughout 'John I'm Only Dancing' she keeps to a standard rock dance style, loosening up with the next track, 'Changes,' during which she clutches her ears and silently enacts primal screams.

'Ziggy Stardust' comes on. Since 'Space Oddity' David hasn't been happy, he isn't famous enough, the lust for fame gnaws at him, rages in him. *Hunky Dory* has been a fizzer, sells only 5,000 copies a month. Okay, a hit with 'Life on Mars,' but David wants more, much much more. He cooks up Ziggy, alien as rock star, a wannabe willing himself into stardom by treating himself as a star. Angie's hairdresser crops his hair at the front, leaves it long at the back and dies it bright red. He gets into Burroughs, into cut up. He's the gender-bending sci-fi fame freak, the leper messiah. London 1971, he records *The Rise and Fall of Ziggy Stardust and the Spiders from Mars.* He has a new manager, Tony Defries, Tony de Freak, Tony Deepfreeze, rapacious, driven, devoted as a mother. Defries turns David into a company, MainMan, and licenses him exclusively to RCA. Defreeze opens a debit/credit account in David's name, the motor driving the MainMan fantasy. In America David tours to conquer. RCA will pay. Tony teaches everyone how to spend a million dollars. At the Beverly Hills Hotel David and entourage run up a tab of $100,000 splashing out on groupies, limousines and champagne. David pays his crude Yorkshire mechanicals the following weekly wage: Mick £30, Trevor £20, Woody £15. Yank Mike Garson, his drug-free scientologist jazz pianist, gets ten times that amount. No one knows how much David makes.

For 'Suffragette City' Caitlin breaks into a catatonic pogo, her arms rigid, her mouth slack. She jumps as high as she can without losing control, her orange garbage bag rising to show the inverted triangle of her purple panties and, on particularly high jumps, her flat pale stomach.

David has fears of being assassinated on stage. David is

afraid of being touched. David won't fly. David writes the same song over and over – verse chorus verse chorus middle eight verse chorus – packaged and marketed in different ways. RCA will pay. RCA, Radio Corporation of America. The music division is a loss-making venture useful as a tax write off. David fellates Mick Ronson's guitar. The crowd loves it. David crosses the stage arms outstretched singing gimme your hands! The crowd surges towards him, creating the famous ripple effect. Tony takes 50% of all earnings.

Caitlin, bored with catatonia, dances a shuffling boogie woogie. She smudges her lipstick with the back of her hand. The bare yellow light fizzes on the orange plastic. She strikes Piaf poses. By the end of 'Suffragette City' she decides she's had enough and, in the silence before 'Jean Genie', flops down on the couch next to Paul, her face slick with sweat.

Paul sits there showing photos from the European trip he recently went on – with Mark'n'Caitlin, of course – to the remaining guests, all female. Mark and I join the group piled onto the couch, part of the same suite as the armchair, and in no better condition. I sink down next to a girl reeking of sandalwood, her face hidden by a tangle of teased black hair. The photos are passed around and cooed over. They're the standard alternative tourist fare: different combinations of Mark'n'Paul'n'Caitlin in cafés, nightclubs and museums. They've been labelled on the back, most probably by Mark, judging from the way he adds details in his high-pitched voice, which is becoming extremely irritating; I wonder how Paul'n'Caitlin put up with it for six weeks. Caitlin'n'Paul make the occasional remark; minor disagreements break out over exact places, times, situations, who was out of it on what, who was more out of it than who. I accept photo after photo, glancing at the images and place names: London, Athens, Inverness, Ireland, Wales, Amsterdam, Paris, Berlin, Budapest, Rome, Brindisi, Paris. We sit there passing the photos to one another in steady rhythm, as if we were an inversion of the automated photo lab that would have done the processing, our hands a conveyor belt, our eyes absorbing the images rather than projecting them.

The roar of a crowd comes over the speakers; 'Diamond Dogs' is David's Orwell pastiche. Holocaust swellagence. David's new religion can be summed up in three words: 'Metropolis', 'Nuremberg', 'Power'. He starts a massive US tour financed by ego and delusion, a lone figure against a backdrop of blood-dripping skyscrapers, his mind full of tanks, turbines, smoke stacks, *ecce homo*, decadence, fluorescent tubing, state police, alleyways, cages, watch towers, girders, beams, Albert Speer. The set costs $250,000, amortised by Defries, later dumped on a whim of David's and donated to a Philadelphia public school. In the manner of classic artists David calls himself Bowie. He's thin, gaunt, but no longer the waif, now the predator, Nero-like, a coke-sniffing vampire prowling a ruined city, his lips sticking to his gums when he gives his trade mark grimace, his skin dried from a coke addiction that devours half his MainMan allowance. 'Diamond Dogs' rollicks and roars in the living room, sound waves bouncing against the tongue and groove walls, thrumming in our ears as we scan and pass, scan and pass, London, Paris, Rome, Berlin, Mark'n'Caitlin at the Virgin Megastore on the Champs Elysées, Paul'n'Mark sharing a hotel bed, Paul'n'Caitlin in wrap-around shades with an equestrian statue...

A photograph is passed to me that is different to the others; it's of a face − slightly out of focus − against a background of bright blue sky. After a few moments I realise it's Caitlin. She's younger and has light brown hair, shoulder length. The tops of her shoulders, bare and smooth, are in frame; she has a healthy tan that's in complete contrast with her current pallor. Her face is striking not so much because of her looks, or the age difference, but because of her extraordinarily warm smile. The hazy focus adds rather than takes away from the intensity of her smile; it suffuses her entire face, making it a warm blur of skin tone against a piercing blue sky. If I were sentimental I'd say her expression was truly beautiful. She must be in love. There's also something unusual about her pose, the way her head hangs forward. The person who took the photo must have lain on the ground while Caitlin crouched over and looked into the lens, like someone staring at their reflection in a pool of water.

I'm about to turn the photo over to see if there are any accompanying words, when it's snatched out of my hand. Caitlin stands in front of me, the photo held by one corner as if it were a soiled article of clothing. Of course, heresy, the pre-punk pre-*Scream II* Caitlin: perhaps also the pre-active Caitlin. She sure isn't smiling now; her face is lit up with the self-righteous anger of an iconoclast. 'You *creep*, you *bastard*,' she screams at Paul, then, offending object in hand, vanishes into the back of the house. Her reaction is a little over the top; revenge for being made to dance to CHANGESONEBOWIE? The ragged guitar riff from 'Rebel Rebel' starts up, followed by crunching percussion. David pretending he's Mick Jagger.

Paul sits there stunned, Caitlin's absence leaving its usual crater in our personal space. After a brief silence he rallies and continues showing the photographs, trying hard but failing to dispel the air of embarrassment. Towards the end of 'Rebel Rebel' the remaining guests say goodbye and leave. Paul hardly listens to them, probably furious at having been chewed out in public, muttering he'll see them at next week's gig. I also say I have to get going. Before I leave I head off to the toilet, leaving Paul whispering indignantly to Mark, who shakes his head like a TV interviewer during a cutaway.

The toilet is just off the back verandah. I relieve myself of the filtered remains of six stubbies of beer, close the lid and sit down, the door near enough for me to press my forehead against, allowing me to adopt the kind of pose I used to strike in public but which I now reserve for moments of unobserved introspection. The shrill sax intro to 'Young Americans' penetrates the bathroom door, followed by David's vocals. I can hardly hear his voice, but I know the song so well that an involuntary chant is triggered off in my mind, one that anticipates the actual playing of the record and creates a weird double-tracking effect as he huffs out the poignant tale of a young virgin's deflowering behind a refrigerator.

Sigma Sound Studios, Philadelphia 1974. David plays the gouster, fucks black women to get the rhythm. Gets into Barry White, Zoot suits, Gamble and Huff. Appears on *Soul Train*. The New York critics hate it, call it plastic soul. The public thinks otherwise; 'Fame' is David's first US number one. US record sales to date: *Ziggy Stardust* 480,000; *Diamond Dogs*, 420,000; *David Live* 314,00; *Pin-ups* 258,00; *Space Oddity* 243,000; *Aladdin Sane* 240,000; *Hunky Dory* 190,000; *The Man Who Sold The World* 120,000. I knock my forehead gently against the toilet door; I want to cry. There must be some way of getting all this Bowie junk out of my head. I feel as if I had been poisoned, years of afternoons in front of the record player unwitting sessions of exposure to low-level radiation, my brain drip fed with sterile data, passive data that lies there, inert, blocking the flow. I feel like a cat taught how to use a can opener, given an unlimited supply of *Whiskas* and left to eat itself to death. How did all this brain junk get in there in first place? I put it there. Pocket money from my parents, Christmas money from my relatives, TEAS cheques from The Department of Finance, dole cheques from the DSS, pay cheques from Pancakes, all spent on records. But it's not only my fault. RCA are to blame. Tony Defreak is to blame. David is to blame.

Indifferent to my concerns, David continues to huff and boogie. He yelps out the montage of now dated *zeitgeist* lyrics – a jumble of Cadillacs, jive talk and blue-collar angst – against the background of a pseudo gospel choir. He chants the same song over and over; the notes change, the themes change, but there's no escaping what it is essentially the same song.

I flush the toilet and go back into the house. Light spills into the dark corridor from the open door of the bathroom, accompanied by the sound of running water. I look in. What I see takes me completely by surprise. I sidestep into the doorway of the opposite bedroom.

The bathroom is large, dominated by an ageing bathtub with rusting feet that stands against the wall opposite the doorway. A bare fluorescent tube floods it with light. Caitlin and Paul are in the bathtub, naked, Caitlin sitting up, her face in perfect profile against the grimy white tiles. Paul stretches out before her, his legs wrapped around her lower torso. His body is lean, the muscles of his thighs and torso clearly defined in the harsh light: he looks as if he'd been skinned. I imagine the top of his spine pivoting against the gritty white surface of the bathtub. Most of Caitlin's body is covered, either hidden by the bath or Paul's body.

She's leaning forward, her head still, her mouth stretched wide, only a small section of his erect penis visible in the gap between her hand and mouth. From time to time her cheeks bulge as, hidden from view, her tongue revolves around his glans. Behind her the water gurgles and splashes. She takes her hand away, like a singer releasing a microphone, revealing a pole of flesh that seems impossibly large for her tiny mouth. Her head starts to move back and forth, her red lips sliding over his penis. Her breasts, no longer concealed by her arm, sway in time with her head movements. Paul blinks at her like a reptile. In the fluorescent light his head seems all skull, the skin stretched over it an afterthought.

Mark sits in front of them on an old wooden chair, his legs flung over either side, his elbows resting on its back. I can make out the tips of his cigarette faintly glowing as he takes a drag, plumes of blue smoke curling into the air.

Stretching out his arms, Paul grasps Caitlin's head. At first it seems he's pulling her further down, or at least guiding her rhythm, but after a few seconds it becomes clear that he's trying to ease her off. Caitlin slowly twines her arms around his and pulls herself forward, taking nearly half his penis into her mouth. A gentle tug of war ensues in syncopated rhythm to 'Golden Years'.

'Golden Years'. Cherokee Studios, Hollywood, August 1975. David is the Thin White Duke. He wears white dress–shirts and black trousers, his slicked-back hair dyed an ever more diluted orange. He's into German Expressionism, Salvador Dali, Fascism. 'Hitler was one of the first rock stars. He staged a country.' David wants to be Britain's first fascist prime minister, he wants to be the first English President of the United States. Fellow superstars suggest that Tony Defries is ripping him off. Angie is in a Swiss chalet, love nest, tax dodge; she rejects David's plans to be the wealthy wife, producing yet more Bowie offspring. David lives in LA, city of greed, trying to find himself, searching and searching and searching and searching. David dumps Defries, cuts out the MiddleMan. He deals directly with RCA, a man now in control of his own destiny, an artist at one with his multinational company.

Mark stands up and goes over to the bathtub. For the first time I notice how upright his posture is; his shoulder blades seem to cut through his T-shirt. He positions himself just behind Caitlin and drops his cigarette butt onto the floor, grinding it into a soggy tile with his heel. He curves his right arm around Caitlin's head and stretches his fingers over her face, covering her eyes, squeezing her lips tighter onto Paul's penis as if they were the labia minora, his middle and index fingers the labia majora. Placing his left hand on her forehead, he steadily pulls back until Paul's member is freed. The swollen glans, a washed out pink in the harsh light, bobs up and down uncertainly. Caitlin leans back with a luxurious smile, like someone in a bath salts commercial, making water splash onto the floor. Mark twists the tap shut then starts to undo his belt. The driving refrain of 'Golden Years' is repeated over and over again, seeping through the wall from the living room. David croons in mock-Sinatra style, doing both lead and backing vocals. Blinking slowly, Paul kneads his penis in his fist.

I decide to leave.

Back in the murky living room David plays to an empty

theatre. An enormous rectangle of light, the after image of the bathroom door burnt onto my retina, floats over the darkness of the room. I stand there blinking for a few seconds, the rectangle pulsing and fading. Images of bodies and water flash through my mind: a rabbit defrosting in the sink; a photo of myself as toddler, naked in a playpool; the enormous change room at Centenary Park swimming pool. From across the living room the yellow rectangles of the amplifier's level meters stare at me like cat's eyes. I go over, crouch in front of them and watch the needles bounce to and fro. I realise that I'm stopping myself leaving the house. At the end of the song, I'll go home at the end of the song.

On top of the turntable are Mark'n'Paul'n'Caitlin's holiday snaps. I thumb through them, and find at the bottom of the pile not just one, but a whole series of photographs of Caitlin's face, similar to the one she snatched out of my hand. I flick through them. Throughout the sequence her head moves across the picture plane, from left to right, from right to left; there must be a whole roll of shots here, taken with a motor drive. With every photograph her smile becomes more and more intense, each one more out of focus than the last until there's just a blur of warm skin edged with dazzling blue. I turn the last one over. Neatly written in ballpoint pen are the words: *Paul fucking Caitlin, Noosa.*

I sit down in Paul's armchair, a decrepit throne, the springs as aggressive as ever. I put down the photos and pick up the CHANGESONEBOWIE cover from the floor. David, cheeks gaunt in sumptuous black and white, gazes pensively at the small price sticker: Target, $6.95. I peel it off and press it onto my wrist, then shove the cover into the nearest box.

On the floor in front of me I notice a pair of headphones. I put them on and plug them into the amplifier, instantly draining the living room of sound, the music diverted through a coiled cable into the chambers of air between my ears and the tiny speakers, sealed shut by a cushion of black plastic. 'Golden

Years' beats against my ears like a fist smashing glass, the refrain sparkling, hypnotic. My hands clasping the slimy armrests, my head swaying back and forth, I start to lip-synch the refrain, crooning with greater and greater abandon...I press the thumb and finger of my right hand together, ready to click them at the exact moment the song ends, a game I often play with myself. I concentrate, press my fingertips tighter and tighter...

All around me sit the red plastic boxes stacked with albums, the result of years of Paul's sorties to music stores, to the Record Market, Rocking Horse, Palings, his fingers running over cardboard square after cardboard square coated with hysterical imagery. The covers protect the delicate plastic discs from dust and moisture, their tightly coiled grooves etched with voices and guitars and synthesisers and drums and compressed again and again and again, transferred from microphone to twenty-four track, from twenty-four track to masters of metallised polymer, from masters to factory, from factory to retail outlets, from retail outlets to hi-fis manufactured by Sansui, Technics, Sanyo, Sankyo, Philips, Rotel, Pioneer, Sharp, Omega, Hitachi, an invasion of decoding machines made by cheap Asian labour. How many records are there in the world? How much frozen desire is just waiting to be reconstituted by the decoding machines housed in leisure spaces all over the planet? If all their grooves were unravelled and put end to end, how far would they stretch? I imagine myself shrunk and injected into that endless vinyl groove, hurtling along a stream of energy, my tiny body, hard as diamond, breaking through walls of fingerprint grease, crushing boulders of dust, David and Elton and Ringo and Dione and Aretha and Thelonius and Miles and Neil and Debbie and Roger and Rotten Bowie particles swarming all over me, shouting all the while in petulant fury *the sound isn't clear enough, the bass isn't deep enough, the treble isn't bright enough, I can't hear enough, I just can't hear enough...*

The song is about to end but I snap my fingers a moment too soon, the last chords echoing in my ears like laughter. The tone arm glides over to the terminal section of groove, then rises and floats to its resting place. The orange record label slowly comes to a halt. RCA will pay.

The house is silent. Crushed beer cans, overflowing ashtrays, dog-eared paperbacks. Record covers tilted back like headstones.

I wonder if Paul has cum yet.

Fifteen

As she walks up the platform, her husband beside her, the Japanese woman finds the wind on her ears intensely irritating. Since the departure of the train the wind has become less erratic, building into a cold, steady breeze that blows into her face, causing the tips of her sensitive ears to burn and itch as they are buffeted by all kinds of invisible matter, a large proportion of which is made up of stale, already-breathed air, stripped of its oxygen and charged with residues of toothpaste, food and whatever else may have found its way into passengers' mouths, not to mention the fragments of skin and hair that, at every second, fall from their bodies, like over-ripe fruit, or the dust from ageing masonry, and either blend, if small enough, into the breeze, or fall to the ground where they are pulverised into tiny units by the never-ending army of heels, ready to be picked up by the air flows that traverse the enormous network of tunnels, these flows determined in part by the London Underground's air conditioning systems, a subterranean network of clumsy mechanical lungs, or perhaps rather a single enormous lung, constructed from ducts, grilles, fans, cables, computer-controlled thermostats, a stationary breathing machine that interfaces with the thousands of its mobile, human counterparts.

The Japanese woman is particularly sensitive about her ears, considering them one of her most beautiful features. When she was no more than five or six, while playing with her mother's make-up – the lipstick, mascara and rouge only occasionally hitting their target – she noticed how nice they were and, subsequently, was always disappointed that no one complimented her on them, this being all the more surprising since she was complimented on nearly every other aspect of her appearance. After months had passed without comment, despite her best efforts to draw attention to them (pulling her hair back, cocking her head at fetching angles, demanding to have them pierced), she was forced to content herself with the knowledge that she and she alone knew how beautiful they were, over the years this fact becoming a treasured secret, a hidden sign that only the select few would ever notice, if they were truly perceptive about beauty. What she loves about them is their smallness, their elegant shape and proportions, the thinness of cartilage that is almost transparent; but, more than all these put together, it is the lobes she is especially proud of, which, unlike the majority of lobes, don't dangle free, as if they weren't connected properly, as if their owner had been born not quite finished, but are neatly joined to the skin of her face, a characteristic she noticed in her husband-to-be on the Twister mat and which was a contributing factor in her consideration of him as a future partner and father of her children, even though he had not been perceptive enough to notice this sign of distinction in either himself or her.

In a protective reaction against the wind, the Japanese woman presses her lips tight and pulls the lapels of her jacket closer; she feels she can control the wind everywhere except her ears, which are helpless, completely exposed to its burning coldness. She inwardly curses herself for not having remembered her scarf and glances over at her husband who, of course, doesn't seem in the least affected by their surrounds; he holds his head high, his gaze alert yet detached, as if he were long-distance driving, staring ahead at some point a few feet in front of him delimited by invisible headlights, walking in the way he always walks, no matter where he is, whether he is crossing the living room on the way to the toilet or walking up this crowded train platform, somehow managing to keep strictly to his path despite the unpredictable speeds and trajectories of the passengers leaving and arriving on the platform.

As they continue up the platform towards the Thameslink tunnel exit, the woman links her arm through her husband's and presses close to him. They fall into step, their inner legs flush, swinging forward at the same time, the perfect image of a young couple, the woman dressed in dark grey stockings, short grey woollen skirt and matching jacket, an outfit she had bought from one of the *Grands Magasins* on the Boulevard Haussmann in Paris, Printemps or Galeries Lafayette, she can't remember, the one with the enormous dome of stained glass that towered over the ground floor, a maze of cosmetics counters and cash registers that looked like some kind of geometrical bazaar, the odour of the perfumes, colognes and eaus de vie wafting up to the remaining levels where she had done her clothes-shopping on one of the walkways that swept around the dome's interior, lined with boutiques (Issey Miyake, Comme des Garçons, Kenzo, Chanel, Cardin, Yves Saint Laurent).

Her husband is more casually dressed in a puffy canary-yellow microfibre anorak topstitched with white lozenges, and a pair of tight twin-stretch lycra jeans he bought in Mitsukoshi back in Tokyo, the blue of the jeans deep but curiously bright, powdery, the sort of colour found in children's toys, this childlike effect emphasised by the smallness of the jeans compared to those worn by the surrounding Europeans, as well as by the fact that they are so clean and have been ironed, as if he had been dressed by some doting mother who still wasn't sure, even at this late stage of the century, whether jeans were entirely respectable. The puffiness of his bright yellow anorak is in complete contrast to the tightness of his jeans, which seem moulded to his legs, as if an Asian version of the Michelin man had been skinned from the waist down, his mask pulled off to reveal high cheekbones, flawless skin and a trendy bob of glossy black hair, a hairstyle narcissistically parallel to that of his wife, although considerably shorter, making his fringe end at a point only millimetres above his eyes, the increasingly strong wind blowing down the platform flattening it against his forehead which, because of the warmth of the anorak (lined as it is with some remarkably light but efficient synthetic padding), has become covered in a film of sweat.

From the inner pocket of his anorak he takes out a pair of earphones, the type that consists only of two tiny speakers joined to a length of thin black wire. He reaches into the pocket again, producing a small block of black plastic, a double adaptor for the Walkman that is wedged into the front pocket of his jeans. He puts the small speakers with their bright red foam cushions into his ears, then plugs the jack into the control panel accessible through the pocket's opening. His wife, who does not normally like her husband's taste in music, leans across him, reaches into the same pocket of his anorak, and takes out another set of earphones in the hope that the music will take her mind off the burning sensation in her ears.

He plugs her in, the two of them joined by black wires to a common terminal, his jeans so tight that they clearly show the contours of the Walkman's hard rectangular shape bulging against his muscular thigh, as well as the contours of his genitals, his penis (twisted to the left) and testicles (twisted to the right), vague but nevertheless identifiable lumps in the fabric, the wires protruding from his pocket swaying to and fro as he and his wife walk along, looking as if they were perhaps not only plugged into the Walkman, but into his genitals as well. Once his wife has put on her earphones (hers have blue ear cushions), the Japanese man presses the play button through the denim, squeezing the Walkman as if he were activating some music-playing implant, the noises of the crowded platform (snatches of voices, scuffling feet, the slow heavy clatter of the overcrowded train leaving the station) only noticed once they have been blocked out by the ensuing hiss and rumble of the tape as it drags across the magnetised head, the miniaturised graphic equaliser and amplifier decoding the electrical signal provided by two AA1.5V Duracells, the motor whirring away, turning, by means of plastic gear wheels, the spools of cassette tape in a slow, steady circuit, separated from the Japanese man's reproductive organs only by a shell of black plastic and two layers of cotton fabric.

The tape being played was pirated in India and bought from a stall at the Portobello Road Market, its cassette case now squeezed into the Japanese man's back pocket, the cover depicting a young Englishman in dark, shabby clothes, his overgrown quiff shot against a weak blue sky, the first track of the album a song with a cocky, swaggering rhythm and mannered, cynical vocal, the genre of masculinity presented at complete odds with that embodied by the young Japanese man whose gait is deliberate, purposeful, sober, an advertisement for self respect. He has little conception of what the song is about, being able to understand only some of the lyrics, starting off with the song's introductory wolf howl, followed by *off the...(?) happy stay...(?) get out of my way...(?) off the wrack...(?) easy meet...(?) goodbye, reasonable goodbye (?)*

His young wife, however, finds the music nearly as irritating as the cold wind on her ears. She has no idea what her husband sees in the tuneless singing of this dirty, three-day-growth English boy who strikes her as aggressive, uncultivated, arrogant, and strangely effeminate, her reaction based, like her husband's, on the overall impression given by the music and album cover, neither the wife nor husband realising that the song is the first-person narrative of a male prostitute operating at Piccadilly Circus, who serenades himself with this up-beat rock ballad of depravation, callousness, and the cheapness of human desire and intimacy.

The Japanese woman is relieved to reach the opening of the Thameslink tunnel, convinced that the wind is coming from the black openings at either end of the platform through which the trains arrive and depart, and that her ears will find some respite in the exit tunnels. This impression is immediately contradicted by a slight increase in the air current as she enters the tunnel, bringing with it not only a greater degree of cold, but also a spray of grit that makes her eyes water, this faster speed hinting at worse things to come, as if she were on a boating day trip in some exotic location and found herself caught up in a larger expedition, her boat labouring upstream against a current that becomes stronger at every turn, revealing itself to be part of an enormously powerful river system towards whose source she is heading.

She blinks to regain her focus, imagining the grit that has lodged in her hair, its fine layers an infinitely subdivided space custom-made for storing millions of dust particles, a resource the Underground system produces in abundance. She now realises the pristine state of her hair – so clean that the rays of fluorescent light make it shine like the grooves on a record – will be short-lived, its oils slowly combining with the dirt as the day wears on, in three or four hours causing it to go lank, limp, slightly greasy, ruining her entire appearance, perhaps making her look like some of her British counterparts who, in her private opinion, are for the most part well-groomed, but don't seem willing to make the sacrifices necessary to always look their best, such as washing their hair twice a day if necessary, not to mention what at times amounts to their complete lack of style, of their inability to pick the appropriate hairstyle for their face and body type.

As if to confirm her opinion, the first thing the Japanese woman notices on entering the Thameslink is the poster of the Sun In woman to her right (or it may have been the image that suggested this train of thought to her, the Japanese woman having subliminally noticed it a second or so earlier), the Sun

In woman's peroxided hairstyle the height of banal, the very idea of a spray-on lightener idiotic to the Japanese woman who, even if she had the mousy brown hair of so many Europeans, would not treat it in such a way, making herself look cheap, little better than a sandwich hand or prostitute, the British men in the looks stakes faring much better than the women, as typified by the poster next to it showing the handsome young man wearing a set of headphones, his particular clean-cut good looks, his gentlemanliness, something that could tempt her had she not been married and devoted to her husband.

Without any warning her husband increases the Walkman's volume. The music, which she has found diverting even though it isn't to her taste, suddenly turns from a background presence to an assault of guitars, drums and keyboards, its loudness, coupled with the closeness of the earphones, sealing her off from the outside world, making her feel disoriented, as if she were listening to the soundtrack of a video or film that did not correspond to the events (or, perhaps more accurately, non-events) unfolding around her, making her feel partially absent from this mass-transit continuum that she is not meant to inhabit any longer than the time needed to pass through it, her senses thrown back upon themselves, intensifying the burning coldness in the tips of her ears, a sensation now not only confined to the tips, but also spreading down along their outer ridges, making the tiny hairs that grow there, barely visible, stand up on end.

With her free hand she takes out the earphones and shoves them into a gap beside her husband's Walkman, for a moment having difficulty forcing them into his pocket, the thin black cables coiling out every time she pushes them in, until she hits upon the solution of curling her three middle fingers into a single phalanx and driving them past the bottleneck at the opening of the pocket (caused by the earphone double adaptor) deep into the more generous recess beyond, her nails, long and well-manicured, digging through the fabric of his pocket into his flesh, a mild pain to which he does not outwardly respond (he does not respond to any form of pain, unless extreme), the music playing on regardless to an audience made of a linty wodge of paper – a receipt that has gone through the wash – and his thigh, which flexes against the tight layer of denim as he walks along, his step increasing as he unconsciously falls in with the beat of the music.

Relieved that she is no longer listening to the Walkman (the treble bursts coming from her partner's left ear clearly audible), the Japanese woman and her husband enter the second stage of the Thameslink, the short section with the pink walls and ceiling, its surface area, extended by the countless undulations, a concrete sponge for dust and grime, very much like her hair, although the distribution of space is quite different, the vertical strands of hair creating depth, while the walls and ceiling constitute a vast surface. Her low heels strike on the yellow tiles of compacted stone, its unyielding surface as hard as metal, jolting her spine and altering her posture so that she pitches forward slightly, her husband protected from the tiles by the cushioning crepe sole of his Timberland moccasins, the only effect on him being the small increase in the swing of the shoes' leather tassels. Wanting him to slow down, she clutches tightly at his arm as if in a gesture of sudden affection, as if she needed the comfort of his body close to hers, a well-worn gambit she uses whenever he is walking too quickly.

The couple step over the rubbish which has accumulated in a wind break against the bottom step, the crushed Ribena tetrapack, torn blue foil crisps' packet, red and white chocolate wrapper and piece of apple green A4 paper, which have now been crushed into a single mass by the front toes of the dozens of shoes that have kicked and trodden on them since the arrival and departures of the last few trains, the sticky red Ribena juice providing an ideal binding medium.

They mount the short flight of stairs, automatically following the stream of passengers ascending to the left of the burnished stainless steel railing, the passengers to the right descending, the Japanese woman able to look into their oncoming faces without having to fear running into them (the protocols attached to negotiating fellow passengers at times complicated, people practising a kind of brinkmanship as they see who will be the first to step aside, arrogant men, women with prams or those bearing large parcels the most demanding, always expecting others to get out of their way). She watches the series of faces cascade down the stairs, staggered in accordance with the receding steps, as if they were marching down the face of a ziggurat or other ceremonial or sacrificial building, the light from the crooked spine of overhead fluorescents glowing dully on their faces as they make their way down to the platform at a uniform pace.

As she mounts the stairs the Japanese woman's ears find protection from the wind, the crowd forming a barrier that doesn't allow it to penetrate. The respite, however, is only brief: at the top of the stairs she is met by a sudden gust of wind so powerful that her hair is whipped back nearly horizontal, the departure of a train from the platform sucking a wave of air out with it, as if it wanted to drag her along, the wind surging against her ears and sending cold currents down her collar, a particularly strong blast catching in her eyelashes and for a split second blowing her lids wide open just long enough for a piece of grit to strike and wedge into her eye.

The pain is excruciating. She pulls her husband over to the wall a metre or so from the top step, doing her best to get out of the way of the crowd, which automatically diverts around her, like an organism that responds to a loss of one of its parts by reknitting itself into a new configuration, at the same time telling him that she has something in her eye. Her husband, however, is unable to hear her, his thoughts concentrated on the phrase just sung – *the Piccadilly palaver...(?) was...(?) silly song... (?) between me and those boys...(?) on my gang...(?) remembering palaces...(?) oh so natural order...(?) you couldn't understand...(?)* – and is bewildered by his wife's actions. He takes out one earphone and hooks the cable behind his ear, allowing the tiny speaker to dangle within hearing range, in this way hoping to both understand his wife and salvage some of the music's stereo effects. Hurt and annoyed, she repeats her problem in a tearful voice. She blinks and feels her eyelid drag over something hard, sharp, as if her eyelid were a wiper dragging a stone across a windscreen's surface and cutting an arc into the glass, her blinks at an erratic offbeat to the movement of her dark brown iris, which expands and contracts in time with her heart, the movement of her eyelid embedding the speck of grit in the soft white membrane of her cornea, now hot and flushed as the blood rushes to its tiny veins and her tear duct redoubles its effort to pump enough liquid to flush the foreign body out.

The speck of grit comes from a painting, the work of an art student who had been a passenger on the same train as the Japanese couple but who is now far ahead of them, on his way up the Euston Road exit escalator, his progress quicker due to the fact that, at his point of embarkation, he had positioned himself in the carriage that would stop nearest to the Thameslink exit (give or take a few metres), unlike the less experienced Japanese couple who have yet to master such time-saving details.

The painting is one of a series the artist, a man in his early twenties, executed during a year-long stay in Birmingham, a city he had gone to in order to escape the stresses and expenses of London, and in which he had hoped to come to terms with some of the artistic issues obsessing him at the time, largely of a personal/emotional nature, these concerns suddenly vanishing once he had set himself up in a warehouse in a disused industrial area, to be replaced by themes of industrial decline and social stagnation. At first inspired by a wave of enthusiasm by his new project – the thought that he was using abstraction to depict public, social issues rather than internal, emotional states striking him as potentially innovative – the artist set to work, this enthusiasm waning over time as he found it increasingly difficult to find any kind of affirmation in his subject; this search, he realised, being the implicit goal, but whose attainment seemed more and more remote as he covered hardboard panel after hardboard panel (all of them four foot square) with nebulous layers of oil and acrylic, urban decay and alienation, to the point where he realised that, in the end, he was merely registering his emotional response to this decay, and that no direct political response was possible.

In a cold, impotent rage, he executed the final paining of the series on his last hardboard panel, slowly building up the layers of black, mixing the oil paint with tar, crushed eggshells, pitch, sand, the dirt and soot from abandoned factories. He contrasted mat, granular surfaces of pitch and PVA glue with glossy smears of oil, over these planes of darkness finally drawing a single pink horizontal line two thirds up the picture plane, the effects of this line absolutely delighting him, in particular the way it threw the black shapes into ever more ambiguous relations with one another and relegated them to a background, although one still close enough to react directly on the spectator's nervous system.

With the painting now crooked awkwardly under his arm as he makes his way through the crowded Thameslink, the thought occurs to him that the transporting of the enormous object – filthy and stinking of a mixture of odours, from the eucalyptus of gum turps and the faint reek of (cat, human?) urine to the drier smells of soot, sand and earth – on to the Underground in the build up to rush hour is a kind of artwork in itself, an act of aggression against the passengers in mortal fear of dirtying their clothes, although they need not worry as the surface is more or less stable, although not as stable as the artist may wish, the painting occasionally dragging on the ground, the intermittent shocks causing a small part of the heavily caked surface to slowly crack (the fluctuations in temperature the painting has recently undergone assisting the process), the section finally shattering as the painting bumps up the escalator, all the loosened fragments showering to the floor, save for one tiny piece with sharp, jagged edges that is picked up by the wind and carried by a stream of air that flows down the steep incline of the ceiling of the escalator, gliding effortlessly in a series of perfect arcs around various tunnel corners, picking up greater and greater speed until a perturbation in the air flow hurls it out of its trajectory and into the eye of the Japanese woman, which is now being stared into by her husband, his face appearing to her both in blur and sharp focus as he tries to see what is wrong.

He clasps his wife's face gently in his hands and turns it towards him so that it is out of the wind, which has died back down to a breeze, then prises her eye wide open with his thumb and forefinger, identifying the offending speck to the left of her iris. After a moment's inspection he releases her eye, takes his handkerchief out of his anorak, coils the tip, wets it with his saliva and, prising her eye open once again, starts to poke at it, the fragment eluding him for some moments, his wife complaining he is being clumsy and urging him to be careful. After a few moments of chasing the piece of grit around his wife's eye, at first losing it under her top lid, which he is forced to pull right back, exposing the reddish purple network of veins behind it (so much of the white of her eyeball showing that it looks as if it may pop out, as in one of the grossly exaggerated comic book illustrations of people confronted by something unspeakably terrifying), he prods it into her tear duct, all of these manoeuvres making her eye weep profusely until it is red and swollen.

As he performs this delicate operation, the song he is listening to reaches its stomping finale, his favourite part because he can understand all the lyrics (having had them explained to him by a British classmate), the drama of these final words, sung in milky, plaintive tones, something he can identify with, especially the line that describes life as a battle, as a struggle, which makes him think of all his own battles, his final university exams, the challenges of a new city and a new language, all of these difficulties, successfully overcome; and the line that describes life as being simultaneously endless and transitory, a line that captures so perfectly the tension of his existence in this enormous city, its ability to suddenly switch from certainty to complete instability– all of these sentiments perfectly encapsulated in the form of a sophisticated English rock sound so many Japanese bands at his undergraduate university tried so hard, yet so dismally failed, to emulate.

After repeated attempts, many of them frustrated by the handkerchief that so easily becomes unfurled, he succeeds in lifting off the speck of grit which, only weakly bonded to the fabric by his saliva and the film of salty liquid produced by his wife's eye, is lifted up by the breeze and blown back down the tunnel.

Her pain soothed, the Japanese woman wipes her eye with back of her hand and sniffles. The abruptness with which the surge of wind has turned into a light breeze both astonishes and annoys her: why has she been made to suffer so senselessly, so unfairly? Her husband puts his arms around her, hugs her (the hard shape of the Walkman pressing against her) and, for a brief moment as they turn around to join the lane of exiting passengers, accidentally brushes his ear against hers, the contact of his skin, so exquisitely warm and dry, sending her into a split second of delirium.

Sixteen

My father likes to take his boys for a drive. He comes into the darkened living room where my brother and I are sprawled on the floor in the pool of light spilling from the TV, glued to the Saturday night movie. Out of the corner of my eye I see him, a silhouette in the doorway, tufts of white hair shining through the darkness. He switches the light on and turns our cinema back into his living room. The car keys gleam in his hand as if they could open up the world. 'Let's go for a drive,' he says with a smile half hidden by his pepper-and-salt moustache, his deep voice weaving its way through the dialogue blaring from the TV's tinny speaker. He's wearing a white shirt, a brown cardigan and old cuffed trousers that are too long for him and sag at the knees. The top button of his shirt is undone, showing a triangle of singlet which, unlike mine, has even rows of tiny holes. He rocks the keys gently in one hand, the other thrust into the pocket of his cardigan, a pocket I often check for coins while he takes his afternoon nap. The keys tinkle when he shakes them again, but I keep looking at the screen, unable to take my eyes off the adventures of Lawrence of Arabia, even though I've already seen the movie twice before, once on TV and once at the movies. Lawrence is at the army headquarters in Cairo, talking to a diplomat in a large, high-ceilinged room. He lights the diplomat's cigar then, pinching the match between his thumb and forefinger, watches the flame burn down. Just before it reaches his skin he leans forward and, with a self-satisfied grin, blows it out. The screen then fills with a huge sky underlined by a thin strip of desert. It's before dawn. The sky glows brighter until the horizon line, dead straight, is broken by a dazzling cusp of white light: the rising sun. My father breaks the silence. 'Well boys, if you prefer to watch television, I'll have to go by myself.' My brother springs to his feet. He's wearing his favourite outfit, the blue and white jersey of his football team, Valleys (up the Diehards!) and his loose white Karate pants, a sport he's just taken up. He nudges me in the ribs with his bony foot and tells me to come on or they'll leave without me. I ignore him. The burning sun continues to rise into the TV sky, white on shimmering grey. When I look up a second later they have both gone. Afraid I'll be left behind (it would be just like my brother to tell Baba that I didn't want to come), I jump up and, dressed in my Hush Puppy slippers, which are still too big, and blue flannelette pyjamas, which are too small, scramble after them. My mother stops me before I reach the front door and makes me put on my new dressing-gown. It's dark blue with a gold pattern running through it. My father tells me I look like a Turkish prince when I wear it, and calls me Ali Pasha. With my brother shouting 'C'mon will ya!', my mother smoothes down the lapels and pulls the blue imitation silk cord tight around my waist. As I pass through the shop to the front door the film's theme music, soaring violins, pours out of the TV.

Outside the evening is so quiet I can hear the swish of my dressing-gown against my pyjama pants, then the idling engine of our dark green Holden station wagon, which is waiting by the footpath. Its chrome door handles and bumper bars glow dully under the powerful new street lights. Clouds of blue and white smoke putter out of the exhaust pipe and vanish into the artificial light, leaving a warm, acrid smell. The back door is open and waiting for me. As I cross the footpath I glance down and count at least three shadows fanning out from my feet, at first dirty grey on the concrete squares, then dirty green as I step across the grass. My brother, who has of course grabbed the front seat, leans out of the window and shouts 'Get in will ya!' as I clamber into the back. I pull the door shut a little too hard and the whole car shakes. My brother mutters 'dickhead' under his breath so my father can't hear.

The car's upholstery is a deep bottle green. The first few seconds inside the car are the best; it feels like a special room of our house, fitted with a motor, put on wheels, and used to go wherever we please. 'So, where to, boys?' my father asks. He always asks us where we want to go, even though my brother and I already know: it's a trick to drive into the Valley and buy the papers without annoying my mother. 'To the city,' I nearly shout. 'To the city, to see the temples.' He guns the engine, takes hold of the gear stick and, after a moment's coaxing, pushes it into first. We jerk forward then back as he releases the clutch too quickly. 'Well, I'll think about it,' he promises in his best smooth-talk manner. He sets off into the city-bound lane without indicating and we cruise along the endless bitumen strip, flanked by wooden houses, shops and trees, forever chasing the weak puddle of light in front of us. The curved supports of the street lights arch over the road like the rib cage of an enormous snake.

For a moment I lie down on my back, stretch out on the seat and stare up at the ceiling of white plastic punctured with tiny holes, just like my father's singlet. I pretend the holes are black stars in a white sky. I close my eyes and imagine the motion of the tyres on the road; the wrinkled vinyl trembles against my back. I sit up, rest my arms on top of the front seat, then rest my chin on my hands. I look through the gap left by the heads of my father and brother, my brother's much lower than my father's which, majestically high, smells of hair oil and warm skin. There aren't many cars on the road, and all the traffic lights we approach stay green until we have gone through, as if they know we are coming. Lawrence blew on a match and created a desert, we approach a set of lights and they turn from red to green to let us through; everything is very simple, the world obeys our every command. I listen to the engine, feel the thousands of tiny muffled petrol explosions vibrating up my spine.

We pass through a busy intersection. An enormous white petrol truck swerves into the space in front of us, swallowing us up in its tremendous roar. On the back of its fuel cylinder, gleaming stainless steel, a dark red star has been painted, its tips narrowing out to fine points. The star's centre is filled with black letters that spell the word CALTEX. Every time the truck hits a dip in the road, the star shakes in time with the furious jolting of metal. 'Let's overtake it,' my brother says. My father doesn't answer. Underneath the red star I can make out the words WARNING. HIGHLY FLAMMABLE LIQUID: DO NOT EXPOSE TO FLAME, also painted in red. Obviously in a hurry, the truck's driver surges ahead, sending the lid of its exhaust chimney flapping. Within seconds it disappears from view, lost in the thickening traffic heading towards the city. To our right we pass the Kentucky Fried Chicken barrel, rotating against the sky. My brother sings: 'Say Kentucky Fried Kitten for me, meow meow!' I join in on the cat noises, squealing as high as I can.

My father takes his hand from the gear stick and pushes in the cigarette lighter button. Its face is covered with a white illustration of a cigarette tip, much of it worn away by repeated contact with his nicotine-stained thumb. I love staring at the dashboard; at night it's lit up like a tiny stage. Whenever I sit in the front seat I play with everything I'm allowed to touch. I twist open the vents, I open and close the glovebox and rifle through the junk: a rusty torch, feathery bits of official looking papers, empty cigarette packets, tangled clumps of coloured wire. I desperately want to sit in the front, but there's no point in nagging; my father will just tell me that it will be my turn on the way back. I lean forward and rest my chin on his shoulder, my face pressing against the rough stubble of his cheek, the smell of hair oil and dry skin more powerful than ever. I watch his hands, flecked with grey and mauve marks, the lower joints covered in hair, some of them still black. His hands rest lazily on the wheel, pushing it this way and that in response to the curving road. I study the dashboard. The orange needle of the speedo quivers around the thirty-five mark. To the left of the speedo is the petrol gauge, its orange needle never more than a quarter full, and tonight in its usual place, hovering above empty. Under the speedo is a tiny window showing a long strip of numbers, all of them black except for the last two, which are red. When I get really bored I wait for the number nine and watch it slowly give way to zero, causing the tens to move. If I'm really lucky I'll catch the hundreds moving. Tonight the red numbers stand at eighteen. Once, when I was out alone with my father, I asked what it was called. 'It's the odometer, son. *Odos*, road, *metron*, measure,' he told me in one of his occasional attempts to teach me Greek.

The cigarette lighter pops up from the dashboard with a sharp click. Before my father can get to it, I lunge forward, grab the warm plastic handle, pull it out of its socket and examine the tip. The tight coil of metal glows red in the darkness and immediately starts to fade. My father reaches into his top pocket and produces a crumpled soft pack of Camels. He puts an equally crumpled cigarette to his lips and reaches for the lighter, but I insist on doing the honours. I hold the lighter at such an awkward angle that he's forced to twist his mouth around, puckering his lips and swivelling his jaw. It's only when I take the cigarette between my fingers and pull it over a little further that it makes contact with the lighter. He puffs theatrically, drawing in his cheeks, clouds of smoke spilling out of his nose and mouth, a blue streak streaming from the tip up to the white vinyl ceiling. Brown and grey specks of ash drift into the air and, in the intermittent waves of the street lights, float back down, some of them settling on the blue and gold sleeve of my dressing gown. I hold the lighter close to my face; even though the metal coil has gone a dull grey, it's still quite hot. I slowly put it close to the back of my brother's neck, something I know he will be expecting. Sure enough, even before it's close, he spins around, grabs my wrist and squeezes it as hard as he can, all the while grinning from ear to ear. With the other hand he strips me of the offending weapon and, after releasing me, pushes it back into the socket.

My brother coughs, so my father winds down his window halfway, letting some of the smoke escape. The rush of cool evening air makes his cigarette tip glow and gives me goose-pimples. We're about halfway there. From time to time headlights left on highbeam blind us like tiny suns thrown into our faces, their rays catching on the layers of dust coating the windscreen. As we draw closer to the city centre the road becomes lined with shops and offices that hide the houses stretching out for miles behind them, as if they were a barrier holding back the suburbs. Out of the night sky, which now has a pale violet tinge from the city lights, a petrol sign floats into view, this time an enormous green shield impaled on a steel pole. It has the same curved, triangular shape as those carried by the medieval warriors illustrated in my brother's *Look and Learn* magazines, except this one doesn't sport a cross, or a lion, or a coat of arms, but the lemon-yellow letters BP.

His cigarette wedged in his fist, my father flicks the indicator, setting a small orange disc to the left of the dashboard blinking. At the same time the long ash of his cigarette falls to the floor where it joins the burnt remains of packets of other cigarettes, the grey and white flakes that have collected under the pedals like a bed of crushed moths. We swerve across the lane of oncoming traffic, make a U-turn and pull up next to a fish and chip shop. My father tells us to wait and returns a few minutes later, two Dagwood Dogs sticking out of his hand in a clumsy V sign. The barbecue sauce dribbles down the sides of the mustard yellow batter and gives off a reddish brown glow, like Coke when it's held up to the light. The car fills with the smell of hot spices, deep-fried flour and sausage meat. My father dispatches the first Dagwood Dog in a quick series of huge bites then, with the sleeve of his cardigan, wipes off the layer of steam that has fogged up the window. Once we're on the road again he tosses the stick out the window. He slows down to catch the next traffic light so he can eat the second Dagwood Dog but, despite dropping to a low speed – which prompts furious beeping from the car behind – doesn't succeed in catching the red. One hand on the wheel, the other brandishing the Dagwood Dog, he attempts to eat it, annoyed that he can't finish it off with his usual speed. I glance at the needle of the petrol gauge: it's dropped just below the empty mark.

We pass the hospital and slow to a crawl because of the red traffic light at the top of the hill. The car loses speed and begins to shudder as we go up the incline; my father only changes gears at the last moment. About halfway up the slope we come to a complete stop; he pulls the handbrake to with a loud crick. His hands free, he's now able to concentrate on the Dagwood Dog before it gets too cold: my father hates cold food. He tilts his head to the side and chews noisily. My brother turns to check how far away the car behind us is, at the same time giving me a knowing look: hill starts always mean trouble. I look around too. Luckily, the car behind us is a good distance away. We sit in silence, dreading the moment the lights change. They turn green and my father releases the handbrake. The car, ever so slowly, begins to roll backwards. My father, engrossed by his eating, doesn't seem to notice. In the rear-view mirror I watch the headlights of the car behind us grow bigger, filling our car as if a spotlight had been shone into a darkened room. Our car continues to roll back. With hill starts it always takes forever for my father to put the car into gear, but the Dagwood

Dog is making the manoeuvre take even longer than usual. My brother turns around again; his face is angry and scornful in the light streaming from behind, white pinpricks flashing in his dark eyes as he turns to my father and shouts: 'Hurry up, we're gonna crash!' My father, wrestling with the gear stick, the Dagwood Dog swaying wildly as he tries to push into gear, says in a slightly indignant voice: 'Be patient son.' As we continue to roll backwards the headlights vanish from the rear-view mirror and the interior of our car is dark again. The horn behind us beeps furiously. I turn around and can see the driver, a woman with dark glasses, her body lunging forward as she hits the horn in short, angry bursts, as if she hoped these shrill blasts of air could push our car forward. We continue to roll back, more quickly now. It feels as if we are floating. She stares directly at me, and for a moment I can't tell whether we are rolling back or she's coming towards us. The beeping of the horn becomes as furious as the expression on her face, a glowering mask framed by dark curls. Frightened, I swing around to the front; up ahead the lane is empty, the green circle of the traffic light impatient for us to get a move on. I expect to feel the crash of chrome bumper bars at any second. An image of a crumpled foil wrapper speckled with chocolate crumbs flashes through my mind. My father wrestles with the gear stick. Under his breath he says to it: 'Come on my friend,' as if there were some misunderstanding that could be straightened out with a few soothing words. After glancing up at the rear-view mirror to see how much he's rolled back, he changes tactics. With a couple of short, violent shoves, followed by the grating and clanging of metal from under the car, he succeeds in getting the gear stick into first. The engine roars in our ears as he presses down on the accelerator. As he lets out the clutch the backward rolling slowly stops. But, as we start to creep forward, the car jerks back and forwards violently as the engine surges and falters. 'We don't have enough petrol!' my brother screams. 'Why didn't you get any petrol?' 'Well why didn't you remind me son?' my father replies, unaffected by my brother's shouting. Turning around to me, he says 'Quick son, jump into the front.' This has happened before; the tank is tilting too far back for the petrol to feed into the engine. I scramble into the front seat. My father, brother and I all jump up and down in our seat. My father pumps the accelerator. Suddenly the jerking motion stops and, with a massive roar, the car shoots forward. We climb the hill, within moments cruising through an amber light. My brother turns around to check the progress of the car behind us, and laughs with a truly fiendish delight when he sees it stuck at the intersection, caught by the red.

As we go down the other side of the hill and into the Valley, my father licks his moustache like a cat giving its whiskers a final once over. The Dagwood Dog has vanished; somehow he managed to finish it off while I wasn't watching. 'Well boys, I think we need some petrol.' I jump into the back seat and, pressing my forehead against the side window, keep a look out for my favourite sign. Within seconds it comes into view, a weathered rectangle of wood with an accordion painted onto it, the bellows stretched apart at the top so that it looks like a spread fan. Below the illustration are the words ACCORDION TUITION: REASONABLE RATES, followed by a phone number. I know the number off by heart, and even dialled it at home once, but hung up before anyone could answer. I love the accordion; there's always one at the Christmas dances at Cloudland. We kids rush between the couples waltzing across the wooden dance floor, the floorboards bouncing under the weight of their hundreds of footfalls, the enormous light above them like a giant brooch with glowing purple panels.

We pass through the main intersection of the Valley, past Waltons and Myers, the department stores that furnished our house, and turn into the road that feeds into the city. Up ahead, to our left, is another petrol sign, this time an enormous yellow seashell on a bright red background. We pull into the station, my father taking his usual care not to indicate, and stop with a jolt next to one of the bowsers, a stout robot with a mechanical arm. Immediately the race is on between my brother and me for the petrol hose. I beat him to it, and my brother is left with the menial job of taking charge of the petrol cap. My father remains in his seat and, resting his hand lazily on the wheel, says: 'Only five dollars son. Petrol is like gold now.' I nod furiously in agreement. All throughout the year petrol has gone up and up. My father says it's because of the Arab countries; they have plenty of petrol, but they know how much we need energy and have raised prices. My brother doesn't agree. He thinks that the amount of petrol in the world is running out, and that the Arabs are making as much money as they can before there's none left. My father and brother are always arguing about politics; it doesn't matter what it is, one of them will always take the opposite side. The night has been quiet so far; I'm surprised neither of them has fired an opening shot yet. I pick up the pump. It's heavy in my hand, an enormous toy gun that spurts petrol instead of sparks. Holding the pump, dressed in my blue and gold dressing-gown, I feel like a hero out of fantasy story. My brother oversees my every movement ('pull the hose further along, don't scratch the paint, keep your finger off the trigger') as I manage to get the clumsy nozzle into the tank opening. When I press the trigger the pump jerks in my hand like a mechanical animal as the petrol surges through the pipe, and the numbers of the bowser's meter, which are just like our odometer, only bigger, turn with clicks muted by the scratched glass window. A cloud of vapour billows up from the opening, warping the chrome stripe above the opening, in the same way that the heat of the desert had made the distant horseman, emerging from the horizon, waver and flicker in *Lawrence of Arabia*. A sweet, mineral smell fills the cold air and stings my nostrils; it makes me feel slightly dizzy. The trigger, a metal button, is hard to keep down for more than a few seconds. I pause to rest my thumb, and stare over at the long, narrow slabs of concrete, sealed with black rubber, a fizzing grey pink under the spotlights. I imagine the petrol stored in huge tanks directly under my feet, a watery red liquid flooding underground lungs. I press the button, again feeling the surge of liquid mineral. The powerful sweet smell makes me dizzier. Petrol is short for Petroleum. British Petroleum. Lawrence of Arabia is British. He fought for the Arabs, who were backward and disorganised, when all the time there was a sea of petrol under the desert. Americans call petrol gas, they call bills checks. CAL is for California, TEX for Texas. SHELL means seashell but it also means petrol. GO WELL, GO SHELL. My brother barks at me to stop the pump. I release the button, take out the pump and, a little off balance from the petrol fumes, return it to the bowser with great care. I look at the meter, and see that I've clocked up eight dollars worth. Baba will be furious; he hates having to spend any more money than he has to. My brother notices me staring at the price meter and comes over. 'You've done it now. The old man will hit the roof. Dickhead.' He screws the petrol cap on, and runs over to get the money from my father. I wait for him to rat on me, but he takes the money from my father without a word. As he passes me on his way to the counter, he whispers, 'You owe me three bucks.'

A few moments later we are driving up through the lower part of Queen Street, past the banks, insurance offices, government departments, the odd sandwich shop or second-hand store breaking up the monotony. The city streets are deserted. 'Get ready for the wave,' my brother says. We're approaching our favourite bank, the one with the grey-uniformed security guard sitting at his wide desk in the foyer, on show as if he were part of a shop display. We come level with the bank. He's there as usual, his only company a telephone, his face expressionless, lit by a chandelier made up of pieces of brown plastic, ochre light smouldering away inside. My brother and I wind down our windows, stick out our arms and wave, rotating our hands at the wrist just like the Queen. The grey-uniformed figure doesn't move. My brother claims that last time we passed he saw him reach under his desk, probably to get his gun and blow us away.

We continue up Queen Street into the heart of the city, past shop windows full of clothes, electrical appliances and kitchenware. 'Boys, shut the windows, you'll catch cold,' my father says a little gruffly. Once they're closed he announces in a mock tour guide voice: 'Okay, temple number one.' I've started to feel quite sleepy, so I bounce up and down on the seat to wake myself up. I love the temples in the middle of the city, the way their columns are lit with different colours. We pass the City Hall, a huge building whose bottom section is made up of a long row of tall columns topped by smaller ones. From this broad base an enormous clock tower rises into the sky, crowned by what my teacher says is the largest four-faced clock in the southern hemisphere. The City Hall's stone is a rich yellow in the floodlights. Two metal lions crouch at its entrance, keeping a watchful eye over the drunks in King George Square.

As soon as we have left the City Hall behind, my brother says: 'Stalin was a mass murderer.'

My brother couldn't care less about the temples; he wants an argument. He and my father have been arguing about Stalin for two years, ever since my brother began reading *Time* magazine. My father is silent for a few moments as we turn and drive by the river.

'Stalin, son, was a great man,' my father replies. 'Okay, temple number two.'

We pass the Treasury building, the one I like best. It's like a huge money box, taking up the entire block at the end of Queen street. Dozens of small columns are stacked on top of each other, each row forming a balcony lit from the inside by a different colour: green, pink, yellow, blue. We turn right before the bridge.

'If he was so great how come he killed ten million peasants?'

'It's not true, son. How can anyone kill ten million people? It's all lies.'

The State Library comes into view. 'Temple number three,' my father announces. Its pale stone is harshly lit in white, making it look hard and sharp like plastic. It's a tiny building compared to City Hall and the Treasury Building, with only a single row of medium-sized columns.

'What, so no peasants died?' my brother asks with a sneer.

'Many people died. There was great suffering. But he had to do it, son. He had to do it.'

'Why does anyone have to kill fifteen million people?'

My father pauses for a dramatic second.

'He had to do it to save the revolution.'

We approach the Land Administration building.

'Temple number four,' my father announces.

I hate the Land Administration building. It's a bloated, shapeless box with an imposing façade of stone blocks. There's a row of tall white columns in the middle, the space behind them lit a pale violet. We stop at a red light. For the second time during the drive, my father uses the indicator. While we wait for the light to change, my brother resumes his attack.

'What about the Gulags?'

Gulags. Just the sort of word my brother likes. I can see him crouched on his knees, a *Time* spread out on the floor in front of him, mouthing the word over and over again, a word he will use sometime later in the day as if he had known it all his life.

'Every country has prisons, son.'

'What about the mental hospitals full of political prisoners?'

'Son, this is all Western propaganda.'

Propaganda. A brick wall my father puts up every time and that my brother always crashes against. It's all propaganda. He hasn't figured out a way around it. Yet. I can feel how angry he is.

'That's your answer for everything,' he snaps back.

Silence. My father usually spins out the first stage of the argument a bit longer; he's probably still hungry. The light changes to green, we turn right and are on the way home again. A wave of tiredness overcomes me. By rights my brother and I should swap places, but I decide I'll stay in the back so I can lie down. I stretch out on the seat and stare up at the patch of dark blue sky peeping through the top of the window. After a few seconds I find it harder and harder to keep my eyes open, but know I have to, so that I can see the final temple. The car glides along the smooth city streets. My father and brother continue their argument, but I don't follow it. Finally, my father says:

'Temple number five.'

I haul myself up and press my face against the cold glass of the window and see Customs House, a squat rectangle with a large dome, its columns pink against a lemon-yellow background. The dome fascinates me: it's a dusty, pale green, the same colour I've seen on bronze statues, on the copper coins I find under the till. As I get sleepier I remember my father telling me about cities in Europe completely different from ours, where the buildings aren't boxes made of glass or steel or concrete, but full of temples covered with statues of people and animals, many of them capped with enormous domes much larger than the one on Customs House, which is a tadpole in comparison. Once we have passed it I slump back down on the seat and, lulled by the gentle motion of the car and the murmur of familiar voices, fall asleep.

The slamming of the door wakes me up. My first sensation is of a something wrapped around my face. I open my eyes, but it's still pitch black; it takes me a second or so to realise that I've turned over in my sleep and managed to bury my face in the join at the base of the seat. 'Come on son, we're home.' I feel my father's hand gently shake my shoulder. When I move, the vinyl peels away from my skin, making it feel hot and prickly. Before I get out I remember to check how far we have gone. As my father gets out of the car, the overhead light comes on. I lean over the seat to get a good look at the dashboard. The last two numbers of the odometer stand at thirty: we've only gone twelve miles. I run to catch up with my father. He's walking with slow, tired steps, his heels scuffing the concrete as he approaches the house. I follow right behind him, matching my footsteps to his, letting the heels of my slippers drop and scuff in time with his footsteps. The weekend newspapers, impossibly thick, are folded under his arm. As he opens the front door I grab the papers, duck around him and get in first.

Back in the living room *Lawrence of Arabia* is still going. My brother is sitting on the floor, leaning against the couch. I take up my spot in front of him and unfold the papers. The one on the top is the *Sunday Sun*. I love the idea that we buy the *Sunday Sun* on Saturday: it's as if we can see into the future. The newspaper headline screams a single word: INFLATION. For a second I rub my nose against the black letters and breathe in the sharp tang of ink. The lino feels hard under my elbows, but the sleeves of my dressing-grown are thick enough to make the position bearable. My father comes into the living room, munching on a sandwich. He comes over to me and takes the papers, then stands there, munching his sandwich and watching the TV. He's wearing his reading glasses and two bent rectangles of light, television screens, shine on the lenses. 'Who's that?' he asks in mock surprise. 'Oh, it's my old friend, Ali Baba, and his forty thieves. Well, in this house, I'm Ali Baba, and I've only got two thieves.' He takes another bite out of his sandwich. 'Now boys, don't stay up too late,' he manages to say through a mouthful of bread, before vanishing into the bedroom. I say goodnight to him, but my brother remains silent. I fight my tiredness and manage to wake myself up enough to concentrate on the film.

Lawrence of Arabia and Omar Sharif, mounted on camels, are on a ridge overlooking a vast, flat plain. Omar Sharif explains to Lawrence that it's one of the hottest parts of desert in Arabia. It stretches across most of the screen like the floor of a dried ocean bed, bands of pale grey swirling across its surface. Distant mountain ranges, so pale they hardly stand out from the sky, break up the horizon line, which is so long it seems to follow the curve of the earth. Lawrence has sworn to do the impossible, to lead them across this desert so that, with the aid of the motley Arab army ranged behind him, he can capture Akaba. He wears a Bedouin headdress that makes his British field uniform look silly. Omar Sharif, his reluctant companion, is dressed in flowing black. Once Lawrence has led them across this desert within a desert, he's rewarded with his own Arab army. Omar Sharif gives him the white robes and golden dagger of an Arab Prince. Lawrence wreaks havoc in Turkey, blowing up their railways, strutting victoriously across the roofs of the trains he derails, his adoring army cheering all around him, his white robes, blown by the desert winds, streaming against the powder blue sky. It's my favourite part of the film, and I desperately want to stay awake to see it.

Just as Omar Sharif gives the command to start the desert crossing, a commercial cuts in. It's an ad for Australia's very own petrol company, Golden Fleece. It's not a commercial I like so, to keep myself awake, I roll over to talk to my brother. His eyes, bright with the cathode light, stand out in the darkness. 'I hate seeing 70mm on TV,' he says, waiting for me to ask why. I'm too tired to say anything so, after a brief silence, he answers his own question. 'You only see half the picture.' I'm amazed. It has never occurred to me that half the film was missing. Already I can hear myself repeating these words at school tomorrow, passing them off as my own. With this juicy tidbit of information tucked away in my mind, and feeling deliciously sleepy, I roll back over onto my stomach and look at the TV. Filling the screen is a Golden Fleece logo, the profile of a Merino sheep looking very dull in black and white. By the second commercial I'm too tired to keep my head propped up on my elbows; I fold my arms on the floor and rest my chin on my hands. By the third commercial my eyelids refuse to obey my orders to stay open. As I drift off to sleep, to the sounds of an orchestra serenading a packet of Winfield, I imagine I can still see the sheep's face, its horn twisting round and round like a snail's shell, its tiny chin tucked into the folds of wool piled up around its neck, its mouth a smiling line that curls in at the cheek like a question mark lying on its back. The logo, no longer in black and white but in full colour, shines in the blackness behind my closed eyes, the sheep's head gold on a deep blue background, absolutely my favourite colours.

Seventeen

Trapped against the tunnel wall by the human current redirecting itself around them, the Japanese couple have some difficulty resuming their journey out of the station. The husband unhooks the tiny speaker dangling behind his ear and fixes it back into place, resealing his cocoon of sound, then, fortified by the full impact of the music's swaggering rhythm, clasps his wife firmly around the waist and pushes his way into the stream of people, only for a moment brushing against two other passengers, behind him a man with a thick grey beard, leather bomber jacket and cheap lemon-yellow silk tie, in front a young woman with a McDonald's rucksack and stubby, rust-coloured dreadlocks, the gap instantly forming between them a force field of empty space that, within seconds, finds its equilibrium as the couple move with what has become a single, fast-moving queue stretching from the doors of the train which has just arrived (packed to capacity) to the distant ticket barriers, many of which are not working, at the top of the escalator.

Able to concentrate on her surroundings now that her eye is free from grit, the Japanese woman is amazed to find herself in a newly-built semicircular passageway, part of an orderly stream of passengers that converges towards a vanishing point traced by the overhead fluorescent tubes, so bright they seem to cleanse her of the murk and grit of the previous sections. The light washes down the surface of the smooth yellow walls in even tones, their matt acrylic finish diffusing its glare, eliminating any harsh shadows but still maintaining high definition and contrast, making the Japanese woman feel as if she is on a film set, the faces of the oncoming passengers suddenly more intense, more vibrant, as if they were actors merely imitating passengers, the light homogenising everything it comes into contact with, merging figures and setting into a single display of clean, efficient public space.

As they progress up the tunnel, the Japanese man notices that the tunnel walls do not form an unbroken surface. His eyes catch on the thin strips of bright orange metal that slice the walls into metre-wide, prefabricated panels, each one moulded into the shape of a quarter circle that meets at the apex of the ceiling. He lifts his gaze to the line of overhead fluorescents, to the shining white thread that leads the way out of the tunnel, his eyes counting off the tubes of light in time with his step and the rhythm of the music (the succession of tubes reminding him of the news footage of the thermal imaging of the Iraqi AAA fire, the tracers crisscrossing Baghdad's night sky like rows of luminous green hyphens), this hypnotic state – so pleasant, so satisfying, how many hundreds of hours has he spent absorbed by his favourite tapes, wife on his arm, his eye scanning minimal series, vast fields of repetition? – broken by the sudden appearance of some large blocks of primary colour painted onto the tunnel's walls and ceiling. Surprised at first by these vibrant blocks of red, yellow and blue (their colours remarkably similar to those of his earphone cushions, anorak and jeans), he realises that they are letters, the kind drawn with children's stencil rulers, only magnified many times and rendered with great precision. Glancing up as he passes under them, he reads the S's of this mirror-image sequence separated by the row of fluorescent tubes, the other letters curving down the tunnel walls only visible in intermittent glimpses because of the constant stream of passing passengers. He briefly tries to think what the letters stand for, more out of the habit of registering the countless messages of the urban landscape than any genuine curiosity, but within seconds he has forgotten about them, his attention drawn to a disturbance up ahead.

Jutting out from the stream of bobbing heads is a black, bulbous shape – the cause of some obstruction judging from the way the lane of exiting passengers detours around it – the Japanese man's every step revealing more of it until, approaching the circle of people that has gathered around, he sees it is a policeman's helmet, not black, as he had first thought, but a deep navy blue, the shape like that of some old-fashioned, aerodynamically styled domestic appliance, the back lip of the helmet sweeping over the policeman's neck suggesting that it has been put on backwards. The Japanese couple take their place amongst the spectators, next to a young man in a fawn trench coat and several other people, their bodies forming the limits of a small stage, and watch the policeman question a tall thin man with an accordion strapped to his chest.

The man in the fawn trench coat, initially attracted by the music, which has many resonances and associations for him, has been on the scene for some minutes, watching the small crowd build up around the accordionist like pieces of debris catching against an exposed root, the circle of people around him growing to the point where it has forced the flow of traffic into a mere four lanes, a bottleneck picked up by the security staff on their surveillance cameras (the member of surveillance staff who spotted the disruption on her video terminal – its image changing every fifteen seconds – in no way resembling the preppy young Englishman in the advertisement: she is a middle-aged Pakistani woman, formerly a Traffic Officer whose job consisted of designating illegally parked cars for clamping, and who has been employed by the London Underground security services as part of their drive to implement equal opportunity policy). The man in the trench coat watches with indignation as the police officer interrupts the accordionist's performance with the brusque request that he stop playing and move on immediately. The accordionist, a man in early middle age with dark scraggly hair and beard, complies with the first part of the request, the sudden absence of music throwing the noise of hundreds of footfalls back into sharp relief, and leans back, unperturbed, against the tunnel wall, his arms hugging his instrument, less in a protective gesture than in one of solidarity, while the policeman, his pasty, close-shaven face sternly peering out from beneath his helmet, takes a small spiral-bound notebook out of his pocket and proceeds to interrogate him in a bored voice that underplays his sombre expression, jotting down the man's answers as he delivers his next question, giving the impression that he is writing his own words, or that he is not waiting for the replies, preferring to make them up himself, his helmet, straining against the chin strap, wobbling slightly as the pen skips across the paper, the wind, which begins to pick up speed again, whipping at the notebook's pages and forcing him to clamp them down with his thumb. Once he has finished his questioning, the policeman stows his notebook away and delivers a short speech warning the busker that he had better not be there on his return beat. The light flashes off the ornate silver insignia on his helmet as he turns to join the stream of exiting passengers, the bulbous, dark blue shape swept away on the surface of their bobbing heads.

With a jerk of the shoulders the accordionist pitches himself forward off the wall and, gently pushing the aluminium container in the direction of the Japanese couple with his shoe (its thin black leather, or perhaps vinyl, caked with dirt and falling apart at the seams), resumes his concert, his right hand dancing over the keys, his left pressing tiny buttons, the instrument's casing, red plastic flecked with mother of pearl, shimmering as the bellows draw in gasps of tunnel air and expel them in shrill, raucous blasts representing a spirited, central European (?) melody that drowns out the rock song the Japanese man is enjoying, much to his annoyance, although the effect it has on him is negligible compared to the one it has on his wife: the waves of sound impact on her ears (which have started to burn again) and course straight through every nerve in her body, sending a shiver through her teeth and a wave of goose-flesh up her arms and the back of her neck, the cusps of her goose-pimples swelling and hardening with the instrument's every rasp. This sensory attack − coupled with the accordionist's shameless, subtly menacing gesture of pushing the foil container forward with his shoe, a movement perversely elegant in its execution, taking into account the unwieldiness of the accordion − causes the Japanese woman to tighten her grasp on her husband's arm and pull him away as quickly as possible, the two of them disappearing into the crowd, leaving the accordionist with his eyes fixed on the point where they vanished as if he were staring into a torrent that had swallowed up his last valuable possession, his gaze returning to the empty foil container that, because of the metal greengrocer's weight providing it with ballast, does not move in the current of air now whipping over the yellow tiles of compacted stone.

The man in the fawn trench coat, at first finding the abrupt departure of the elegant Japanese couple amusing (he had caught the woman's expression at the exact moment it transformed from a fixed, passive stare, to one of complete horror), suddenly feels sorry for the musician who, despite the fact he plays badly, very badly, often hitting wrong notes and showing no feel whatsoever for phrasing or rhythm, performs with genuine enthusiasm. Just as he starts thinking about how much he will throw into the aluminium container, the busker stops playing, deftly slips off his instrument and props it against the wall, next to a large red, white and blue bag of shiny woven plastic, which he grabs by the handles and drags to the centre of the small clearing, at the same time signalling people, with smiles and waves of his hand, to wait for his next treat. He kneels down, unzips the bag and rummages inside for a few moments, finally producing two large, creased Pizza Hut home delivery cartons, which he sets down on the tunnel floor and, securing them from the wind with the toe of his battered shoe, quickly weighs them down with a wide range of what is meant to be merchandise; the carton lids, no matter how much he tries to bend them back, continue to flap rebelliously in the wind. With a tentative sweep of his hand, the musician-turned-seller invites the small crowd to inspect his wares, then steps back, dragging the striped bag with him which, emptied of much of its contents, crumples against the wall like a depressed, overweight toddler. He leans against the wall, between his bag and accordion, his arms crossed, his expectant eyes flitting from the faces of the crowd to further up the tunnel, on the lookout for the policeman.

The man in the trench coat decides to inspect the items and squats down in front of the improvised display cases, his weight shifting uncomfortably onto the balls of his feet, the tails of his trench coat flapping against the tiled floor, the powerful, diffused tunnel lighting similar to that of a large department store. He examines the contents of the first pizza box, the odour of cold dough and spices clearly noticeable despite the wind, the fat stains that have seeped into the cardboard not entirely covered over by the most prominent objects, a pile of what look like packets of chewing gum, but could not be, judging from the logo on the side of each, a pig's head in a chef's hat drawn in profile, its eye a minute line creased in delight, its mouth curled in what is probably meant to be the hearty smile of a satisfied chef, but instead looks more like the sinister grin of a butcher, the colour scheme selected not helping matters much, the designer having chosen pink for the pig and a faecal brown for the background, the letters, printed in black, spelling out a language the young man does not recognise, although he assumes that the products described are pork stock cubes, which he finds surprising and also slightly nauseating, as he has heard of beef, chicken, fish, herb and vegetable stock cubes, but never of any derived from pigs. Out of curiosity he squeezes one of the thin rectangular packets, half expecting it to be soft and warm, perhaps even to oink, but finds it stiff and cold and no different to any other product of its kind.

He glances up involuntarily to find the eyes of the accordionist fixed on him, his lips curved in a half smile; perhaps it is the afterimage of the crowd of grinning pigs that has this effect, but the man in the trench coat imagines that the accordionist's smile is tinged with a similar expression, a kind of sinister, greedy smirk, these two expressions, that of the pig and musician, both invitations to buy, to part with some of the cash sitting in his trouser and trench coat pockets. He suddenly finds himself on the verge of asking how much it costs, even though he does not want any, even though he finds the very thought of it repulsive, so insistently do their grinning faces seem to demand that he buy something before he leaves.

He pushes these thoughts aside and, trying to ignore the pain in his toes, which are slowly crushing together as they are pushed further and further forward into the front of his sturdy leather brogues, turns his attention to the next object in the pizza carton, a cassette case turned face down, its antique status clear from the myriad scratches that reflect off the black body of the shell, the clear plastic back window now so cloudy that he has to pick it up in order to make out the list of titles printed on the cover folded inside. He reads:

Side One: Future Legend/Bewitched - Diamond Dogs - Sweet Thing - Candidate - Sweet Thing (Reprise) - Rebel Rebel Side Two: Rock'n'Roll With Me - We Are the Dead - 1984 - Big Brother - Chant of the Ever Circling Skeletal Family.

recognising the titles instantly, which evoke songs he hasn't heard for more than a decade, the album so clear in his mind he could have listened to it that very morning, the experience of coming across something so forgotten yet so familiar in this most unexpected of places leaving him somewhat stunned, as if he were staring at a piece of his own mind, a neural cluster that had been objectified and sucked into the maelstrom of the market, only to be accidentally rediscovered years later in this section of tunnel in a Pizza Hut container.

He turns the cassette case over, eager to inspect the cover illustration, but is disappointed by what he sees; the image that has been triggered off in his mind by the list of titles is the 12-inch album format he possessed when he was an adolescent and had sold years later, along with the rest of his record collection, to raise money to go overseas, the memory of the album cover clearer and more vibrant than the tiny faded reproduction he holds in his hand, its potency dulled and distanced not only by the size but also by the scratched, bleary window of plastic, the physical equivalent of the years that have passed, that separate him from the time he stayed for hours in his bedroom, lying on the floor on his stomach, chin propped up on elbows, speakers blaring only inches away as he gazed at the cover, an airbrush illustration of David Bowie, who gazed back at him, cool, self-contained, his enlarged right pupil carefully rendered by the illustrator – one of the distinguishing (divine? demonic?) marks that contributed so much to his aura, to his other-worldliness – his cheeks gaunt, his body, the colour of dried blood, stretched out naked on bare floorboards, his thin, sinewy arms propping up his equally sinewy torso, the rest of the figure continued on the back cover (which, as an adolescent, he had ritually spread open only once he had put on Side Two, there being a race for him to get from the turntable back to his position on the floor in the few seconds it took for the stylus to negotiate the first section of blank groove), the two panels forming a long rectangle that reminded him of his favourite cinema format,

70mm, the remainder of Bowie's body revealed to be that of a dog, the illustrator's choice of the colour of dried blood now clear, evoking the skin of a flayed animal, or of rotting flesh, or of very short fur through which the pinkness of skin peeps, the twisting base of the figure's thorax giving way to an elongated belly that in turn gives way to lean, muscular haunches, the shanks thin and elegant, the space between the legs a dark hollow, the genitals, formerly prominent, having been airbrushed into oblivion by order of RCA executives, this decision, rather than robbing the illustration of its potency (in the great tradition of Kens and Barbies), adding to it, emphasising its androgyny, making it more of an abomination that it would have otherwise been, his (the man in the fawn trench coat's) adolescent curiosity about what was hidden in the black triangular space so aroused that it gave birth to a game during which he would conjure up the most fantastic genitals imaginable: combinations of male and female, human and animal, plant and animal, human and mechanical, mechanical and electronic, or further combinations of all these, this game not the only one he used to play with the cover, but the warm-up for a much more compelling game, one that involved running his eyes from one end of the flayed figure to the other, Bowie's bland gaze fixed on him as he tried to determine the exact point where the human became dog and the dog became human, with each scan more dog visible in the human, more human visible in the dog, until he himself would look in a small, circular make-up mirror pilfered from his sister's room (still smeared with her lipstick and rouge) and see himself as a dog, and then in that dog see himself as a human.

The tiny face of the dogman stares at him through the scratched plastic window, demanding to be bought. He opens the case to check the quality of the tape, and at a glance can tell it's worthless: the colour of the tape itself, a light brown, indicates dubious quality, as does the rusting of the metal screws holding the shell together. Yet, even though he knows that the songs are as puerile as the sensibility that produced the cover image, that the sound quality will be appalling, its treble washed away over the years, its mid-range frequencies absorbed by a layer of muddy bass, that the tape has probably been mauled and scrunched and concertinaed by the bent capstans and worn, clogged pinch rollers of who knows how many cheap cassette players, that, worst of all, he is giving in to the kind of nostalgia that he has seen befall other members of his generation and that he on principle despises, in spite of all these things he succumbs to the irrational, embarrassing imperative that he must have the tape, and that he must have it now.

The pizza cartons bring him back to his senses, a surge of wind having sent the lids flapping so that they seem to be attempting to bite him. He rises from the crouching position, his knees throbbing as they unlock, the lining of the tails of his trench coat collecting a film of dirt as they sweep across the yellow tiles and, holding the *Diamond Dogs* tape as if he were offering it to the accordionist, takes a step forward into the little clearing formed by the ring of standers-by, all eyes turning on him and the tape he holds in his hand. The fluorescent light washing over him in a diffused, even film, he feels self-conscious in the small clearing. The accordionist too is looking at him and, from the suppressed grin on his lips, the man in the fawn trench coat realises he has made a terrible mistake, the kind of mistake that is nearly impossible to rectify; he is showing too much enthusiasm for what is, after his own feelings and personal history have been subtracted from it, a next-to-worthless object. The lids of the pizza boxes continue to snap at his feet as the accordionist takes a step towards him, his thumbs hooked into the top corners of his trouser pockets, tufts of light brown hair discernible in his scraggly beard, traces of the porcine smile on his lips. Both men stare at the cassette cover, DogBowie staring, oblivious, up at the ceiling.

With polite aggression the man in the fawn trench coat asks: 'How much?'

The accordionist reflects for some moments, scratching his chin.

'Five quids,' he declares in a heavy German accent.

The man in the trench coat pouts and waves the tape in little circles.

'David Bowie is a has-been,' he answers as patronisingly as possible.

'David Bowie is a genie,' retorts the accordionist, offended, his smile souring into a grimace. The man in the trench coat refuses to bow to these cheap tactics.

'The tape is old, from the mid-seventies...'

'Probably original,' cuts in the accordionist.

'... and is probably wrecked. Look, I know this album. There's only about thirty minutes of music on it. You'd be lucky to get a pound for it.'

The accordionist, even more offended, takes a deep breath, and in clearly articulated words that cut straight through the steady wind, replies:

'Then you must know that *Diamonds Dogs* is classic. It is the Bowie *Gesamtkunstwerk*. Only his Berlin albums are so good.'

The accordionist crosses his arms – probably more angry at the idea that anyone could put so low a value on a work by the master, rather than out of a sense of thwarted gain – and gazes haughtily around the small crowd of onlookers, his expression asking whether he should condescend to sell anything to this idiot, his eyes coming to rest, for the first time since their transaction began, on those of his potential customer, who is taken aback by the accordionist's anger and apparently sincere worship of David Bowie, recognising in it the same blind fan mentality that had taken hold of him as an adolescent. The man in the trench coat begins to find the whole situation faintly disturbing; not only has this fetish object from his past, the tape, rematerialised, but also the feeling of idol worship that accompanied it, a taste he had long abandoned but which he can now see in the glint of the German's eye and his offended stare, this hero worship identical in form, but present in a different body, age group, even language, like an infinitely flexible parasite capable of colonising any mind. For a split second he imagines the German must be either a distant relative or best friend from childhood he had forgotten about, or a member of a David Bowie brotherhood he had forgotten he belonged to. He wants to get away as quickly as possible, away from the disgusting mixture of intimacy and estrangement the German embodies, but can't bring himself to leave without the tape, for which he flatly refuses to pay five pounds.

'I'll give you one pound fifty,' the man in the trench coat announces with all the offensive casualness he can muster.

'Four quids and this is a cheap price.'

'Two pounds.'

'Three pounds. Already you rob me.'

'Two pounds, final offer.' The man in the trench coat does a half turn, threatening to leave, to vanish into the endless stream that carries away the vast majority of the accordionist's potential customers.

'Okay, okay. Two pounds.'

He produces two £1 coins from his trouser pocket and hands them to the accordionist, at the same time slipping the tape into his deeper trench coat pocket. One of the coins, however, does not reach its destination: the man in the trench coat lets go of it prematurely and it falls short of the accordionist's outstretched hand, hitting the yellow tiled floor and, with remarkable speed, rolling down the slope towards the platform, the wind pushing it along, vanishing from sight as it negotiates a path between the obedient feet of the exiting passengers, the image of the sovereign tumbling round and round, the thin rubber sole of a woman's shoe crashing down on it and flattening the coin onto the tunnel floor, the face of the sovereign protected from its filthy surface by the coin's perimeter of raised metal.

Both the accordionist and the man in the trench turn to retrieve the coin – the accordionist swearing under his breath in German at the ineptitude of these Britishers – but stop once they notice the swift approach of two police helmets bobbing towards them on the sea of heads, one slightly lower than the other. In the few seconds left to him the accordionist hurriedly collects the pizza containers and aluminium fast food tray and shoves them into his bag crumpled against the wall, a black paper envelope slipping out of one of the cartons and dropping onto the floor unnoticed. Before he manages to pick up the accordion the police have arrived, the officer with the pasty face accompanied by a policewoman.

The man in the trench coat has in the meantime stepped back and once again joined the crowd that has, since the arrival of the police, instantly doubled in size, further narrowing the pathway for human traffic, and drawing the attention of every passer-by to the accordionist's dilemma. In the space framed by the dark blue backs of the police officers he watches the accordionist indignantly protest his innocence, his arms waving against the virulent yellow backdrop of the tunnel wall which has painted onto it, the man in the trench coat notices for the first time, blocks of bold, primary colour, obviously parts of letters, which he is unable to read because of the bodies blocking his line of vision. The policewoman, in a sign of impatience, places her arms behind her back and joins her hands, this gesture repeated only a second later by her colleague. She then unclasps her hands, detaches the mobile phone from its hip holster and raises it to her ear, the message she delivers obviously frightening the accordionist who, after listening for a few moments, falls silent and slumps back against the blocks of primary colours painted onto the tunnel wall. She replaces the mobile phone and, stepping forward, grasps the accordionist gently by the shoulder, the policeman left to pick up the plastic bag and the accordion, which he slings over his shoulder, the bellows stretching out and filling the tunnel with a shrill, drawn out wheeze. They form into single file, first the accordionist, then the policewoman, who no longer has her hand on his shoulder, and finally the policeman, who deftly slips the accordion onto his chest, looking like a member of the policeman's band.

Once they have left, the man in the trench coat is free to retrieve the black envelope, which has been blown up against the base of the wall. As he approaches to pick it up he once again notices the blocks of primary colour curving down the left wall and pauses to try to decipher them. It takes him a moment or so to realise that they are letters printed in reverse and set on their side:

⌐

ᒬ

the teeth of the E rendered in postbox red, hanging off a spine of sky blue, the L above it the navy blue of the police uniform. He is about to continue deciphering the letters stretching across the ceiling when a gust of wind threatens to blow the black envelope out of reach; he slaps his hand down on it, too enthusiastically, judging from the painful impact of the stone floor underneath, and straightens himself up, leaning momentarily against the wall to watch the flow of traffic, which has resumed as if no one had been arrested there only seconds earlier, as if there had been no accordion, no accordionist, no Pizza Hut containers, no pork stock cubes, no police officers, no mobile phone, the two orderly lanes of traffic, one ascending to the exit, the other descending to the platform, having resumed their stable, monotonous rhythm, the only evidence that the event did take place the David Bowie tape stowed away in his pocket (which he can't wait to pop into his Walkman), and the black envelope which, on closer inspection, is no envelope at all, but a Boots photo pouch containing two standard 3" x 5" prints, its negative sleeve as empty as a ransacked tomb.

Eighteen

Every now and again, to cheer myself up, I drop into this second-hand record store to visit my old record collection which, years ago, I sold to go overseas. I cross the threshold and, responding to the SHOPLIFTERS WILL BE PROSECUTED sign that hangs from the ceiling, leave my overcoat and briefcase behind the front counter. Everything in the shop is filthy. Ridges of black dust trace the floral swirls embossed into the ancient wallpaper, once white but now nicotine yellow. The carpet is a soiled maroon, the blobs of chewing gum ground into its pile dully reflecting the weak fluorescent light. The manager sits at the front counter, going through a large pile of CDs brought for trade-in by a cocky young man waiting in front of him. The manager is old, very old, positively decrepit; his eyes are rheumy, he's lost most of his hair, his hands tremble slightly as he deals the CDs onto the counter, yet there he is, peering through his black-framed spectacles and totting up the current market value of some contemporary British grunge. The young guy leans against the counter, his backside thrust out. He's smirking, confident he'll wrangle a good deal from this old codger. His hair, short and spiky, looks like plastic: he's dyed it black on black. The long fringe, reinforced with gel, flicks out at the manager like a lizard's tongue. I feel like telling him to wipe that silly smirk off his face: he'll be ripped off just like I was.

The store is just one, large single room, like an enormous bedsit. Sagging chipboard racks fill the middle of the room: each compartment is full to bursting with second-hand records, their battered, dog-eared covers sticking out like cards in an unevenly stacked deck. I do my usual circuit of the shop, trying not to bump into the crammed boxes of records on the floor. I glance over to the wall on the left, which is covered in shelves of cassettes, the stacks on the uppermost shelf piled high, disintegrating into total disorder as they climb the wall, making it impossible to take one out without the risk of bringing others crashing down. On the right wall are the CDs. They look totally out of place, neatly herded into custom-made racks that foil any attempt to present them untidily. The whole place smells of grit and cigarette smoke, plastic and dust, of paper and cardboard slowly eating itself away; it smells of things that have died of loneliness. I try to not breathe too much when I come here.

There are a few other customers, all at the racks, all of them male, the older ones browsing through the classical records, the younger ones flicking through the rock. I take up a place between my fellow shoppers at the rock section. We lean forward and stare down in silent concentration as if we were standing at a urinal. I start to go through the albums. They're in no particular order, and the bin is packed so tight I can hardly tilt the covers forward. Splotches of type and colour pass before my eyes; I keep a lookout for something familiar. Every record I turn releases a little puff of evil-smelling dust that makes my eyes water.

The young guy to my left is a sensitive looking soul with pale skin and a dark scraggly beard. His hair is pulled back in a little pigtail held together by a thick red rubber band, the type banks use to secure bundles of notes. His fingernails are dirty, and there's a phone number written on the back of his hand in blue biro. He doesn't bother checking every record, pulling forward handfuls at a time, willing to let chance play a role in what he might find.

The guy to my right couldn't be more different. He checks every album and flicks them forward at a furious pace: he's leaving nothing to chance. He's tall and thin, with cropped blond hair that makes his big ears seem even bigger. Not only is his flicking fast, it's accurate. Every now and again he pauses, or rather comes to a dead stop, this brief second filled with a burst of intense concentration I can literally feel. Pause, scan, assess, reject; pause, scan, assess, reject: before I know it he's halfway down the bin, and I haven't managed to get past the first five covers. I realise I have to lift my game: guys like him will pick the whole place clean within minutes. He'll be running a small country by the time he's thirty.

I focus my efforts and start to sift. After a few moments I see that the grouping of the records isn't completely random: at times patterns emerge. I hit a crop of compilation albums: *Red Hot Hits. Summer Sizzle. Disco Feverbeat. 80's Overload. Chartstoppers. Dance Party.* Next to me the guy with big ears stops longer than the customary second, whisks out a record and rests it on the top of the others. George Harrison's *Thirty Three and a Third.* I feel a small thrill of recognition– one of my old collection! The price sticker says two dollars, which is an absolute bargain. The album is truly awful, a real dud. The hit single, 'Cracker Box Palace', had one of the most stupid film clips I've ever seen, which is an achievement, given the nature of the form. George, the naffest of smiles stuck on his face, swans about the vast gardens of an imposing Victorian estate, frolicking with badly costumed elves and garden gnomes; the whole thing is a fiasco, an ill-advised foray into 1960s psychadelia that, by 1976, is long past its use-by-date. I can't recall any other song on the album, even though I would have dutifully listened to it at least fifty times. Nevertheless, the sight of the cover fills me with jealousy. Big Ears picks it up and puts it in the front of the bin: he's going to buy it. Why does all the luck go to this kind of geek?

I resume looking, and hit a seam of Middle of the Road; Barbra Streisand, Elton John, Barry Manilow, Neil Diamond: it's all too depressing. I get halfway down the bin, then look up for a moment's respite. A guy in black jeans, black shirt and black pointy boots stomps past on his way to the counter, a serious expression on his face, his arms clutching records as if they were trophies. Everybody seems to be getting something except me. I search with increasing desperation.

The shop becomes crowded, making it difficult to get access to a rack. One guy, too impatient to wait his turn, goes so far as to squat down behind me and reach between my legs to get at a box he must think is particularly promising. Big Ears hungrily eyes my rack: he's finished his, managing to score some Paul McCartney, *Wings Over America*, a triple live album set. I feel my energy start to flag, from the lack of air, from the effort involved in scanning the mass of covers, from having to compete with absolute fanatics. The guy with the pigtail moves to the next rack, I move to his rack, Big Ears moves to my former rack. He soon whisks out *Ringo's Rotogravure*. Another of my orphaned children is now in the possession of the wrong parent. How did I miss it? Hit single, 'Photograph', probably a promo deal with Linda; after all, her dad is Eastman of Eastman Kodak. He stows it away with George and Paul, polishes off the rest of the rack in under two minutes, then stares ruthlessly over at mine, pressuring me to move on. The guy with the pigtail is advancing at a crawl, so there's nowhere for me to go but down.

I crouch down and peer into the tier of records hidden away in the racks underneath. The dust, coupled with the smell of shoes, makes the lower stratum a real challenge. Big Ears leans over the top of me as he lunges into my former rack, pressing his leg up against my back and side; his body quivers in time with his flicking. Balancing uncomfortably, my toes crushing into the tips of my shoes, I start to flick. I hit pay dirt within seconds: Nils Lofgren's *I Came to Dance*. The opening lyrics, forgotten for ten long years, come flooding back: it's Nils in rebel mode, politely telling his agent where he can stick his advice on how to reach the dizzy heights of stardom. Yes Nils, we know, you'll never be Bob Dylan, that you never miss a beat. That's it Nils! Stick to your guns! Do it your way! Don't take shit from anyone! Poor Nils. A good-looking guy, even if he's a bit short. Things went well for a while (successful transition from child prodigy axeman to solo career), but it all fizzled out after *I Came to Dance*. A mediocre record, but worth acquiring again. I squeeze the cover; the stout cardboard is a sure sign that it's an American pressing. I couldn't have done better– an import! The sticker says four dollars: not too bad. A leg presses up against me from the other side, blocking out some of my light. Someone else kneels down just behind me and goes through one of the boxes. I glance down and see fingers scrabbling at the covers like the legs of an enormous blind insect. Big Ears twists and gets up on tiptoe so he can reach the back of the top rack; I feel his groin push against my ear.

There's no light left for me to see by so, with *I Came to Dance* clutched under my arm, I stand up. In the few seconds I haven't been looking, the shop has filled up considerably. A group of schoolboys in blue blazers, some of them in shorts, others in long trousers, is scattered about the store, attacking boxes of records, the cassette shelves or, in some cases, each other. The guy with the ponytail moves on to the next rack; I only just manage to beat Big Ears to the one he's just left. I resume flicking. *Journey to the Centre of the Earth. Slade Alive. Barry Crocker's Greatest Hits. Sheena Easton. The Ferrets. The War of the Worlds. Howzat. I, Robot. Melodic Memories*; I keep flicking. I'm well into the swing of it now, flicking with all the precision, all the dexterity of my rival. Within seconds I'm a quarter of the way down the rack, not one record left unscanned. Nothing but crap, crap, crap. I suddenly hit a former treasure: *Death of a Ladies' Man*. Leonard Cohen is there on the cover, looking suave, supercool, hanging out in some seedy bar with a woman on each arm, the debauched soul who has survived the excesses of his depravity and grown older and wiser. As I study the cover I can hear the wistful, droning vocal of the title track: bitter spoonfuls of Leonard's most dirge-like reflections on the futility of love, sung in thin, high vocals against a background of strings, synthesisers, and whatever else Phil Spector thought might render the atmosphere as bleak as possible.

I don't even stop to think: Leonard is stowed under my arm along with Nils. This second find goes to my head, and I realise a kind of hysteria is overtaking me. Embedded in these racks, like chunks of gold in a riverbed, are dozens of fragments of my past lying in wait to be discovered. I flick faster and faster. My fingers start to hurt. I can feel guys squeezed in all around me, groping past each other to get to the racks, each pretending the other doesn't exist, totally absorbed in the procedure of flicking, scanning, assessing.

Loud voices from the shop entrance make me look up: a large group of guys, all dressed in faded jeans, checked shirts, and topstitched boots is standing at the threshold, checking the place out. One of them saunters over to the nearest box, inspects a few records then, turning to his mates, shouts: 'It's bloody cheap!' As if a starting gun had been fired, they descend on the racks. They continue talking to each other as if no one else was there. One of them mentions something about having only an hour left in Sydney: they must be from the country. Some of them push straight in to get at the records; others are a little less aggressive, standing behind and gradually inching their way in. One of the cowboys pushes in to my left, dislodging the guy with the pigtail: his hairstyle must mark him as an easy target. My new neighbour narrates his findings to himself in a mumble, occasionally turning and reporting back to his mate waiting behind him: *Leo Sayer, Linda Ronstat, Pilot, Kenny Rodgers* (whisked out and passed to his friend), *The Nolans, The Tubeway Army, The Bay City Rollers, Willy Nelson* (whisked out), *Sweet, Pussyfoot, Slade*, every name recounted in a muted twang that sends a whiff of beery breath into my face.

Hoots of joy come from the back of the store: one of them has found a whole box of Country and Western. He hauls it onto his shoulder and over to the front counter.

The air becomes stiflingly hot and I start to sweat along with everyone else. I flick faster and faster, my gaze bouncing back at me cover after cover; I feel slightly dizzy. I search for a familiar face, or setting, or a certain combination of colours. At times I come across face after face after face, some covers just an expanse of flesh with no limit other than the cover's square frame. Rising out of these planes of flesh are huge noses, lips whose every crease can be seen in minute detail, the performers' foreheads covered in an identifying row of type that spells out a name or a title or both, or sometimes only a single, striking word that fuses both album and artist. I flick and flick. There are thousands of people spread onto these covers, being scanned by a shop full of men hungry for noise.

The cowboy to my right quits his rack with his spoils; he's immediately replaced by two schoolboys who cram in together, their hands barely able to make it out past the sleeves of their three-sizes-too-big blazers. The schoolboys shove and jostle each other, and me in the process, calling each other loser every other second. Neither of them is the sporty type, and one is definitely the class nerd: glasses, bum fluff, the look of someone who loves to spend hours in their bedroom classifying mountains of trivial information. Every album they pause to look at is treated to a hearty sneer: this seventies graveyard is much too daggy for them. Within seconds they are gone. I grab their slot as quickly as possible.

Going through the next rack is the guy with the pigtail, his face relaxed, positively serene, seemingly oblivious to the crush of people in the store, to the noise that has got louder and louder since the arrival of the country lads. The roar of distorted guitars suddenly fills the room. The sound is even more shrill than usual, the store's cheap speakers unable to pick up the bass frequencies. I notice Big Ears again; he's moved to my former rack. We start to go through our racks at exactly the same moment, the music locking us into a common rhythm. Every few seconds we surreptitiously glance into each other's bins. I plough through a seam of soundtracks: *The Last Emperor.* *The Lord of the Rings. The Godfather. Never on a Sunday. Tommy. Lawrence of Arabia. The Student Prince. A Clockwork Orange.* Images from the films go through my mind: Alex Delarge strapped to a chair and made to watch films of unspeakable violence and perversion, his eyes forced open with metal clamps, a nurse filling them with drops that run down his cheeks as he writhes and screams *it's a sin! it's a sin! it's a sin!* Michael Corleone sitting in a low, massive armchair, the room as dark and as ornate as a Catholic church, his face sombre, grave, as if chiselled out of granite. The Pinball Wizard (Elton John) at his machine, standing on five-metre platform shoes, playing before an ecstatic crowd of mainly nubile young women. Pu Yi mounting the stairs of his makeshift inauguration platform, the sky lead grey, the belching smoke stacks of the industrial town in the distance the only sign of his new realm, the puppet state that the Japanese have made of Manchuria. The giant stone head of a (Nordic?) idol floats across a misty landscape of green rolling hills; it lands and out jumps a bearded, ageing Sean Connery, gun in hand, his hair tied back in a long ponytail, dressed in a cross between red hotpants and a guerilla outfit.

The roaring guitars fall silent, only to be followed by a deafening drum solo. It quickly finishes and the sound of violins pours into the room, a lush, romantic theme. The violins begin to speed up, the tempo becoming faster and faster with every second. The heavy metal guitar breaks in again, playing a rasping, monumental riff. Soon both heavy metal band and orchestra are thundering over each other at breakneck speed. My fingers fly over the tops of the records, my joints barely able to stand the effort required to keep up with Big Ears, whose tendons, I'm now convinced, must be made of high-performance synthetic cables. I hit a stretch of pure chaos:

Bawdy Ballads. The Exuberant Harpsichord. Roumanian Folk Songs. Samantha Fox's Greatest Hits. War Crimes. Solo Guitar. Let's Get Physical. The Street Kids Sing. The Six Wives of Henry VIII. David Soul. The orchestra and heavy metal band begin to slide apart, imploding in an orgy of pure noise.

The music stops. So do I. My heart is racing and the tips of my fingers tingle. To my amazement Big Ears has stopped too. The whole store is silent. Suddenly there's an enormous crash behind me. I turn around, ready for anything. A huge chunk of the cassette wall is missing, as if a mortar had been fired at it. Two of the country guys burst out laughing: it's impossible to tell who the culprit is, or what caused it. The manager looks up, mildly curious. Another heavy metal track starts. He turns the music off, perhaps thinking that it was the vibrations that sent the cassettes crashing to the floor.

I look down at my rack and notice that I've stopped at an album I'd completely forgotten I ever owned: John Lennon's *Shaved Fish*, forty minutes of user-friendly existentialism released at the height of his post-Beatles fame. The immortal chorus to 'Number Nine Dream' starts up in my head, John singing a (mock?) Japanese refrain in his best stoned lullaby voice, as if he were sending us to sleep from his home somewhere far, far away, in the misty regions of rock star nirvana, the words always complete nonsense to me but which sounded like:

Ah! bowowkowa pussy, pussy
Ah! bowowkowa pussy, pussy

The price, however, is far from appealing: $6. Six dollars? It's ridiculous! The album is ancient, the cover faded, the corners dog-eared. An Australian pressing from the mid-seventies: in technical terms, the lowest of the low. I slide out the record itself; there's always the chance that it may be in good condition. Scribbled onto the Apple label in gold pen is the name Tanya. I tilt the record under the weak light to get a better look at its surface. Tanya sure didn't make much of an effort to look after her records. The vinyl is dull and lifeless, coated with a layer of dust that still manages to allow all kinds of deep scratches to show through. The edge of the record, the empty band that represents nothing but hiss and crackle, is covered in fingerprints, most of them smudged, but some of them still clearly defined, the recent ones probably made by careless browsers. I slip the record back into its sleeve and am about to put it in the rack when I notice that Big Ears has stopped flicking and is staring intently at the cover. His long thin arms rest on the top of his rack. They tremble slightly, like the exhaust pipe of an idling car. George, Ringo, Paul...he's got them all except for John, who I now hold in my aching, grime-covered fingers.

I look Big Ears in the face for the first time: until now he's been either a profile or a blur. I'm astonished at how young he is; his blond eyebrows don't seem to have fully formed yet, and his face is lean, its planes terrifyingly clean and simple. Even though he's tall for his age, he can't be more than fifteen. He continues to stare at the cover, his pale blue eyes a paradox of blankness and urgency. I find myself feeling sorry for him. You can tell that this is *important* to him, important that he scores each of the fab four in consecutive racks. I decide to put *Shaved Fish* back in the rack for him to pick up later; it seems to be the least embarrassing way to make sure he gets it. As soon as he sees that I've replaced it, he goes back to his flicking as if nothing had happened.

I look over to see how the guy with the pigtail is going, but he's left. In his place is a young woman in a low cut T-shirt with horizontal blue and white stripes. She has a pale face and heavy eye make-up. Her hair is a mop-top thick with henna; it has the colour and texture of fine rust. To avoid contact with the bodies that threaten to crush against her (all those disgusting boys), she squeezes her arms in as much as possible; they push her breasts forward, giving her a cleavage worthy of a character out of *Les liaisons dangereuses*. The cover of the album she inspects sports a line illustration of a large, bright yellow banana – *The Velvet Underground*, a cult classic.

I suddenly feel quite exhausted. My fingers are numb, my heels ache, my head is clogged with dust and the noise has started to build again. I decide to leave before they put on any more heavy metal. I review my selection of records, *I Came to Dance* and *Death of a Ladies' Man*, then fondly put them back in the rack. There seems no point in buying them again. I know them off by heart, I've squeezed every drop of goodness from them, what's the point of gnawing on old bones? I feel a twinge of sadness as I shove them back into the rack, as if I'm releasing animals bred in captivity into the wild for the first time. As soon as I leave my rack Big Ears jumps in. I hover for a second to see if he goes straight for *Shaved Fish*. He does.

Getting out of the shop doesn't prove to be as easy as getting in: there's a bottleneck near the entrance caused by the manager's off-sider, a young, skinny guy with lank brown hair. He crouches on the floor gathering up the last few fallen cassettes into a cardboard box. He's wearing his favourite heavy metal T-shirt, its illustration a snarling demon with huge fangs crushing a knight in silver armour in its taloned left hand. A small audience has gathered around him, consisting mainly of the country lads and schoolboys and, to my surprise, the guy with the pigtail, who holds a Queen album, *A Night at the Opera*, clasped to his chest. What's he doing with something as gaudy and processed as Queen? He should be buying something soulful, melodic, preferably Celtic: Van Morrison, The Hot House Flowers. But Queen?

The country guys leave in a large group, clearing the crowd a little. I make my way over to the counter to get my bag and jacket, but am blocked by the young guy with the gelled fringe, who is still trading in his CDs. I hear the manager give him his final price – fifty bucks: take it or leave it. In a rare display of weariness the manager takes off his glasses and rubs them with the corner of his shirt: there must have been some serious haggling going on. The guy with the fringe huffs and blows and mutters 'fuckin' rip off' so that half the shop can hear, then gives a curt nod of assent. The manager, unfazed by this fit of pique, puts his glasses back on, rings up the money on the ancient cash register and hands him a limp $50 note. The young guy crumples it into his back pocket and slouches off into the street.

I retrieve my bag and jacket from behind the counter and, as is my custom when I leave the store, look up at the security mirror bolted halfway up the wall. The entire shop is stretched across its convex surface, a tiny, murky room with curved walls, packed with Lilliputian figures foraging through a garbage tip of stale fame, failed come-backs, unsuccessful debuts, plodding, inspirationless mid-career fodder. I look for a glimpse of myself as I pass the mirror, but the store is still so crowded that the only person I can make out with any clarity is the manager, sitting at his counter. There he is, positioned at his cash register, staring patiently into the mirror, keeping a watchful, paternal eye on his stock and clientele.

Nineteen

He takes the first photograph out of the pouch. The instant he touches it, he feels guilty about the thumbprints that will be left on its shiny surface. Because of the wind, which has picked up speed again and blows with a steady force, he grips the small rectangle of paper tightly, holding it at an angle that allows the stream of air to sluice around and stabilise it. He wonders whether he should not wait until he is somewhere more sheltered to look at the photograph, but immediately rejects the idea; all his life he has been impatient, tearing open the bags of his purchases as soon as he is out of the shop, unable to delay a further inspection of the book or tape or record now that it is exclusively his. He turns his back to the wind, which becomes stronger every second and exerts a persistent pressure on his back, as if it were trying to push him back down into the bowels of the Tube network, back into the chaos of rush hour that continues to build to its climax. The faces of passengers pass him in a steady succession, reminding him of the times when, as a child during long drives, he would lie in the back seat of the car and watch the overhead street lights whiz by, each enormous bulb an eye that glanced at him for a split second, no glance lasting long enough to get a good look at him, although, had the street lights been able to communicate with one another, they might have been able to piece together a portrait. The glances of passengers now flicker over him as did the street lights, each person forced to scan him in order to judge if they might bump into him, many of them having to veer slightly to the right in order to avoid doing so. Face after face drifts by, some only partially visible, covered by scarves tucked up high or hats tilted low, others fully bare, pale masks of flesh exposed to the corrosive blend of fluorescent light and freezing wind.

To make himself as unobtrusive as possible he leans against the tunnel wall. He is about to look at the photograph when one of the inner flaps of the black pouch is blown out from under his fingers by an eddy of wind, hiding the image from view. Printed on the flap is the head of a little girl, a frame of shiny auburn curls surrounding her exuberant, freckled face, her pupils two glowing red discs, the effect like that used in horror films to indicate that a given character has been possessed by some kind of evil power. A caption underneath the little girl's face explains how, with the aid of a new flash design, the problem of red eye can be avoided by using a camera programmed to give off a half-flash before the actual taking of the photograph, this preliminary flash having the effect of closing the pupil – which is often open wide in low-light situations – and preventing light from reflecting off the retinal membrane, the source of redness. It is with some difficulty that the man in the trench coat succeeds in turning back the flap, the wind binding it to the surface of the photograph with surprising tenacity. Now that he can see the photograph he tries to examine it again, but immediately meets another obstruction; most of the image is obscured by a puddle of white cast by the overhead lights onto its glossy surface. He tilts it this way and that, careful to prevent the wind from creasing it, the puddle of light sliding over the edge once he brings it closer to his face.

The photograph depicts the ruins of a Greek temple on

the summit of hill, shot from a low angle so that its weathered marble columns shine brilliantly against a still, cloudless sky. Some of the columns support blocks of marble that, catching the sun, flare against the field of blue like the remnants of a footpath suspended in sky, this field of blue becoming impossibly rich, almost metallic at the picture's edges, where it also acts as a backdrop to the man in the fawn trenchcoat's thumbs which, compared to the sun-drenched marble columns, seem cold and lifeless. The overhead lights throw into relief the fine grooves of his thumbnails, their striations bearing a structural similarity to the fluting of the columns, whose ridges are in some places so worn that it looks as if bites had been taken out of the stone, although often they are still clearly defined, the fluting increasing the marble's surface area and thus the amount of sunlight that catches on the columns' bleached, granular surfaces, allowing it to refract endlessly throughout the remains of the temple.

The quality of picture resolution and colour saturation suggests that the photograph was taken with a medium-priced point-and-shoot camera, its lens not quite up to an accurate representation of the temple's perspective: only the front corner column forming the centre of the composition seems to be vertical, while those on either side tilt slightly towards it, as if someone had reached into the photograph and, with their thumb and index finger, squeezed them towards the middle.

The temple is surrounded by a dry, rocky forecourt strewn with large chunks of fallen stone that lie on its shimmering expanse like beached sea animals. A low fence of crooked aluminium poles strung with yellow rope, tiny in comparison to the columns, has been erected around the temple's base, marking it off limits to the small crowd of tourists present, although there is nothing to stop the more enthusiastic temple-goer from slipping through. However, none of the tourists sprinkled about the forecourt seems inclined to break the temple's sanctity, apparently content to view the building from a respectful distance.

Standing on the broken steps that lead up to the temple's façade are various people posing for photographs. It takes a moment for the man in the trench coat to realise that they are all women. They are dressed in a variety of casual summer outfits, although one particular style is more prevalent than others: a combination of cotton shorts and matching T-shirt, principally in white but also in beige and other pastel colours. He shifts his attention to the forecourt where, sure enough, there is group of people roughly the same size as that on the steps, consisting mainly of men. Many of them are visible only from the back, their extended elbows indicating that they are holding cameras to their faces and are in the process of photographing the women on the steps. All the women are smiling, their facial expressions – or rather single facial expression – a fixed grin, serving not only the purpose of convincing faraway friends and relatives that they are enjoying themselves, but also distancing themselves from each other, each caught up in a moment of purely individual happiness that can only be shared with the temple and camera. Because they are forced to stare into the setting sun, many of them are squinting; on a closer look at some faces, it is possible to read their expressions as those of intense pain, their smile more a grimace, the slits their eyes have become indications of some unpleasant scene they wish to blot out.

Pride of place in the middle of the façade has been taken by a tanned young woman dressed in a sleeveless light-green top – the straps of her bra peeping out white against her smooth, brown skin – and a matching pair of shorts that seem impossibly clean, perhaps just ironed. Her head is framed by a square block of marble, a remnant of the temple's interior wall which, luminous, forms a backdrop for her portrait. A long wave of honey blond hair sweeps from right to left over her head. Even though her smile forms part of the collective grin of the women on the steps, her expression is made more radiant, more dazzling, by the background of shimmering marble that somehow charges her expression with the energy of its surface.

The wind has become so strong that the man in the fawn trench coat has some difficulty in putting the photograph away; as soon as it is no longer being held at an angle that allows the air to flow evenly over it, it blows free of his left hand and, pinched ever more firmly between the thumb and index finger of the right, flaps wildly like a tiny flag. He stuffs rather than slides it into the black holder. He glances up once again at the advancing columns of passengers. Because of the wind blustering in his ears, he can no longer hear their voices (although some couples and pairs still appear to be talking, as if in a mute show), nor the impact of their footfalls, not even the distant clatter of trains; everyone is now moving in a vacuum of silence filled by the sluicing roar of the wind. Even though he knows he should wait until he is somewhere more sheltered (the wind having begun to penetrate the fabric of his trench coat, the nape of his neck, despite his high collar, beginning to go numb), he can't resist taking out the next photograph for inspection.

It depicts the same scene, the same stillness, the same double moment comprising a two thousand-year-old structure frozen for one/one hundred and twenty-fifth of a second. There is, however, an important difference. The foreground of the photograph is dominated by the head of a man with short black hair. Although he is turned towards the camera his face can't be seen, as it is hidden by the camcorder he clasps in his hand, a sleek device that covers his face like a mask of black plastic. The word SONY, its letters bright silver, is situated at the level of the man's forehead: below this the rim of the lens housing, a fainter silver, traces a distorted circle in the darkness. His slender fingers curl around the camera with so much familiarity, so much intimacy, that the black plastic body seems to be an extension of his face, the lens a cold, hungry mouth, greedy for images. The arm with which he holds the camera, tanned and covered in sparse but thick black hairs, stands out against his beige T-shirt. The time on his watch, clearly visible, is five thirty-three. The forecourt and steps are hidden from view and the temple itself, which in the previous image dominated the photograph, is now relegated to the background, the relative size of the man's head reducing it to a mere feature of setting.

The powerful gaze of the lenshead draws him in and he stares into its blackness, discovering a glowing fleck of purple, a ray of sunlight caught in the lens' coating. He continues to look into the lens as if he were playing a staring game to see who blinks first. The lenshead stares back at him, a lidless eye, a pupil without an iris. The man in the trench coat pretends he is being filmed and imagines how he must appear to the camera, his face a muddy smear against the yellow tunnel wall. He imagines that the camera is recording, panning around the tunnel just as it has panned across the temple site, image after image converted into standardised units of energy: the ruined temple; the chunks of broken marble scattered about the forecourt; the woman in the olive-green shorts; the columns of commuters, (only a few seconds earlier so orderly, but now breaking up under the impact of the relentless wind); the prefabricated yellow panels; the discarded crisps and hamburger wrappers that skid along the tunnel floor; the advertisements for foot powder, eye drops, Israeli holidays and police force recruitment that adorn the tunnel and platform walls; the clanking train carriages; the Tube line maps; the loops of worn rail that shine silver in the train's headlights: the man in the trench coat imagines the camcorder weaving its way through thousands of kilometres of tunnel as if it were a surgical camera exploring the insides of the human body, drawing all these images through its lens in rhythm with the steady, inexorable motion of the its tiny motor.

He suddenly finds something objectionable about the stare of the lenshead: behind that mask of black plastic there is something aggressive, invasive, self-seeking. It seems that everywhere he turns he is being stared at. The passengers that scan him as they pass, the surveillance cameras that are trained on him at every twist and turn of the tunnel, and now this man with the camcorder. Why should he subject himself to yet another impersonal gaze? He is about to put the photograph back in its pouch, but before doing so he places his thumb over the lens and, with a feeling of childish satisfaction, presses down until the paper creases, as if he were breaking the lens, as if he were blinding the rapacious eye that stares at him with such insolence, such contempt. He takes his thumb away, tilts the photograph under the light and stares at his thumbprint, at the concentric loops of oil and particles of dead skin traced on the photograph's glossy surface. Then, tired of the image, tired of the tunnel, tired of the pointless exercise that his day has become, he slides the photograph back into its pouch and stows it away in his coat pocket, next to his copy of *Diamond Dogs*.

He turns into the wind to resume his journey out of the station. To keep the wind out of his coat, he clenches his fists and scrunches up the material at the end of his sleeves, creating an airlock. As he makes his first step to leave, he notices something pulling at the sole of his shoe. He tries to step forward, but is held back by its surprisingly strong grip. Balancing on one leg, he kicks his foot free. He kneels down to see what had obstructed him, the wind threatening to blow him over as he crouches, the tails of his trench coat flapping against the floor and sweeping up layers of dirt with its lining. Stuck to the floor are two strips of white paper, one crossed over the other, the corner of the topmost strip curling back: it had been this section of adhesive-coated paper that had caught on his shoe. Across the length of both strips the words AIR FRANCE, followed by the code AF 076801, have been printed in black. Underneath this sequence is a bar code, its striped lines of varying widths jagged at the edges. Printed length-wise in bolder, elongated characters is the sequence, LHR AF 810. It takes him a moment to realise that they are baggage tags, although how they have come to be stuck on the tunnel floor completely escapes him. The loose corner of the bag tag blows back and forth in the wind like the tongue of a panting animal.

He stands up and smoothes down the protruding corner with a sweep of his shoe.

The wind surges, a sudden bluster that almost blows him off balance. Passengers' scarves, untucked hair, coat flaps, carrier bags and anything else that has not been secured are blown nearly horizontal. Those who are on their way down to the platform are pushed along even faster, while those who are leaving the station are slowed to a crawl, forced to battle for every step, the wind, now no longer a surge but a steady gale, blasting directly into their faces, hurling tiny fragments of debris into their eyes, rushing against their ears and making it impossible to hear anything other than the inarticulate howl of the city which, more and more often, makes clear who is really in control by its sabotage of the simplest acts of everyday life.

The man in the fawn trench coat purses his lips and squints, reducing the tunnel to a slit of brilliant yellow light swarming with blurry figures. He huddles forward and clasps the lapels of his coat, pulling them as tight as possible. He joins the chain of exiting passengers and staggers forward, pressing his shoulders into the wind as if he were pushing an enormous load. The wind surges again: shocks of cold air flatten his hair to his scalp, making is shiver. He continues to push, only barely managing to make headway. His trench coat fuses to his body like a second skin: the surface of its fabric ripples with the rush of air. He pulls his collar higher and manages to lessen the wind's impact. As if in response it gives one great, final surge. He breaths in icy draughts: his whole head seems to be at the mercy of the wind that has finally succeeded in penetrating his ears, nose, mouth, and is free to roar through the network of tunnels and passageways under his face. He tries to step forward, but the wind is now so strong that it is nearly impossible.

Acknowledgements

Every effort has been made to contact the copyright holders of material used in this book. However, where an omission has occurred, the author and publisher will gladly include acknowledgement in any future editions.

The following pieces are reproduced with kind permission of the companies listed below.

Chapter One: Microsoft Excel advertisement by Microsoft Australia Pty Ltd.

Chapter Three: Film review of *Freedom is Paradise* by Tony Rayns in *Time Out* Magazine (1991) by *Time Out* Magazine Ltd.

Chapter Nine: Text from Californian Corn Chip packet by United Biscuits (UK) Pty Ltd.

A note on this edition

This novel was originally published by Allen & Unwin in 1997. At that time, I was able to quote a number of song lyrics as the cost of getting permissions was modest. Unfortunately, these kinds of permissions have become prohibitively expensive, and I have not been able to include them in this edition. The changes made are minor, and do not detract from the book in any way.

Also, I would like to point out the meaning of two acronyms used in Chapter Four that will have lost some currency, but that have a strong resonance for my generation. The CES refers to the Commonwealth Employment Service, the Federal government's employment agency 1946–1998. It was replaced by the Howard government with a system whereby private employment providers worked in concert with a new government agency. TEAS refers to the Tertiary Education Assistance Scheme, the financial support given to higher education students so they could pursue their studies. The scheme was in operation 1973–1986. It was abolished by the Hawke Government and soon replaced with a combination of AUSTUDY and the tuition fees scheme known as HECS (Higher Education Contribution Scheme). The abolition of these government schemes and entities (and others like them) marks a significant turning point in Australia's transformation into the more market-driven society we know today.

Anthony Macris is an Australian writer and Associate Professor of Creative Writing at the University of Technology, Sydney. His first novel in the Capital series, *Capital*, Volume One, won him a listing as *Sydney Morning Herald* Best Young Australian Novelist 1998, and was shortlisted for the Commonwealth Writers' Prize (Southeast Asian section) Best First Book 1998.

His book reviews, articles and features have appeared in *The Sydney Morning Herald*, *Griffith Review* and *The Bulletin* for over a decade. He is also the author of *When Horse Became Saw*, his family's inspirational story and a powerful evocation of the world of autism, which was shortlisted for the 2012 Prime Minister's Literary Awards: Non-fiction category.

His second novel, *Great Western Highway: A Love Story (Capital, Volume One, Part Two)*, was published by UWA Publishing in 2012.

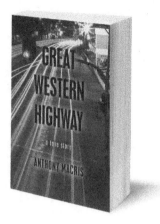

Never before have you felt so close to history. Yet so irrelevant to it.

Thirty-something Nick is walking down Parramatta Road's six lanes of thundering traffic to see his former girlfriend Penny for the first time since they agreed to be 'just friends'. By the novel's end, he is racing back up that same road so he doesn't lose her.

Nick and Penny's awkward romance is played out against the backdrop of high capitalism and the rise of the digital age. Bombarded by advertisements, slogans, news, wars, politics and consumerism, just a little silence is hard to find. Even in the bedroom with the woman he wants so much to love, Nick's mind spirals off to other times and places.

Through him we revisit the Gulf War watched on a rented TV in the London flat he can't afford; we meet the girl who broke his heart; and veteran political journalist Kerry O'Brien interviews Margaret Thatcher like never before. In the hyperbolic, media-driven world they inhabit, can Nick and Penny somehow find ways of being, and maybe even being together?

Great Western Highway, Macris' second novel following the award-winning *Capital Volume One*, brilliantly charts our troubled journey into the free-market renaissance that has completely reshaped the way we live, and love.

'A young man, blessed with a sharp intelligence but not much in the way of intuition, struggles to make sense of the women he is involved with and of the never-ending cascade of images forced upon his attention by global culture. *Great Western Highway* offers a striking record of what life is like when the barriers between public and private space are everywhere giving way.' JM COETZEE

www.uwap.com.au